BETSY

BETSY

PAUL HERNDON

BETSY

iUniverse books may be ordered through booksellers or by contacting:

iUniverse
1663 Liberty Drive
Bloomington, IN 47403
www.iuniverse.com
844-349-9409

Because of the dynamic nature of the Internet, any web addresses or links contained in this book may have changed since publication and may no longer be valid. The views expressed in this work are solely those of the author and do not necessarily reflect the views of the publisher, and the publisher hereby disclaims any responsibility for them.

Any people depicted in stock imagery provided by Getty Images are models, and such images are being used for illustrative purposes only. Certain stock imagery © Getty Images.

ISBN: 978-1-6632-4577-9 (sc)
ISBN: 978-1-6632-4972-2 (hc)
ISBN: 978-1-6632-4578-6 (e)

Library of Congress Control Number: 2022919640

Print information available on the last page.

iUniverse rev. date: 01/09/2023

CONTENTS

PREFACE

This is a work of fiction based on a true situation that existed in the small community of Adams, Tennessee in the early nineteenth century. At that time the activities of the Bell Witch attracted world-wide attention. The "Bell Witch" was the name given to the spirit or entity that haunted John Bell and his family over a number of years.

During that time, investigators came from all over the United States, and even from Europe, in an attempt to solve the mystery of the Bell Witch. Even the famous General Andrew Jackson visited the Bell home to witness the manifestations of the Witch. Today, much has been written about the Bell Witch. The story has appeared in collections of ghost stories and in anthologies of American folk lore. In my estimation, some of the accounts are rather far-fetched.

In his later years Richard William Bell, who appears as a minor character in this story, wrote an account of what happened in his father's house during the time it was "haunted" by the Bell Witch. In so far as I know, that manuscript was never published, but it was included in two books later published by people who were contemporaries with the Bell family. One of these writers, Charles Bailey Bell, was a descendent of John Bell, and in the course of his writing he was able to consult with Betsy Powell, John Bell's daughter, concerning the truth of his manuscript. The other writer, Ingram, had been a newspaper editor in Springfield, Tennessee, at about the time the Bell Witch was making itself known.

One problem the modern researcher encounters is that all

the early literature pertaining to the Bell Witch was written by "true believers." None of the writers ever seemed to doubt the supernatural origin of the Witch. In my opinion, no one today can say with any degree of certainty just what did happen at the Bell home.

I first heard about the Bell Witch while growing up on my father's farm in Robertson County during the 1920s and 1930s. Our farm was located about fifteen miles west of the Adam's community. I was introduced to the story by the child of a tenant farmer who lived on my father's farm. I had been raised to believe that there was no such thing as ghosts, and I was a skeptic from the start. Nevertheless, I developed a vivid interest in the story and tried to learn more about it. I was told that the best source of information on the subject was a book entitled *The Bell Witch*. I was also told that the Bell family descendants had bought up and burned all the copies they could find in order to shield the family from the embarrassment caused by the time of "their family troubles." This brought my first efforts to learn about the Bell Witch to an end.

With the passage of time the Bell family seemed to have had a change of heart and actually developed a kind of pride over their family history. They no longer objected to publication of the accounts of the Bell Witch.

One day while in a bookstore in Nashville, I saw a copy of a reprint of Ingram's book lying in a bookstore window. I rushed in to buy a copy. Later I found a copy of Doctor Charles Bailey Bell's account of the Bell Witch in an establishment that caters to tourists along Interstate 64.

In time I read both books through several times. Little by little I began to get distinct impressions about what really happened in that distant past. No one, and I least of all I, can say that my impressions are true, but this novel is my attempt to get my theory down on paper albeit in fictional form. I have tried to stay as close to truth as the demands of fiction would allow.

In the final analysis, it is my contention, as revealed in this novel, that John Bell's daughter, Betsy, was the source of the occurrences of "supernatural manifestations" during the time of the Bell Witch incidents. There is some evidence that some of her contemporaries suspected Betsy Bell's involvement in the occurrences that plagued John Bell and his family.

There is no proof, of course, and my contentions can certainly be challenged. If not accepted as factual fiction, I hope my effort will, at least, serve to provide an entertaining read.

1

THE VISION

It was August, and along Red River the heat was oppressive. A few miles east of the small town of Adams, Tennessee, the house of John Bell stood on high ground amid a grove of pear trees. Shielded from the direct rays of the sun, the house was several degrees cooler than the surrounding area. Nevertheless, all windows and doors were thrown open to invite cooling breezes that sometimes blew from across the river.

In an upstairs bedroom, Bell's youngest daughter stood by an open window gazing into a small hand mirror. Her face had a strange intensity. Her eyes were pale blue, the mouth rather small, and drops of perspiration beaded her upper lip. Her name was Elizabeth, but everyone, except her father, called her Betsy. At the moment, she was examining a patch of brown freckles that bridged her small nose.

"Betsy, you should always wear your bonnet when you are out of doors," her mother had told her a thousand times.

Betsy was anxious to please her mother, whom she adored, but in such heat, a bonnet was most uncomfortable--hence the freckles. The freckles were hopeless. Momma would be upset, but that could not be helped. Now she examined her eyebrows. They were brown and rather heavy. Touching her finger to her tongue, she smoothed out the left one. Her eyes met their reflection. Then something strange happened. As each eye locked on its counterpart in the mirror, she saw her father turning into the lane that led past the house from the main road between Springfield and Adams. That intersection was less than a mile away but hidden from view by woods. Still the vision was clear, and it was as though she was hovering in air looking down. John Bell was astride his favorite riding mare, and under his left arm he carried a package. For some reason, she knew that the package contained material for a new dress for her mother. The material was dark blue with bluish purple figures--totally unsuited for her mother's complexion.

"Oh, Poppa!" she exclaimed with irritation.

As suddenly as it came, the vision vanished. It left her troubled. Nothing like this had ever happened before, and she had no way of understanding the experience. Still, she was certain that what she had seen was actually happening.

She turned to the window. She focused on the point where the road disappeared behind the trees. The mirror slipped from her fingers and dropped unnoticed on the floor. A pasture lay between the house and the woods, and a rail fence separated the pasture from the road. In the August sun, heat waves were simmering, and entwined within the rails, the trumpet vine was blooming. Close by a blue bottle fly buzzed insistently, the sound magnified by the eerie silence. She paid no attention to the fly.

A horse and rider came into view suddenly. Betsy's eyes widened. She drew a sharp breath. Her hand flew up to cover her mouth. Her father rode serenely with a large brown package under his arm.

"Miss Betsy," a liquid voice called from below. "Yo Momma want you to com'ere dis minute."

"Yes, Nanny," she answered, "I'm coming."

She turned from the window and ran from the room.

She found her mother in the front room. It was a large room and served as both parlor and bedroom for her mother and father. She slipped through the door, eyes downcast, and she did not look her mother in the eye. That was typical behavior for Betsy. She rarely looked anyone in the eye.

"Oh, Betsy, those awful freckles. Have you been wearing your bonnet?"

"Most of the time," Betsy said.

"You must always wear it when you go out in the sun. A young girl's complexion is terribly important."

"Yes, Momma."

"Nanny needs your Sunday dress, so she can iron it for church tomorrow. Your father will be home soon."

"He's coming up the drive now," Betsy said.

A quick glance out the window confirmed Betsy's statement.

"Oh, gracious," Lucy Bell said. "He'll be upset if everything isn't ready."

"I'll get the dress now," Betsy replied. "Nanny can iron it while he's stabling the horse--and Momma..."

"Yes, Dear?"

"If you don't like blue and purple, don't let Poppa make you keep that dress material he bought you."

"What on earth are you talking about, child?"

"Nothing, Momma."

She flew up the stairs and down the short hallway to her room. Since her older sister, Esther, had married, she was the only one in the family to have her own room. It was a very small room, but all hers. As she reached the door, she saw Nanny bending over to pick up the mirror she had dropped.

"Dat chile leave her things all over de house," Nanny said. "Dat a real nice mirror and she leave it on de floor."

The sight of the mirror reminded Betsy of her vision. She wanted to think about it but realized the immediate need to placate Nanny. The surest way to get into trouble in the household was to have Nanny report some misbehavior or act of carelessness to her father. Such reports were few and far between, but the times it did happen were to be remembered. Unseemly conduct by Betsy or any of her brothers and sisters was always sternly rebuked.

"I'm sorry, Nanny," she said contritely. "I was in such a

hurry to see what mother wanted, it just slipped out of my hand."

"When yo get so you mind yo momma so good?" Nanny grumbled, but the apology had robbed her of her anger.

"Momma said for me to get my Sunday dress for you to iron."

"Sho can't iron it ifen you keep it locked in yore trunk."

Betsy unlocked her trunk and handed a white dress to Nanny.

The old Negro woman shook the dress out and gave it close examination.

"Dat seam need sewing, and Marster gonna be wanting he supper," she said as she left the room, Betsy's dress in her hand.

"Nanny" was the children's name for the family's oldest slave. Her real name was Chloe. Lucy Bell's father had given Chloe and her oldest son, Dean, to Lucy as a wedding present. Lucy had been a Williams, and at the time of her marriage to John Bell both the Williamses and the Bells had lived in North Carolina. When Lucy and John moved to the Tennessee frontier, Chloe and Dean went with them. As a result, Chloe was separated from the man who fathered her son, but since that time Chloe had given birth to eight additional children by an assortment of men. Nevertheless, Choe's white owners considered her morals to be impeccable.

Betsy had heard Chloe tell stories about her childhood in Jamaica and of voodoo rituals she had witnessed there. It occurred to Betsy that Nanny must know something about visions. She followed the slave down the steps and to the large log kitchen out behind the house. The arrangement of having the kitchen separated from the rest of the house was not unusual since it served to protect the main house from fire, flies, and the oppressive heat of the open cooking hearth. Having slaves to fetch and carry dishes from the distant kitchen kept the arrangement from being an inconvenience to the white masters.

Nanny lived in a room over the kitchen and the building was her domain. On most plantations, the detached kitchen was a place where idle slaves congregated. Not so in Nanny's kitchen. Any slave who wandered into her path was either swatted with the flat of her broom or put to work. A slave on the Bell plantation who was so lucky as to have an idle hour avoided the kitchen like the plague.

Nanny laid Betsy's dress on the ironing board and went to choose one of the irons arranged in a row where they would be heated by the glow from the coals. She lifted one with a heavy pot holder. First, she wiped away any ashes that might have accumulated, then spit on her own finger and gingerly touched the flat surface of the iron. There was an explosive sizzle, which Nanny judged to indicate the right temperature.

Betsy's Sunday dress was simple in accordance with the standards of the time for eleven-year-old girls. Still, it had enough pleats, bows, and lace to make it complicated to iron. Nevertheless, Nanny could have ironed it in her sleep. She arranged it deftly on the ironing board then tried the iron on a scrap of white cloth. Satisfied that the iron was clean and of the right temperature, she moved it over the fabric of the dress with long quick sweeping strokes.

Betsy had followed Nanny into her abode and now perched on a nearby stool. The temperature of the room must have been a hundred thirty degrees. Sweat popped out on Betsy's forehead, and she could feel a large drop sliding down her back. Nanny's face was bathed in perspiration. An odor of cooking and perspiration permeated Nanny's abode, but it was an odor Betsy was used to.

"Nanny you know about voodoo," she said. It was a statement and not a question.

There was a pause in the rhythm of the iron. Chloe gave her young mistress a quick cautious glance.

"A little, I reckon."

Chloe thought back on memories that had grown dim over time. She had been born in Jamaica, and while a still a young woman, she had been a voodoo priestess. Her talents in the occult had been recognized by blacks all over the island.

When her master learned about her taking part in a forbidden ritual, he had whipped her severely and locked her in a stifling hot room. Her future was ominously bleak at that time, but fortunately a slave trader happened to show up in the area looking for house slaves for the Carolina plantations. Her master took advantage of the moment and sold her to the trader, saying nothing about her involvement with voodoo in order to get as good as price as possible. A few weeks later, Chloe arrived in North Carolina, Jamaica far behind her and her voodoo past unknown. Soon, she learned that many slaves in North Carolina practiced voodoo but she had learned her lesson well. Like many slaves Chloe possessed insights and skills unsuspected by white people. But previous experience obliged her to keep her skills and knowledge to herself.

"Could them that practiced voodoo see things happening in other places?" Betsy now asked.

"Chloe looked at Betsy. Her old eyes were muddy brown, and no one could fathom their murky depths.

"Some of 'em could," she answered.

"How did they do it?"

"Dem dat do it don't know how dey do it."

"What could they see?"

"Different things."

"Could they see whenever they wanted to?"

"Some could. Voodoo woman I know say she could call up de sight, but she never know what she liable to see."

"How did they get the power?"

"Doan get it. It's a gift. Dem dat have it never know where it come from. Why for you asking all these questions?"

"I was just wondering," Betsy said.

Suddenly she jumped from the stool. "I think I hear Momma calling," she said as she ran from the kitchen.

Inside the main house, she ran up the stairs and went to her room. The mirror was still on the table where Nanny had laid it. She picked it up and stared intently. Her eyes probed their own depths, but she saw nothing beyond her own image. In a way she was deeply relieved, but she also experienced a twinge of disappointment.

She laid the mirror back on the table and picked up a Bible that rested beside it. She turned to the twenty-second chapter of Exodus. The previous Sunday, Reverend Gunn had asked his congregation to read the chapter, and Betsy knew she could expect to be asked some questions about it this Sunday. She read slowly, pointing out each word with her forefinger and forming the words silently with her lips. She had a retentive memory. After she read something, she would be able to see the printed page in her mind and quote it from memory.

She came to the eighteenth verse: 'Thou shalt not suffer a witch to live.'

She reread the verse and looked up with a deep frown on her forehead. Was that it? Was she a witch? If so, was she condemned to hell? Surely not. God could not be so unjust. She had not sought the power. And come to think of it, was she so sure that she had actually seen the vision of her father? And would she ever have such an experience again?

She heard Nanny's heavy tread on the stairs and went back to her reading. Nanny came in with the freshly pressed dress and hung it in her wardrobe.

"Yo got clean petticoats?" Nanny asked.

"Yes, Nanny," she answered without looking up from her reading.

When she had finished the chapter, she carefully closed the Bible and replaced it on the table. The back door opened, and she heard her father's heavy tread. She listened apprehensively as he moved toward the front room.

"Lucy," she heard him ask, "is everything ready for tomorrow?"

"Yes, John, I believe so," her mother answered.

The door to the front room closed, and Betsy was no longer able to follow the conversation.

As the sun sank behind the trees in back of the house and twilight descended, the air cooled slightly. Those who worked on the farm began to converge on the area around the house. Slaves trudged from the field to begin their night chores. One by one Betsy's brothers came to the house. In addition to her sister who had married, Betsy had six living brothers. Her brother, Jessie, had also married and had started his own household. Her brother, Drewry, was not married, but he had bought land across the river and during the week he stayed in the cabin he had built for himself. He was expected home tomorrow. The other brothers, Zadock, John Jr., Richard William, and Joe E. still lived at home.

In preparation for the family supper, Harry, the house slave, came through the rooms lighting candles, and the slave women brought dishes from the kitchen to the dining room table. From the bottom of the stairs, her father called Betsy to supper.

Meals at the Bell household were a ritual. John Bell ruled at the head of the table. He was a tall, slender man, with a white head of hair. In December he would be sixty-five. He claimed no religious denomination, but he was a man of absolute faith and uncompromising morals. He was honest to a fault, his word was his bond, and his reputation was unblemished among his neighbors.

John Bell was an intimidating presence at the table. His wife, Lucy, sat at the opposite end of the table, and the children sat along either side. John Bell smiled fondly at his wife and ran his eye along the table mentally noting the presence of each child. No fork would be lifted until he gave the signal.

"John, how did the tobacco suckering go today?"

"Fine, Poppa," John Jr. answered. "We finished the field across the road."

"Very good, but I had hoped that you would get a start on the west field. Are you sure the slaves aren't loitering?"

"Yes, Poppa, I'm sure."

"Zadock, how are you doing with the reading of the law?"

"Fine, Poppa. Colonel Wilson says I'm ready to start reading contract law."

"Good, but remember a Christian gentleman is bound by his word. Let your yeas be yeas and your nays nay."

"Yes, Poppa."

"Elizabeth, I see you have been neglecting to wear your bonnet out of doors. Are you ready for the worship service tomorrow?"

"Yes, Poppa."

Is your dress ironed?"

"Yes, Poppa."

"And the Scriptures? Have you read the chapter Brother Gunn assigned?"

"Yes, Poppa."

"Perhaps you could edify us all by reciting something you read."

"Suffer not a witch to live," she said.

"Very good, Elizabeth. Be sure you remember that."

Now he looked at his wife at the end of the table.

"Mrs. Bell, you have given me fine sons and daughters. As the Scripture says, `Bring up a child in the way it should go, and when he is old, he will not depart from it.' Perhaps you would like to tell the children about your little surprise."

Lucy Bell smiled, but the smile was artificial. She seemed deeply troubled. She gave Betsy a puzzled glance. "Why, yes," she said, "your father brought me material for a new dress--it's blue with purple flowers."

Betsy could feel her mother's eyes, but she refused to meet the look. Instead she looked down at her plate.

At the head of the table, her father said, "It has been a fine day. Now, let's all give thanks for God's great bounty."

2

THE SERVICE

Sunday mornings were always a time of hectic activity in the Bell household. Breakfast was served at sunup. Afterwards Betsy retired to her room in preparation for her bath. Harry brought a large, galvanized wash tub into her room, placing it near the center of the room, well away from all windows. Nanny and two other slave women with buckets of tepid water followed Harry into the room. Nanny shooed Harry out and closed the door. Betsy undressed and stepped into the tub for her weekly bath.

As time to leave for church drew near, the pace increased. Betsy fussed with her dress and hair. Household slaves scurried from room to room on errands for various members of the family. By nine thirty the family was ready to go. Nanny's son, Dean, drove up to the front door in the family surrey. The boys rushed from the house in a mad scramble to get the seat up front beside Dean. Betsy descended the stairs for her father's final inspection, and Lucy rushed about the front room looking for her lace handkerchief.

Five minutes later the family had found seats in the surrey, and Dean clucked to the horses. They flew down the drive behind a smartly stepping team. A light wagon, fitted with straight backed chairs, followed the surrey. This was for the accommodation of the slaves. John Bell was not sure that the Negro had a soul, but he was not willing to take any chances. The

Scripture admonished: 'Preach the Gospel to every creature.' Presumably this included the Negro, assuming they had souls to benefit from it. But if it turned out that they didn't have souls, they would surely benefit in this life from the edifying messages delivered by the various ministers in the county.

At that time there was a good relationship among all the denominations in that part of Robertson County, and people from one church frequently attended services at other churches. One advantage John Bell had in not expressing a sectarian preference was that he was presently on the board of deacons of three different congregations, all of different faiths. That included the congregation they had decided to attend this morning--the Oak Grove Methodist Church.

The church served the spiritual needs of about 100 families in Robertson County, and a number of families of Todd County just over the state line in Kentucky. Sometimes, however, a greater number of people might attend a Sunday morning service, when members of other congregations showed up.

The pastor of the Oak Grove Methodist Church was Thomas Gunn. He was the father-in-law of Bell's son Jesse, and today the Bell family felt perfectly at ease attending Reverend Gunn's church.

By surrey it took the Bell family forty-five minutes to get to the church. Along the way they passed the Gardner farm. Joshua Gardner was three years older than Betsy, and they went to the same school together. Everybody said that Josh was sweet on Betsy, and she knew that her

parents expected her to grow up and marry him. Now as the surrey stirred up a cloud of flour-fine dust along the road that passed the Gardner farm, her father examined the fields they were passing with an appraising eye.

As they passed a small field of dark green tobacco, her father said, "Elizabeth, I talked to Joseph Gardner yesterday. He tells me this field belongs to young Joshua."

"Yes, Poppa," she answered without looking either at him or the tobacco.

Betsy wasn't sure how she felt about Josh. She supposed she liked him well enough, and she certainly expected to get married someday. A girl`s measure in life depended on the kind of marriage she made, and all the girls she knew looked forward to the day when they could have suitors.

Betsy supposed she would like having a suitor and getting married. Her older sister Esther had certainly enjoyed being courted and had acted like a giddy ninny during the time she was planning her marriage.

But Betsy didn't really want to think about it now.

"That is fine tobacco," her father was saying. "It speaks well for young Joshua. It's hard to find such a young boy who is willing to work hard."

"Betsy is sweet on Josh," Richard William giggled. Richard William was four years younger than Betsy, and he was at the age when he could be obnoxious to an older sister.

Betsy was about to protest his teasing, but it proved to be unnecessary. Her father pointed a stern finger at Richard William. "Young man, according to the Scriptures, marriage is an honorable estate. It is not for you to make light of your sister's emotions for the man she intends to marry."

"Yes, Poppa," Richard William said in a subdued voice, eyes downcast. He was thoroughly cowed by his father's rebuke.

Betsy was vindicated, but she wished her father wouldn't take her feelings for Josh Gardner so much for granted.

They were fast approaching the drive up to the Gardner house. Just before they reached that point, a horse and rider came out of the drive and into the road. It was Josh, and it was obvious that he had been waiting for them.

The road was narrow, and Dean had to rein in the horses, and for a moment everything came to a standstill. Josh was blushing, and Betsy knew that he was embarrassed by his own audacity. Nevertheless, Josh gave no ground. A cloud of dust swirled up around the surrey and its passengers.

Josh now remembered to doff his hat. He tried to flash an engaging smile. To Betsy it looked like a silly grin.

"Good morning, Squire Bell," he said.

"Good morning, Joshua," Betsy's father returned.

"Mrs. Bell," Josh continued his salutations

"Good morning, Josh," Betsy`s mother responded.

"I reckon you all are going to church."

"That's right," John Bell said.

"Oak Grove, I `spect."

"Yes."

"Thought I might ride along with you."

"Is the rest of your family coming?" Lucy asked.

"No. Mom's poorly, it'll just be me this morning."

"We're glad to have your company," John Bell assured him. "Would you like to tie your horse behind and ride in the surrey?"

"That would crowd you. I'll just ride alongside."

John Bell might have insisted that Josh ride in the surrey had he not noted that Josh's observation about crowding was accurate.

"As you wish," he said.

They traveled at a fast pace. The noise of the surrey made ordinary conversation impossible. John Bell and Josh were the only ones who conversed, and they had to shout to be heard above the noise. The two men talked about the weather and the conditions of the crops.

Betsy was somewhat put out. Josh had not even looked in her direction, but she knew perfectly well that he had waited on her account. She was not sure what there was about him that she did not like. She could not figure out what it was.

As they neared the church, the road became more crowded. Buggies, wagons, surreys, men on horseback and pedestrians were in front of and behind them all headed toward the oak grove that had given the church its name. The dust became thicker and Betsy found it difficult to breathe. As they approached the church, a buggy coming from the opposite direction turned into the lane in front of the Bell family surrey. Lucy caught her breath in excitement.

"It's Jesse and Martha," she cried.

The young man and girl in the buggy waved.

"Hi, Momma, hi Poppa," Jesse called. "See you down at the church."

They drove into a park-like area shaded by great trees. The ground under the trees was bare of vegetation, attesting to its constant use as a parking area for the vehicles of the arriving church goers. The church ground covered several acres. There was a small cemetery nearby.

Dean let the family out in front of the church then he took the surrey to the parking area. He would unhitch and care for the horses before retiring to that part of the church yard reserved for the slaves.

Betsy had barely set foot on the ground before they were joined by Jesse's wife Martha.

"Momma, Poppa Bell," she cried and embraced first Lucy and then John.

"Where's Jesse?" Lucy asked looking about the yard.

"He's taking care of the horses," Martha told them.

Betsy remembered that Jesse and Martha did not own a slave. Her father had offered to make them a present of their house boy Harold, but Jesse had refused.

"No, please, Poppa," he had replied to the offer, "I wouldn't feel right owning a human being."

"Nonsense," John Bell had countered. "God made the Negro to serve the white man. He gave us the responsibility to feed and clothe them and teach them useful skills."

"Yes, Poppa, but that responsibility is not for me. I've talked it over with Martha and she agrees."

"Well, I hope you are not going to become one of them... uh them..."

"Abolitionists, Poppa," Jesse finished his father's thought, then replied, "No Poppa, I have no intention of telling others how they should order their lives. I speak only for myself."

The family had now congregated outside the church and everyone talked at once. Josh Gardner hovered at the edge of the group hoping to be included in the conversation. Only occasionally would he cast a sidelong glance at Betsy before turning back to the group.

"Ain't me he's interested in," Betsy thought. "He just wants to be one of the family."

Her sister Esther now came into view, and Betsy left the grownups, running to meet her. They squealed like young girls are wont to do when reunited and threw their arms around each other.

"How are things at home?" Esther asked.

"About the same," Betsy told her.

"Poppa as fussy as usual?"

Betsy smiled and nodded.

"Elizabeth, have you been diligent at your crocheting today?" Esther said in a gruff voice mimicking their father.

Both girls giggled.

"You and Ben are coming for dinner today, aren't you?" Betsy asked.

"I guess we'll have to," Esther replied. "You know how Poppa is about having the family together on Sunday."

The area in front of the church was getting crowded. Church going served as a social as well as a religious function. Friends met, people got news of the community, men talked about crops, and women swapped recipes.

When it was time for the service to begin, Mrs. Broadberry began playing loud and commanding music on the piano. The women were the first to their pews. They were followed by their men folk and finally by the slaves slipping through the door to file up a narrow stairway to the large balcony that had been built for their accommodation.

Services started with singing. After the third song John Bell was called to lead the congregation in prayer. John Bell was given to much praying that morning, and his prayer lasted forty-five minutes. Betsy counted sixty-two times that her father used the phrase, "Our Heavenly Father." Her father's prayers were as instructive as most sermons, and he asked God to have mercy on fourteen kinds of sinners some of which Betsy had no understanding of.

What on earth was a fornicator, she wondered.

That word was frequently used in prayers and sermons, but when she had asked her mother what it meant, Lucy had blushed and told her she was much too young to understand.

"How am I supposed to keep from sinning, if nobody will tell me what sin is all about?" she wondered to herself.

Since the service had started, the sun had climbed higher, and even the shade of mighty oaks could not keep the building from growing steadily hotter. While her father was praying, the temperature reached a hundred. Betsy felt rivulets of sweat sliding down the skin under her dress, and the room now had the smell of buildings of the era. It was a mixture of body odor, the perfume of various brands of powder, and the scent of the oils used on the floor.

A handheld fan was a part of every woman's summer attire, and now they fluttered all throughout the congregation in a last ditch effort to stave off heat strokes.

After the prayer, there was another song then Brother Thomas Gunn stepped to the podium. He was as thin as a scarecrow and might have been tall had he not stooped. His hair was thin and gray. His seamed face had a kind of other worldliness look in it, and folks said there was a sweet radiance in his smile.

His sermons were possessed of a kind of sweet logic, and he was adored by his congregation. This was unusual in a day when congregations tended to judge their preachers by their thundering oratory and dramatic posturing.

Because of his soft persuasive voice, Betsy had heard some of the slaves refer to him as "old sugar mouth." The designation seemed so appropriate that she had giggled for a week whenever she thought about it. But she dared not repeat it. Her father would have disapproved of any levity directed toward a minister of the gospel and doubly so since Brother Thomas was indirectly a member of the family.

Brother Thomas reached the podium and stood for a moment while the congregation put away their hymnals and settled down.

Now he asked, "Those of you who read the twenty second chapter of Exodus we assigned last Sunday kindly raise your hands."

Betsy and about a third of the congregation raised their hands. Brother Thomas thanked them and praised their diligence. Then he explained how the chapter set forth the laws for the people of God and rules of a Christian's conduct toward his neighbors.

"Those laws are as good today as they were in the time of Moses," he proclaimed.

Starting with verse one, he expounded on the chapter verses in some detail. Betsy, who had not been paying attention, now perked up when he read verses sixteen and seventeen.

"If a man entice a maid that is not betrothed, and lie with her, he shall surely endow her to be his wife."

"If her father utterly refuse to give her to him, he shall pay money according to the dowry of virgins."

When Betsy had read those verses at home, she had been puzzled over their meanings. She was not entirely sure what the word "entice" meant. And what harm could come from a man and a maid lying down together?

Hoping for enlightenment she turned her full attention to Brother Thomas. She was soon disappointed. After reading the two verses hurriedly, Brother Gunn went to the next verse without comment. Sex, even though frequently mentioned in the Bible, was not thought suitable for public discussion.

But he was entirely comfortable with the eighteenth verse: "Thou shalt not suffer a witch to live."

Perhaps to make up for his cursory treatment of the previous two verses, Reverend Gun plunged into a lengthy discussion of the sin of witchcraft. While he was ready to concede that perhaps modern Christians should not actually put witches to

17

death, he was positive in his warning to Christians about not having anything to do with witchcraft or those who practiced it.

"And when Moses warns the Congregation of Israel about witches, just what is he talking about?" he asked the congregation.

"Is he talking about ugly old women?" he added.

Reverend Thomas now spent five minutes assuring his listeners that many ugly old women had souls of radiant beauty.

"Is he talking about women who ride across the sky on brooms?" he continued.

"No!" Brother Thomas answered his own question.

He proceeded to explain how witches could trade their virtue for dark powers, but he warned the congregation that witchcraft was more insidious even than those common perceptions.

He posed other questions that he answered himself. Betsy fidgeted in her seat. She was not interested in what a witch was or was not. She wanted assurance that it had nothing to do with seeing visions.

"But we do not have to guess about the nature of witches," Brother Thomas assured his listeners. "The answer is in the Bible. Now we turn to the twenty eighth chapter of First Samuel."

He now described King Saul's visit to the Witch of Endor: "Saul went to this wicked woman and asked her to use the tools of the Devil to raise up Samuel from the dead so Samuel could show him the future."

"And there we have it," he announced as he finished the story.

Betsy didn't see it at all. There had been nothing about visions.

Reverend Thomas continued his sermon: "Witchcraft is seeking to uncover what God has chosen to keep secret. For each of us, God has chosen to draw the curtain over what is to be, and when we use witchcraft and black magic to penetrate the veil, we defy God's will and take unto ourselves powers God has not seen fit to give us."

18

Having satisfied himself on the point of witchcraft, Brother Thomas moved on to other verses, and an hour and fifty-two minutes after he had stepped up to the podium, he closed his Bible and called for the closing hymn.

As the congregation filed out of their pews, men looked at the large clock in the back of the auditorium and assured each other that they had just heard a scholarly discourse. While they were moving along the aisle toward the door and later as they waited in the yard for slaves to hitch up the teams, John Bell moved among the more prominent members of the congregation whispering to each of them.

When Dean finally arrived and the family had bordered the surrey, they learned that John Bell had invited almost a third of the congregation to the Bell household for dinner that afternoon.

3

SUNDAY DINNER

M ore than a hundred people filled their plates at the Bell table that hot Sunday afternoon. In addition to those John Bell had personally invited, there were the Sunday regulars. These included Jesse and his wife Martha and Esther and her husband Bennet Porter. Drewry from across the river always came over on Sundays, and the Reverend Thomas Gunn, while not exactly a Sunday dinner regular, was nevertheless a frequent visitor since his daughter had married into the Bell family.

Today Josh Gardner was also among those John Bell had invited. On the surface he was just another guest, but it was a tacit encouragement for him to start calling on Betsy.

There was no way of accommodating so many inside the house, so dinner was served out in the yard. A long table had been placed under the shade of the largest pear tree. Hovering in the background, the slaves brought dishes to the table and were ready to spring to the assistance of anyone who needed anything. The slaves would also be responsible for cleaning up once the meal was over.

The meal consisted of several hams taken from the Bell smoke house and a dozen chickens fried in a large wash kettle after the family had returned from church.

The meats were augmented by a variety of vegetables, breads, pies and cakes. For the thirsty there was coffee, milk, buttermilk, summer apple cider, and cool spring water. Lemonade, a treat that Bell had provided at considerable trouble and expense was also offered.

The men could count on something more substantial. As each family arrived, Bell took the man of the house aside and escorted him down to the spring house. There in the deep cool shade of mighty oaks, the guest was handed a water dipper and invited to drink from John Bell's own whisky still. No one, including the Reverend Gunn, saw anything wrong in such hospitality. The temperance movement was far in the future, and alcohol was considered a gift from God, and, when taken in moderation, a tonic for health and good spirits. But any man who became drunk was an abuser of his host's hospitality. And if a man became a habitual drunkard, he would be ostracized by the good people of the community.

Whiskey was not offered to the women and children. It was believed that the taste of whiskey was too harsh for the palate of refined ladies, and children were considered too young to handle it wisely.

Among those considered too young to be invited to the spring house was young Josh Gardner. While the men imbibed at the spring house, Josh wandered aimlessly about the yard trying to find them.

Seeing him so ill at ease, Lucy called Betsy to her side.

"Honey, why don't you take Josh to the front room and entertain him until dinner is ready."

Betsy shrugged in resignation. She had no desire to talk to Josh Gardner, but her training required unquestioning obedience to her elders. She went to find Josh.

"Do you know where your Poppa went to?" he asked once they were alone in the front room.

Betsy knew where the men where and what they were doing--just as she knew why Josh had not been invited. But she also knew that her mother expected her to be tactful.

"He's around," she told Josh. "He'll show up once dinner is ready."

21

"I can't seem to find any of the men," Josh complained.

"They'll show up too.

Betsy had taken a seat on the sofa, but Josh paced the floor, frequently pausing in front of the window to peer out into the yard.

"Poppa pointed out your tobacco patch to me this morning," Betsy said in a desperate effort to make conversation.

"Oh, he did? Did he say what he thought about it?"

"He said it was fine tobacco."

"Oh, yeah? Gee Golly, did he really call it fine?"

"That was what he said," Betsy assured him.

"You know I have almost two acres. Pa says that when I sell it, I can keep the money.

"Really," Betsy enthused. "What will you do with it?"

"Buy a mule, maybe."

"Oh, really," Betsy said. "Ye gad," she thought to herself, "how utterly dull."

If she'd had money, she would buy a horse.

Josh had stationed himself at the window. He was looking out on the yard, searching for some sign of male companionship. His back was to Betsy.

"I guess you are aiming to be a farmer," she said in a final effort to get a conversation started.

"Yeah," he said without turning. "I figure we will fix us up a house somewhere between here and Poppa's. One thing about farming, land is cheap, and it don't take much to get started."

The inference was not lost on Betsy, and she was about to say something about him taking so much for granted, but by the time she got her mouth open, Josh had seen the men returning from the spring house and suddenly exclaimed, "Yonder's your Poppa," and he rushed out of the room.

The meal took up most of the remaining afternoon. Heavy set women and men with generous paunches filled plates from the table and went to find chairs in shady spots. The young folks, including Betsy, sat on the grass and ate picnic style. Children ran through the yard and stable, pausing only long enough to snatch goodies from the table to eat on the run. Josh Gardner did not eat with the young people. He had taken a chair among the older men.

There were the usual mishaps to be expected at such a gathering. Glasses of lemonade were tipped over. Somebody spilled their cup of coffee on Mrs. Thomas Gunn's Sunday dress. Two children got stung by bees, and one child fell out of a tree down in the orchard. Anna Porter snagged her dress and tore a hole in it.

As the sun moved toward the western horizon, stomachs refused to accept more nourishment and bodies cried out for rest. Some families gathered their children and started for home. But Betsy knew that some would stay until dark. She was tired herself, and since Josh continued to hover around the older men, she slipped into the house and went up to her room. A cross breeze through her windows made the room tolerable. She was getting ready to lay down for a nap when she heard someone on the stairs. A moment later Esther appeared at the door.

"May I come in?" she asked.

"Sure, it's your room too," Betsy said--it seemed only yesterday when they shared the room together.

"Not anymore," Esther said as she stretched out on the bed. Betsy sat down beside her and leaned back against the headboard.

"I still wake up nights and wonder how come you are not in the bed with me," Betsy said.

"Seems to me like I been married forever," Esther said.

"Esther, can I ask you something?"

Esther looked up at her younger sister. "I guess so," she said cautiously.

"What's it like being married?"

Esther looked up at the ceiling, the trace of a frown on her forehead as she considered how to answer the question. She had gone into marriage totally unprepared, and she did not want that to happen to her sister. But there seemed to be no polite words to describe the intimacies of marriage.

"It's nice," she said lamely. Then she added, "...if you love your husband."

"Don't you love Ben?"

"Yes..." Esther said, but Betsy noted the hesitation in her sister's voice.

"But?" Betsy encouraged.

Esther looked up at her sister seeing the questions in her eyes.

"Please, Betsy, you've got to promise you won't say a word about what I tell you. If Ben, Momma or Poppa ever found out..."

"I promise," Betsy said.

"Well, it's just that being married isn't what young girls expect. It sure wasn't what I thought it would be."

Betsy nodded encouragement.

"Understand," Esther continued, "I do love Ben. But you remember how it was when we were courting. He was so attentive, and he would hardly touch me. He acted like I was made of glass and would break if he wasn't careful. Now, sometimes he goes for a whole day and hardly notices me, then that same night he suddenly wants to hug and kiss and put his hands all over me. We fuss a lot. Then there's the housework. I do have Prissy to help, but one slave can't do everything, so I have to do a lot of the work myself."

"Does Ben love you?"

"Oh, yes, I'm sure of that. Sometimes I wish he didn't so much. Men love differently from a woman. But he's really a fine person, and I know he's going to make a fine father, although he's too much like Poppa."

Betsy was puzzled. "How can he be a father when you don't have any children?"

"That's another secret," Esther told her. "I think I might be going to have a baby. So far, I haven't even told Ben."

Betsy's interest perked up. "That's something else I want to ask you about. How do you get a baby?"

Esther blushed. "You really ought to ask Momma about that."

Betsy rolled her eyes toward the ceiling. "When I ask her anything like that, she gets redder than you do and tells me that there is plenty of time for me to find out after I'm married."

Esther knew that what Betsy said was true. She had never been able to get even the basics out of her mother before her marriage.

"Well, it's awfully hard to talk about," she told her sister.

"Then how am I ever going to know anything," Betsy wailed. "Poppa is already talking about me getting married, and here I am not knowing anything about what I'm supposed to do."

Esther pressed her lips together in determination. "All right, I guess it's up to me to tell you. Do you know where babies come from?"

"Kinda," Betsy admitted. "I wasn't supposed to, but once I watched Blackie have kittens. Do babies come the same way?"

"Yes," Esther admitted. She was relieved to find out that Betsy knew as much as that. It would save having to make some delicate explanations.

"But what I don't understand, is how the baby gets inside of you."

"It grows there," Esther said evasively.

"How come it don't start growing until you get married?"

"Well, it can't start growing until your husband plants the seed inside of you."

"How does he do that?"

Again, Esther blushed. This was the detail she had been dreading. But she gritted her teeth and plunged on, determined that Betsy would be better prepared for marriage than she had been.

"You've seen your baby brother without any clothes on, haven't you?"

"Sure, I've helped Momma with Joe E."

"Remember that little thing that boys have?" Esther held

up her little finger so Betsy could not help knowing what she was talking about.

Betsy's eyes went wide with astonishment. "You mean what they wee wee out of?"

Esther nodded. Her own eyes had grown large because of the enormity of the communication that was passing between her and her sister.

"Your husband puts it inside of you and the seed runs out and a baby starts growing," she said.

"Don't it hurt?" Betsy asked.

"It did at first," Esther admitted.

Betsy's face was a study in incredulity. But she realized that she was learning things that would set her apart from all the girls she went to school with when they entered the world of adulthood.

"You don't have a baby. Has Ben done that to you yet?"

"Oh, sure," Esther said with a nervous laugh. "He does it almost every night."

Again, Betsy's face showed her surprise. Just when she thought she had learned all there was to know, here was a whole new dimension added to the picture.

"Why?" she asked.

"Men like it. Ben says it feels good."

Betsy made a wry face. "Do you mean that if I marry Josh Gardner, he's going to expect to do that to me? Every night?"

Esther nodded.

"And I'm supposed to let him?"

Esther nodded.

"Even if it hurts?"

"It only hurts at first. Later you get so you don't mind it, except sometimes when you are tired and want to sleep."

"I don't think I would have to worry about Josh doing something like that. He don't even like to be around me."

"Why, Betsy, why do you say that? I'm sure Josh likes you very much. After all you are a very attractive girl."

"Like today. I could hardly get him to talk to me," Betsy explained.

"He's just shy."

"All he wants to do in hang around Poppa and the grownups"

"Josh is very young, Honey. It's going to take a while for him to grow up. Right now, the approval of adults is very important to him."

"And when he does say something, it's about farming or the weather."

"That's because he's a man," Esther explained. "Ben's like that too."

"Don't you get so bored listening to talk about tobacco, corn and other crops?"

"Sometimes, but that's just part of being married."

"I don't think I'll ever get married," Betsy declared.

"Betsy, what a terrible thing to say. You have to have a husband so you can have children."

"From what I'm hearing, I ain't sure I ever want any."

At this point, they heard a heavy tread on the stairs. Feeling guilty about their conversation, they stopped talking.

Bennet Porter, Esther's husband, appeared in the doorway.

"What you girls gossiping about?" he asked.

"Just talking," Esther said quickly, giving Betsy an imploring look not to reveal what they had been talking about.

"We were talking about Brother Gunn's sermon," Betsy said on impulse.

"I bet you can't remember a thing he said," Ben challenged.

"I can so. He talked about not suffering a witch to live, and about King Saul visiting the witch of Endor."

"I don't reckon we got any witches around here, so there's no need for you two to worry," Ben assured them.

Betsy wondered what Ben would say if she told him about her vision.

"Don't you reckon we ought to get started for home?" Esther asked.

"That's how come I'm up here--looking for you," Ben answered.

Esther arose from the bed. "I'll gather up my things," she said as she shoved Ben out the door and got him started down the steps.

When he was beyond hearing, she turned to Betsy and whispered, "Now remember, give Josh some time and he'll turn out all right. He's a fine boy, and he comes from a good family. They've got good land and have a fine reputation in the community. Just remember, you could do a lot worse than Josh Gardner."

Five minutes later Betsy was alone.

4

THE SECOND VISION

From her room Betsy could hear Esther and Ben taking leave of the family, and shortly afterwards, she heard the clop of the horses' hooves on the driveway. By the time the buggy reached the road, the sun was setting, and a long twilight was descending. Except for occasional laughter from the remaining guests, the house was quiet. The room was growing darker, but she did not light a candle. It had been a long day, and she had many things to think about. The revelations from Esther about sex and marriage had been quite disturbing. She needed time to sort out her feelings. She tried to imagine Josh planting his seed inside her. She still had no clear idea of how it was done, but the thought filled her with a vague disgust. Her father's praise of Josh as a suitor and her sister's approbation of Josh as Betsy's future husband failed to make a difference in the way Betsy thought about him. In her eyes Josh was an awkward lout. She didn't like the way he smelled, talked or acted.

She found the idea of human mating, as she had learned it from Esther, to be deeply disturbing. She was repulsed by the thought of Josh doing something like that with her. She could just barely imagine Esther and Ben or Jesse and Martha mating. But it was almost impossible to think that such things could take place with people like Reverend Gunn and Mrs. Gunn. Even Betsy's most vivid imagination could not conjure up a picture of such ridiculous indignity.

A more disturbing thought occurred to her. Mating intimacy must have occurred between her mother and father. The thought made her ill. In her eyes her mother was a saint, and mating could have happened only as a result of her father's aggression. That, she believed, would explain her mother's timid disposition. Betsy had always been in awe of her father and dreaded his displeasure. But now, for the first time, she felt resentment and anger.

Betsy's mother called from the foot of the stairs breaking Betsy's train of thought.

"Betsy, are you coming down for supper?"

"No, please, Momma, I'm still stuffed from dinner."

"Very well, Dear," her mother said.

Betsy closed her eyes and tried to sleep. It would not come, so she thought back on Reverend Gunn's sermon, and she thought about the vision she had experienced yesterday.

She attempted to compare her vision with what Reverend Gunn had said about witchcraft. As she understood the Reverend Gunn's sermon, the sin of witchcraft had to do with the attempt to foresee the future. Her vision had nothing to do with the future, and she had certainly raised no dead spirits to learn about the future.

She began to doze off. Suddenly she was looking into a strange room. She had never seen a room exactly like it before. It looked like an ordinary bedroom, but somehow it was different. She could not tell exactly how it was different.

It seemed that she was looking down from one corner of the ceiling. The room contained a bed, a straight-backed chair, and a china wash basin standing on a small table beside a matching ewer. There was also a plain dresser and above that, a mirror on the wall. The room was dark, lit by a single candle. A man stood in front of the dresser reading a letter by the light of the candle. His back was too her, but she could see his face in the mirror. He was slight of stature and only a few inches taller than her own five feet four inches. But his body was well proportioned. His hair seemed to be brown and slightly wavy. The face would have

30

been ordinary if it had not been for the eyes. In the candlelight she could not be sure of the color of those eyes, but they were dark and brooding. For the moment, he was obviously angry. He suddenly crumpled the letter he had been reading and flung it across the room. He pounded the surface of the dresser with a clinched fist.

"Damn it to hell!" he almost shouted. "That sanctimonious old windbag."

Now he looked into the eyes staring back at him from the mirror.

"It's all your fault!" he exclaimed. "You have to show them all how clever you really are."

He seemed to reach a decision. Turning from the dresser, he looked about the room. He went to a dark corner and returned with a canvas bag. He started filling the bag with clothes taken from the drawers in the dresser. Only once did he stop. Pointing a finger at the reflection in the mirror, he said, "Remember, Lad, from now on you are a proper gentleman and a most devout churchman."

The vision was gone as suddenly as it came. Betsy now saw only the darkness above her head. She quickly left the bed and went to the window. She heard the usual night noises, and a lone wolf howled down in the woods beyond the pasture. Its cry was long and mournful. Nanny had once told her that when a lone wolf howled, somebody in the community was going to die. She shuddered. Again, she was certain that she had seen something that was actually happening. Every detail had been vivid. But this vision was different from her first one. In the first she had seen her father less than a mile from home. This time she was sure that she had been looking upon a scene many miles away. Although the young man in the vision seemed somehow familiar, she was certain that she had never seen him before. In her first vision, Betsy had known what was in the package her father carried. But in the second, she had no idea of the contents of the letter the young man had been reading.

31

Neither could she imagine what he was referring to in the few words he had spoken.

"Anyway, it had nothing to do with the future," she told herself. She finally went to sleep.

A few days after Betsy's second vision, a violent thunderstorm struck the area. Rain poured by the buckets and several lightning bolts struck near the house. One bolt split off the fork of a large pear tree so that it fell against the north side of the house. The bolt left smoke and an acrid odor that reminded Betsy of Brother Gunn's description of fire and brimstone that burned in hell for sinners.

But the storm did no real damage. The rain revived thirsty tobacco plants, and it cooled off the atmosphere by a good twenty degrees. Instead of hovering above one hundred, temperatures now ranged in the tolerable eighties. The cooler weather was a great blessing for the slaves since it was nearing the time to cut tobacco. Barns were emptied and bare earthen floors swept clean. Scaffoldings were erected, and sticks for hanging the plants were hauled out to the fields.

Soon all preparations for tobacco harvesting had been made and the slaves returned to their regular chores while waiting for the plants to take on the yellow speckling that marked fully ripe tobacco.

The rain slowed the ripening process, and two full weeks passed before John Bell judged the crop ready for harvest. Once John Bell gave the word, the slaves, armed with tobacco knives, moved into the fields and began harvesting.

John Bell was everywhere, spurring his mare into a fast lope as he moved from field to barn, watching every phase of the operation with a critical eye, and shouting instructions to his sons who were in charge of the field hands.

Cooler weather brought pleasant days for Betsy. Since the house work was done by the slaves, there was little for her to do except pursue her own pleasures. School would start in the middle of September. Her school dresses were ready, and she would use school books handed down by her brothers. Eventually she got bored and got permission to spend a week with Esther. The visit was pleasant. They did not renew the subject on sex and marriage.

The day after returning home, she was summoned to the front room by her father. She found him seated in his rocking chair with an open Bible in his hand. Her mother was seated across the hearth. There was no fire, but the habit of sitting in front of the fireplace was too strong to be broken, even in hot weather. Her mother pretended to be busy with her knitting, but Betsy knew that she was uncomfortable with the coming discussion. Betsy took the chair indicated by her father who noisily cleared his throat before starting.

"Well, Elizabeth, did you have a good visit with your sister?"

"Yes, Poppa," she answered, keeping her eyes firmly fixed on her hands folded in her lap.

"Is Esther well?" her mother interrupted.

"Yes, Momma."

She refrained from mentioning Esther's earlier expectation of having a baby since that expectation had proved to be false. Esther had asked Betsy to say nothing about it.

"Well, Elizabeth," her father now asked, "how old are you?"

"Almost twelve," Betsy told him.

John Bell looked at his wife and smiled. "Well, Mother, I would say that twelve is old enough for a young lady to start keeping company, provided the visits are well chaperoned."

Betsy looked up, shock and fear in her face. Her eyes appealed to her mother, but her mother refused to look in her direction.

"Very well, John," her mother said in a low voice, "if you think so."

Now Betsy realized that her father was looking at her, and she dropped her eyes back to her lap.

"Elizabeth, young Josh Gardner came to see me today," he said as if he were about to bestow a great favor upon Betsy.

"He asked my permission to call on you. He assured me that

his intentions are entirely honorable. He seems to be a most dependable young man, and I would say that his prospects are promising. I gave my permission with certain understandings. I want to outline those to you: He is to call on you only on Sunday afternoons. You are not to meet clandestinely, and of course you must both understand that you cannot expect to marry until you are at least fifteen years old. At that time, marriage will be a matter for you to decide, though I can't imagine you finding a more suitable young man."

While her father had talked, Betsy's panic had turned to anger. Her own father was willing to turn her over to Josh Gardner for the kind of treatment that Bennett Porter was forcing on her poor sister. She wanted to stand up and shout, "How dare you."

Instead she kept her eyes glued to her folded hands.

"Do you fully understand my conditions, Elizabeth?" her father asked.

"Yes, Poppa," she answered without raising her eyes.

"Very well, young Joshua will accompany us to church next Sunday. After the service he can come home with us for dinner. Your mother will arrange for you to entertain him here in the front room. Your mother or one of your brothers will be your chaperon."

"Yes, Poppa," she said as she stood up to leave the room.

"And Elizabeth," her father called after her, "I suggest that you read the thirty first chapter of Proverbs. I think you will find it most instructive."

"Yes, Poppa."

Sunday was only two days away. It was barely time to prepare the house for a visitor. In the flurry of activity, Betsy was reminded of the preparations that had preceded Bennett Porter's visits to court Esther. The front room was scrubbed from floor to ceiling. Dresses were ironed-- the white one for Sunday Service and a blue one for the afternoon.

"Be sure to go to your room to change just as soon as you have dinner on Sunday," her mother advised. "A young girl is never more attractive than when she has on a freshly ironed and starched dress. Oh, and be sure to keep your bonnet on while you are in the sun."

Betsy took the opportunity to protest. "Momma, why do I have to keep company?"

"Because every young girl has to sooner or later, Dear." her mother said.

"Well, couldn't it be later?" Betsy asked.

But her mother was no longer listening. She was hurrying out to Nanny's kitchen to discuss the menu for Sunday dinner.

Just at that moment, Richard William came through the room. Casting a sidelong glance at his sister, he fought to suppress a giggle.

Betsy whirled on him. "You say just one word, and I'll tell Poppa," she threatened.

Richard William beat a hasty retreat, but once beyond the room Betsy heard the giggle bursting through his restraints. She flopped down in her mother's rocker. Large salty tears streaked her cheeks.

Josh met them at the same place he had on the previous Sunday. This time he hitched his horse behind the surrey and crowded in beside Betsy. As the Bell surrey came wheeling into the church yard with the horses at a brisk trot, there was not a soul that failed to notice Josh Gardner seated beside Betsy. From that moment on the exact nature of their understanding was the sole topic of conversation. Betsy saw the knowing looks and could have died of embarrassment.

As though to forestall the necessity of answering questions, all the Bell family entered the church on arrival, and by the time Mrs. Broadberry started to thump on the piano to summon the faithful only the Blacks were outside to answer her call. Those who had pews near the Bells were the envy of all. Later they were able to report that Josh sat next to Betsy and tried to share the same hymnal--a gesture that Betsy refused to cooperate with.

That morning Reverend Thomas Gunn announced that on account of a special request, he was changing his sermon. He then proceeded to read and discuss the thirty-first chapter of Proverbs, and Betsy knew that her father had talked to him about her keeping company with Josh. As far as Betsy was concerned, it was a day of humiliation, disappointment and shame. Her new relationship with Josh had been practically shouted from the rooftops.

Brother Thomas also informed the congregation that the opening of school had been indefinitely postponed. According to Brother Thomas, the school teacher, professor Pendleton, would be dealing with family matters due to the death of his father and would be tied up for most of the coming winter. The School Board (which included Betsy`s father) would have to advertise for a suitable replacement teacher, and school would open just as soon as a suitable candidate was found. The news was another severe disappointment to Betsy. She was a good student and found school stimulating and a welcome break from the routine of farm life.

That afternoon she and Josh occupied the front room while her mother sat by the window tending to her knitting and pretending not to notice what the young people were doing. Josh had not improved on his ability to carry on an interesting conversation. He talked at length about his tobacco, and his plans for cutting and curing it. Three times he explained why buying a mule was a wise investment. He explained that when he had his own animal, he would no longer be dependent using his father's mule to do his plowing and planting. Soon, Betsy was so bored and sleepy that she could have died. She yawned and looked out the window. Josh seemed oblivious to her boredom. The minutes dragged by like hours. Finally, as the sun neared the horizon, Josh announced that it was time for him to start for home.

The next five days flew by swiftly. She dreaded the coming

Sunday. It seemed to Betsy that Monday came and suddenly it was Friday. At least she was not having any more visions. Time and boredom erased the vividness of her past visions, and some of her anxiety over the possibility of being a witch diminished.

⁂

On Friday afternoon Betsy was working on her crocheting under the supervision of her mother. Suddenly there was a firm knock at the front door.

"Would you mind seeing who that is, Dear," her mother asked. "My lap is full, and Nanny is out back."

"Yes, Momma," Betsy said as she laid aside her crocheting.

There was a second rap, this time more insistent. Betsy ran out of the room and down the hall. She opened the door expecting to see one of their neighbors.

The young man standing on the porch was a stranger. While awaiting an answer to his knock he had been watching the slaves at work in the field across the road, and his back was to Betsy as she opened the door. When he turned to face her, Betsy could feel the blood drain from her face. Her eyes went wide, and she caught her breath.

"Oh, hello," the young man said, "I wonder if you could tell me where I could find John Bell?"

Betsy saw that he smiled with his eyes as well as his mouth. Looking beyond the man, she saw her father riding toward the gate that opened onto the road. She pointed dumbly.

The visitor looked in the direction she was pointing.

"The one on the horse, that's Mr. Bell?" he asked.

Betsy nodded. She could not trust herself to speak.

"Well, thank you. I'll catch him down on the road."

The young man jumped nimbly from the porch and untied the horse he had been riding. As he spurred the horse into a fast lope, Betsy watched in fascinated horror.

"That was him," she said aloud to herself. "He was the one I saw in my vision."

"Who was it, Dear?" her mother asked as Betsey returned dazed to the front room.

"Just somebody looking for Poppa." she said. She retrieved her crocheting.

5

THE NEW TEACHER

After Betsy had pointed out her father to the young man, he rode out to meet him. The two riders met in the road and eyed each other with frank curiosity.

"You're Squire Bell?" the young man asked.

"That is correct," Bell said as he continued to stare at the stranger.

"My name is Richard Powell," the young man said. "I have been told that you are the person to see about the position advertised in the paper."

He drew a clipping from his pocket and offered it to Bell. The older man waved it away.

"I happen to be chairman of the board for our little school and am its largest supporter," Bell admitted.

Until that moment, John Bell's stare had been direct, almost to the point of rudeness, but like many of his mannerisms, it failed to convey his true impression. His impression of the visitor was favorable. He had the bearing and manner of a gentleman. He was young but seemed mature. Bell was sure he would make a favorable impression on the people in the community.

"And we are looking for a teacher," Bell added.

"I wonder if I might be considered for the position?" Richard asked.

"Would you like to come up to the house where we can discuss the matter in comfort?" Bell asked.

In the front room, Betsy had positioned herself so she could watch the road through the front window. The stranger and her father stood in the road talking for perhaps ten minutes. They started toward the house.

Betsy suddenly laid aside her crocheting. "Momma, I'm not feeling well. Would you mind if I went to my room?"

Lucy looked up with alarm. Betsy had been acting strange for over a month. Now her face was pale, and her eyes had the look of a frightened rabbit.

"Go ahead, Dear. Perhaps you need a short nap."

Betsy almost flew from the room, and Lucy could hear her feet as she ran up the stairs. Lucy was worried. She remembered that her oldest daughter, Esther, had started her periods when she was only a little older than Betsy was now. So perhaps it was just the vapors that now bothered Betsy. But still that did not explain how Betsy had known in advance about the dress material that John had purchased. How on earth had the child known? John swore that he bought the material on impulse and had not mentioned it to anyone. Still, John was forgetful, and perhaps he had forgotten that he had said something to somebody. In the small community, the news of such an expensive purchase would spread like wildfire, and Betsy could have possibly gotten the news from someone in advance.

If that was not the case, then there was cause for alarm. Lucy could not help but wonder if someone might have put a hex on her daughter subjecting her to the control of an evil spirit. Lucy knew that she should not be thinking of these things. Her religious and cultural upbringing obliged her to reject any kind of belief in the "dark forces." But she had lived all her life around Blacks and had absorbed many of their beliefs and superstitions. She was certain that Blacks knew things that White people were not aware of. If the Negro was only a generation removed from a primitive culture, the White man had not progressed much further. Because of Lucy's worry about her daughter, she resolved to have a talk with Nanny.

While she indulged her concerns, the door opened, and John Bell ushered an attractive young man into the room.

"This is Mrs. Bell," he told the young man. "Mother, this is Professor Richard Powell. He is here to discuss the possibility of teaching in our little school."

Had Richard Powell known his host better, he would have known that he already had the job if he wanted it. In bestowing the title of "professor," Bell had unwittingly revealed the way his mind was working.

Richard bowed low over Lucy's hand. "I'm honored, Madam," he murmured.

Lucy Bell looked at him closely. Such manners. She had not seen such manners since she had left North Carolina. Now Lucy realized that Betsy must have seen him when she answered the door and wondered if his presence may have had a bearing on the way her daughter had just behaved.

She quickly gathered her crocheting, and making apologies started to leave the room. Her husband called after her.

"Mother, I think you can count on Professor Powell being our guest for supper."

"Oh, no!" Richard said hastily. "I could not impose."

"Nonsense," John Bell countered. "A guest is no imposition. Nanny would have to cook supper whether you stayed or not. Besides, if you plan to be our new instructor, it will give you the opportunity to get acquainted with your patrons."

"Well..." Richard hesitated. As a matter of fact, he had no idea where his next meal was coming from. It would be foolhardy to protest too much.

The two men continued talking alone in the front room. John Bell went to some pains to describe the position the Board had to offer.

"We are a community of simple farm people, Professor Powell," John Bell said. "Not all see the advantages of education. As for myself, I had only the rudiments of learning. But, with no thought of boasting, I have done very well by my family. I must say that I am largely responsible for the little school we have. I

41

donated the land and supplied the timber for the building. My slaves did most of the construction. The building is modest, but adequate for our needs. I would guess that you will have up to fifteen students for the coming session. Each parent makes a donation toward the support of the school. That with my own donation should give you an income of nearly two hundred dollars."

"And how long is the school term?" Richard asked.

"We usually run the school for five months," Bell told him.

The salary was a little better than Richard had expected. By careful saving, he should have enough money to be in Natchez by early spring to get a start in that city.

"It seems satisfactory," he said.

"There is one matter," Bell said. "Do you object to providing instruction to young females?"

Richard wondered how he was expected to answer that question. He decided to hedge. "I haven't given the matter much thought," he said.

John Bell hastened to explain. "I am aware that many scholars feel that instruction is wasted on women and that it may even give them dangerous notions of equality with men. But I must say that my own experience causes me to question those scholars. As it so happens, Mrs. Bell was educated by her family, and a more obedient wife you could never find. In fact, it was she who urged me to establish our little school. All my sons have matriculated there, and my youngest daughter will be one of your students. According to our last instructor, she is an apt scholar."

Now on sure ground, Richard hastened to emphasize his agreement. "As it so happens, my mother also had the advantage of an education. It was she who first taught me my alphabet."

John Bell had long made up his mind to hire Richard Powell. The two men continued their conversation until dusk made it necessary to light the candles.

Up in her room, Betsy lit her own candle while thinking about the stranger. A part of her wanted to go downstairs and meet him. His popping up at the door like that had scared the wits out of her, but at first glance she had seen that he was different from all the other men she knew. When she watched him mount his horse, he had shown the grace and poise of a dancer. Other men plodded along with a flat-footed gait that seemed to anchor them to the soil they cultivated. His smile had radiated warmth and good humor. He must be terribly old, but she knew that she would like him.

On the other hand, his sudden appearance was a vivid reminder of the terrible power that had been thrust upon her. She had comforted herself that her visions were of no serious consequence. But now the sudden appearance of the man, after seeing him in her vision, seemed to indicate somehow that she had the power to see the future. It was the kind of power that witches had. It was the kind of power that would damn her to hell. The Bible plainly said so. It was all so unjust. She had not sought the power. She did not know when the visions would appear. What would all this eventually lead to?

While fearfully pondering her dilemma, her father called to her from the bottom of the stairs. "Elizabeth, come here. I want you to meet your new schoolteacher."

She trembled with dread, but years of training robbed her of any will to resist the commands of her father no matter how much she wanted to.

"Yes, Poppa," she answered.

Her father introduced her to the stranger. The stranger's name was Richard Powell. She liked the name, and now as everyone sat around the supper table she and her family were entertained by Richard's stories. He was the most entertaining guest she could remember. Her father liked his stories, and her mother positively glowed from Richard's attention. Betsy remained an entertained observer and did not speak.

"So, you are Elizabeth?" Richard Powell acknowledged after her father's introduction.

She had merely nodded, not trusting herself to speak or even meet his gaze. He made no further effort do draw her out.

It hardly occurred to her that she would have daily contact with him at some point if he was going to be her new teacher. He seemed to have a way of making the world less drab. After supper, Betsy returned to her room in an almost euphoric state.

Noting the lateness of the hour, John Bell suggested the new schoolteacher stay the night and get an early start in the morning.

After a token resistance, Richard allowed himself to be persuaded. He was given a bed in the room across the hall from Betsy that was normally occupied by Richard William and little Joe E. The two young boys were moved to a pallet on the floor so the guest could have the bed to himself.

The boys had long been asleep, as Richard lay in bed thinking. Much had happened quickly. His mind raced both forward and backward. The coming school year had little to do with his plans for the future. This was to be no more than a temporary stop on the road he hoped to travel.

He was a city man, and the bigger the city the better. But the next five months were essential to the realization of his plans, and he would need to make the most of the time. Teaching was one occupation he had never tried, but he resolved to do his best. The experience might even be pleasant, especially since Elizabeth was attractive and would make a drab school room tolerable.

Five months in the wilds of Robertson County would give him time to escape his past and replenish his wallet. Now, he was six weeks beyond his twenty-sixth birthday. He had been born in Cobleskill, New York, where his parents were appearing in the local theater as members of a cast of a traveling variety show.

His father had been a noted ventriloquist much in demand by the traveling variety shows that had been popular at the time. His mother was well educated for the times, and she had supervised his education while he was a child. He had learned the alphabet by the time he was four and able to read simple sentences by the age of five. According to his father, his mother had come from a good family. Richard was certain that his mother had forsaken a secure and pampered life to follow the man she loved. She had never regretted it. Richard's fondest dream was to find such a woman for himself when he married.

As Richard grew older his father tried to train him to take his place in the theater. The idea was abandoned when it became clear that he had no great talent as a ventriloquist or as any other kind of theatrical entertainer.

Deciding that Richard had a limited future in the theater the elder Powell packed him off to boarding school.

"If he can't be a performer he might as well become a scholar" Richard Powell Sr. had announced.

Richard was orphaned at the age of eighteen when his parents died in a cholera epidemic while on tour in the Northwest.

Fortunately, the school they sent Richard to was good one. By the time he had graduated, Richard had a better than average education. Still, Richard figured that he had learned most of what he knew about life from his parents and his association with fellow show people.

The show people with whom Richard associated were often uneducated and often outcasts from "decent" society. But they possessed a wisdom as old and as sophisticated as that possessed by the builders of the ancient Pyramids. They were wiser and more cultured than many who scorned them. Often necessity made them keen observers of humanity and forced them to know the foibles of the human mind. "Ordinary" folks saw these show people as unwholesome and of dubious character. But Richard had found them to be kind and gentle human beings.

By nature, Richard was good natured, and most people considered him likable and outgoing. Through his association with show people, he acquired the gift of gab, a bounding self-confidence and the ability to present himself to others in a favorable light.

Upon leaving school he found it easy to get a job. A fast learner, he could soon do any task his employer set before him. He professed to be a "free thinker," and with the uncompromising principles of youth, he refused to associate himself with the hypocrites of the times—those holier-than-thou "decent" people who attended churches.

Unfortunately, it was a time in American history when many people where suspicious and dismissive of theater people, and many upstanding citizens considered theater people to be not much above charlatans and prostitutes. Church attendance was often the proof of a man's moral fiber, and employers felt that the private lives of employees were legitimate concerns for their businesses.

At first, Richard had taken no great pains to hide his past from friends and acquaintances. He had been proud of his association with show people, and he would occasionally entertain his friends with a bit of amateur ventriloquism and other performing tricks he had learned from his association with show people. He did not hesitate to expound on his philosophy as a free thinker which at times included anti-religious sentiments.

These views were often unpopular in conservative society and often inimical to gainful employment. After losing a couple of jobs in this manner, Richard became more circumspect about revealing his past and philosophy to others. He continued trying to fit into society beyond the theater.

Still, his past seemed to have a way of catching up with him.

He had obtained a good job in Louisville, Kentucky, as a bank accountant, and he had been working there for less than six months when a customer recognized him as "that actor fellow" who had been dismissed from a commercial firm in another city.

The exposure created a furor. With visions of dark plots and missing funds, the bank president immediately held an investigation.

The investigation failed to turn up any irregularities, and the head teller of the bank, who had hired Richard, testified that Richard was a conscientious and hard-working employee. Nevertheless, the bank president was convinced that he had nipped some nefarious scheme in the bud, and even if Richard were innocent of all potential guilt, the bank could not be seen as the employer of a man who had such an unsavory background. The bank fired Richard and reprimanded the head teller who had hired him.

The dismissal was crushing. Even worse, Richard's engagement to a girl of a good family was terminated because of the scandal.

The last straw was the letter Richard received from his fiancée's father terminating the engagement and alluding to Richard's unsavory character. Richard flung the letter away in disgust and railed against the injustice. For the first time in his life Richard hated his fellow man. He looked at himself in the mirror and swore to himself that he would fight back. He swore that he would go so far away that his past could never catch up to him. He swore that he would play the game of deceit and hypocrisy and that he would even join the hypocrites in church when necessary.

So, Richard left Louisville, intending to relocate in some city far away where his past would never be known. He decided to go to Natchez, Mississippi, where he had heard there was a demand for bright young men to be clerks in the numerous commercial cotton-shipping companies.

His immediate problem was lack of money. Having expected to marry into money, he had spent recklessly to impress his fiancée and her family. Now the only money in his pocket was his last week's salary. By the time he reached Nashville, he realized he would have to find a job and work long enough to finance the remainder of his trip. He spent a penny for a paper and read the advertisements. Nothing was promising. Then in the stagecoach office he found a discarded copy of a Springfield paper and saw the advertisement of the Adam's school board for a teacher. He had no idea where either Springfield or Adams were located. After making inquiries, he took an afternoon stagecoach, making an overnight dusty trip to Springfield. He spent the last of his money to rent a horse and made his way along a maze of country lanes to Adams. He arrived at the Bell home on Friday afternoon.

6

SETTLING IN

After spending the night at the Bell house, Richard now faced a number of problems in light of his new appointment as the local schoolteacher. The most pressing problem was getting his rented horse back to the livery stable before he could be charged extra rental. The next most pressing thing was his total lack of funds. He guessed that it would be more than a month before he got his first pay. In the meantime, he needed a place to stay, and he had to get the schoolhouse ready for the new term. It all seemed an impossible task.

Fortunately, Lucy Bell guessed that he might need help.

"I do believe that was a livery stable horse that Professor Powell was riding," she said to her husband as they were getting dressed the following morning.

"I would hope so," John Bell responded. "Even Elizabeth would not buy an animal in that condition."

"Then he should return it to the stable before the rental bankrupts him," Lucy continued.

"Is there any reason he can't return it today?" John Bell asked.

"No, except if he returns the horse, he has no way of getting back here from Springfield"

"Is that my concern?" Bell asked.

"Yes," Lucy answered.

John was startled. Lucy rarely took issue with his

observations and opinions, but when she did, she would not allow him a moment's peace until he allowed her to have her way. Today he was in no mood for argument.

"What do you think I should do?" he asked Lucy.

"Loan him your saddle mare. He can lead the rented horse into town, deliver it to the livery stable, and ride back home."

"I was planning to ride over to Drewry's," John Bell grumbled.

"The walk will do you good," Lucy said primly.

"I suppose I could put it off 'til Monday," he conceded.

Richard had spent a good part of the night worrying about how he was going to return the horse back to the livery stable. When Bell offered him the loan of his saddle mare, he was too relieved to even put up a token protest. As he rode out of the stable lot on John Bell's mare, leading the rental horse, he saw Betsy leave the house heading to intercept him at the gate. He reined in the mare at the gate and looked at Betsy. After Betsy's muteness last night, he was not sure she could talk. But judging from her smiles over his entertaining stories, he knew that she could hear well enough.

"Good morning, Elizabeth," he said as she reached the gate. She stood by the gate staring at his face.

"They're blue," she finally said.

He looked about puzzled. "What's blue?" he asked.

"Your eyes," she answered. "It's the first time I've seen them in good light."

"Yes, I guess they are blue," he said. "Anyway, it's good to know that you can talk."

"Of course, I can talk. What made you think I couldn't?"

"Until just now, you haven't spoken a word since I've been here."

"Everyone else has been so busy talking I haven't had a chance," she said primly.

"Well, it's nice to hear your voice," he said. "Now could I get you to open the gate?"

She unchained the gate and allowed it to swing open but continued to block his way. Reaching into her apron pocket, she drew out a silver dollar.

"Momma said to give you this." she held out the coin.

"I can't take your mother's money," he protested.

"You got any money?" Betsy asked.

"Certainly," he blustered.

"Show it to me," she challenged.

"I will not."

"Because you haven't got any."

Suddenly he laughed and reached for the coin.

"Your mother is right. I really can use it. Tell her I will pay it back."

"She already knows that," Betsy said as she stepped aside so he could ride through the gate.

"Bye, Elizabeth, I'll see you tonight," he called as he rode past.

She made a face.

"What's the matter now?"

"Nobody calls me Elizabeth, except Poppa."

"Oh, what do they call you?"

"Betsy."

He nodded. "I like that, all right, I'll see you tonight, Betsy"

As he turned the horse into the road leading to Springfield, he felt lighthearted knowing that Betsy was perfectly normal.

"Betsy," he said aloud to himself. "It suits her to a tee."

At about the time Richard rode out the gate, Lucy Bell went to the kitchen. She pretended to inspect the laundry, but her real motive was to have a talk with Nanny. In the years of master-slave relationship a cautious trust had grown up between the two women, and they had developed a kind of code to cover those topics that could not be discussed openly.

"Nanny, do you think Betsy looks peaked?" she said, opening up a conversation with Nanny.

Nanny interpreted Lucy's question as, "Nanny, I'm worried about Betsy."

"Looks fine to me," Nanny said without raising her eyes from the task she was performing.

Lucy heard Nanny's reply as, "I'm not sure what you are talking about."

"You don't think she's too pale?"

Nanny interpreted it as, "Haven't you noticed that she's been acting strangely."

"All white folks look pale to me."

To Lucy it was, "You are going to have to be more explicit."

"I do hope there is nothing wrong," Lucy said.

To Nanny it was, "I'm really worried, tell me what I ought to do."

"She's nothing but a chile," Nanny said.

Lucy interpreted this as, "What can you expect, letting Mr. Bell push her toward marriage at her age?"

"Mr. Bell expects so much of his children," Lucy continued.

To Nanny it came out a, "I advised against it so soon."

"A mother knows her chile best," Nanny said. To Lucy it meant, "Who else besides you can help her?"

"Joshua is a fine boy," Lucy defended. "He's going to amount to something."

"Dat Mista Richard seems like a mighty fine fellow," Nanny said, meaning that, "Richard is the one she is really interested in."

"Of course, Mr. Powell is much older than Josh," Lucy said meaning, "Mr Powell is much too old for Betsy."

"How old was Mista John when you two wuz married?" Nanny rejoined.

No translation was needed. John Bell was much older than Lucy, and that was a fact for which she had no answer.

Lucy decided that the conversation was not getting to the point she had originally intended, and her next question was direct, "Nanny is it possible that somebody has put a hex on Betsy?"

"No'am, but maybe *she* hex somebody."

Lucy was now both frightened and puzzled. "What do you mean, Nanny?"

"She ax me about visions."

"Why?"

"She didn't say why, maybe she see one."

"Did she say she saw a vision?"

"No'am"

"That's all just superstitious nonsense, anyway, Nanny," Lucy said sternly, and she changed the subject completely asking Nanny about her plans for Sunday dinner. But when she left the kitchen, she was deeply worried about Betsy.

The news that John Bell had found a teacher for the school spread quickly through the community. According to the rumors that were growing by leaps and bounds, John Bell had engaged a distinguished scholar and a graduate of Harvard. Few in the community knew where or what Harvard was, but the sound of it was impressive.

That night, when Richard returned from Springfield, he found that his standing in the community was quite high. Everyone went out of their way to be friendly. As he passed the Post Office, the Postmaster came out to tell him about Mrs. James who ran a boarding house and who would be glad to furnish him room and board providing he had no other place to stay. At the general store, the storekeeper assured him that his account would be welcome. He was amazed at how much difference could come from being a working member of the community. Within the space of a single day, all his problems had been solved.

That fall John Bell was well satisfied with the way things were going. As he rode about his plantation, he saw positive signs of progress. The area around Adams still showed many of the aspects of a frontier. It had been only 36 years since James Robertson and John Donaldson had brought the first settlers to Middle Tennessee, and even now there was Indian country not far to the west. Fortunately, those were friendly Chickasaws who had given no trouble to white settlers. Nevertheless, when Bell brought his family from North Carolina, he had traveled well-armed since outbreaks of Indian fighting were still frequent in Middle Tennessee. Even now the Creeks and Cherokees were considered a threat to the settlers.

He had bought a thousand acres, much of it fertile river-bottom land, but at the time of his arrival less than fifty acres had been cleared by the previous owner. Now, just eleven years later, he had three hundred acres available for pasture and cropping. He owned twenty slaves. Most of them were generations of the slave populations owned by the families of John and Lucy Bell. But a few of the slaves were acquired by John Bell's careful purchase.

In the early days he had worked in the field beside his slaves, and now he insisted that his sons do the same. This had nothing with democracy. Only by working beside the slaves could the master gauge their strengths and weaknesses.

Like most of the plantations in the area, the Bell plantation was almost self-sustaining. Tobacco was the cash crop, but he grew enough flax and cotton to provide most of the fiber his family and slaves needed. He grew corn and wheat to provide meal and flour. He had his own liquor still, a grist mill, a loom, a spinning wheel, a vat for tanning hides, and evaporation pans for making maple sugar. Now that the plantation was getting into shape, he began thinking about expanding his cultivable land.

Beyond the needs of the plantation, John Bell had been thinking about other activities in which he could get involved for the good of the community. He had toyed with the idea of getting into politics. Not as a candidate, however. He believed that his rudimentary education and lack of knowledge of the law closed off that avenue. But he knew that often the real power in the political arena lay behind the throne. He relished the thought of being a king maker. He told himself that he did not want power for himself, but to create opportunities for his sons, friends and neighbors. He was already someone that people could come to in time of trouble. Because of his many positions on local boards and committees, he was already a community leader. Moving up to leadership on the state and national scale seemed a natural step.

Betsy's understanding with Joshua Gardner had been a step in the right direction. He could now count the large Gardner clan among those who patronized him. Then finding Professor Powell as deftly as he had done was another stroke of good fortune that further enhanced his esteem within the community. The people in the community were still marveling over how he had managed to find such an accomplished man to be the community schoolteacher in such a short period of time.

On Saturday, John Bell rode into Adams to Mrs. James' boarding house--where Richard had taken lodging—to invite him to accompany his family to church on Sunday and after the service to come to the house for Sunday dinner.

Richard's reception at the church was enthusiastic. In the churchyard all gathered around to shake his hand and ask questions. Later the Reverend Thomas Gunn had him stand to be introduced to the entire congregation.

It was at church that Richard first learned about Betsy's understanding with Joshua Gardner. He had been thinking a lot about Betsy, and learning about Betsy's engagement to Joshua was, in a way, a vast relief. Richard knew that a man in his position would have to be a simple-minded twit to even give a whiff of getting involved with a child and a student. Betsy's engagement would make it much easier to avoid that possible scenario.

For her part, Betsy appeared to be quite happy in church. Her understanding with Joshua had imparted a new status to her. She was the envy of all the young girls, and the older women included her in their conversations. Betsy wished that her understanding was with Richard Powell instead of Josh Gardner, but she would have been less than human had she not enjoyed all the attention she was suddenly getting.

Sunday dinner at the Bell place afforded Richard the opportunity to make the acquaintance of some of the important men in the community. In addition to the Bell's sons and in-laws, he was able to talk more with Reverend Gunn. He also met Brother James Johnson who appeared to be a special friend of John Bell. Before dinner Richard had accompanied the men down to John Bell's springhouse for "refreshments."

Richard saw little of Betsy that day. She and Josh were relegated to the front room for their chaperoned courting. But from what little he did see, he had doubts about Betsy's real interest in Joshua. The boy seemed a pleasant enough fellow, considering that he was a farmer and a clod hopper. But he certainly was not the kind of man to handle a girl like Betsy.

"But this is none of your affair," Richard told himself.

In the coming week, Richard learned that being the schoolmaster entailed responsibilities far beyond the classroom. In a community with a high ratio of illiterates, he was the person many called on to read a letter and prepare replies for signature. He was expected to arbitrate disputes and serve as the community dictionary and encyclopedia. He was expected to be expert in religious matters -- each person taking it for granted that his religious views were compatible with their own. He was asked questions that ran the gamut of local concerns. Before the week was out, he had taken a cram course in tobacco culture and the day-to day problems that beset the farmer.

"Fessor, me and Ollie Dickens been arguing about how many yards of canvas we need to cover a bed ten paces long. He says we need twenty yards but seem to me like fifteen oughta do it."

"Fessor, ever since my sister moved to Philadelphia, I been wondering how you spell it."

"What I been wondering, fessor, is where did Cain in the Bible get his wife. Brother Gunn says we got no business wondering what God didn't see fit to tell us. But it seems clear to me he would have had to marry up with one of his own sisters, since t'warnt no other people on earth in them days."

Richard resisted the temptation to laugh at some of the questions that people asked him, and he wisely reminded some callers that in matters of religion their best authority was their minister, just as doctors and lawyers were better experts for medical and legal questions.

Nevertheless, Richard enjoyed being the center of community attention, but at the same time realized that he was under public scrutiny and was being tested by many in the community. He had to be careful not to upset anyone, overstep the bounds of his authority, or expound on any of his more liberal viewpoints in front of the people he met. The wisdom of that course was proven a few days later when he was visiting John Bell. John Bell complimented him on the favorable impression he was making in the community. "Brother Gunn mentioned to me last Sunday that despite your great scholarship you are also a man of becoming humility."

In the middle of October, John Bell told Richard that with the tobacco harvest nearing completion, the sons of the farmers could soon be released to attend school, and that he could expect to open school around the first of November.

Richard went down to open up the schoolhouse and inspect the place where he would be working. It was a simple building.

Inside he found the accumulated dust of the last seven months. Being orderly by nature, he set to work sweeping and dusting. Heat would come from a large open fireplace set in one end of the building. Outside he found a supply of firewood sufficient to last about half the school year.

The furnishings were extremely crude. His own chair was a straight-backed, cane-bottomed affair. After testing it out Richard knew that would be teaching from a standing position for most of the school day. For a table, there was a split log that had been smoothed as much as possible with a draw knife. Two holes bored at each end held crude legs that raised it to a proper height for writing. For the students there were only benches, and he supposed that they were expected to do their writing on slates in their laps. On one wall a previous teacher had fastened a large roofing slate that could be used as a board to illustrate particular points in the lessons for the class as a whole.

Leaving the building to air out, he went to the general store to see what might be available in the way of supplies. Paper was then much too expensive to be wasted on scribbling children, but the store had slates, slate pencils and a few textbooks that included readers, spellers, an arithmetic and an elementary geography.

After completing his preparations, he now only had to wait for the cutting, hanging and curing of the tobacco to be finished for the season.

7

BETSY ACQUIRES A
PIECE OF STRING

E arly in October Lucy Bell got a letter from Victoria Trump.
Victoria had been her closest childhood friend back in the
days when she had lived in North Carolina. The letter was
newsy, causing Lucy to recall names and incidents she had long
since forgotten. Victoria had married a Dr. Randell, and he had
recently moved to Nashville to set up practice. Now Victoria
was inviting her to come to Nashville for a long visit as soon
as possible. Lucy was highly excited about the possibility of
visiting her childhood friend. After talking with her husband,
Lucy posted a letter accepting Victoria's invitation and began
packing.

Lucy decided that taking Betsy along on the visit would do
Betsy a world of good. Since they would return home before the
start of school, there was no reason why Betsy could not come
along.

On the day of their trip to Nashville, mother and daughter
loaded two large trunks and a basket of food into the surrey.
Dean had been relieved of other duties so he could serve as their
coachman.

The distance from Adams to Nashville was approximately
fifty miles. It was considered an arduous trip, but it was not
unusual. Since the roads were dry, they wheeled along behind

a pair of fast gaited horses. Leaving at dawn, they arrived at the Randell residence just after dark.

The trip was quite an adventure for Betsy. She had been too young to remember the family trek from North Carolina. Since that time, she had been only as far as Springfield and Guthrie, Kentucky. She had never traveled as far as Nashville.

What she found most enjoyable was that the Randell's had a brood of children, including a daughter named Elvira who was the same age as Betsy's sister Esther. The two girls took an immediate liking to each other. Elvira was still unmarried, but before leaving North Carolina, she had become engaged to a local boy by the name of Calvin Sander. Their parting had been tearful, but according to Elvira, Calvin had vowed that he would come visit her in the fall. She expected him to arrive at any time. Elvira hoped to get her father's permission for them to get married so she could return with Calvin to North Carolina.

"If you can stay for a few days, you may get to meet him," she told Betsy.

But before Calvin arrived, there was an incident that was to have more impact on Betsy`s future than anyone could imagine at the time.

In Nashville, schools had already opened, and all the younger Randell children attended school each day. One afternoon while walking home from school, they stopped a few blocks away to help themselves to apples from a tree that overhung their path. The owner of the tree, a Mr. Heever, was an ill-humored man by nature and had already had trouble with other apple stealers. Seeing the Randell children picking his apples, he rushed from the house and pelted them with stones. A rock hit the youngest child hard enough to leave a bruise, but otherwise the children were not hurt. They got home in a state of high indignation, as only children can feel when they believe they have been treated badly. In their view, apples hanging over a pathway were free for the taking. Still, they dared not tell their parents about the incident. From experience they knew their parents were apt to side with an adult in any affair involving children. However, they confided in Elvira and Betsy. Both girls sympathized with the children and agreed that old Mr. Heever was a mean old man, but since there was nothing they could do, they advised the children to keep away from the tree. The matter was temporarily forgotten.

Calvin arrived a few days before Betsy and her mother were scheduled to start for home. He came in the night after the young folks had already gone to bed. With guests in the house, sleeping conditions were crowded, but Elvira and Betsy had a bed to themselves in an upstairs room with two of the younger children who had been shifted to pallets on the floor. The younger children were fast asleep, but Betsy and Elvira were still giggling and talking when they heard a horse stop in front of the house. Elvira reached out to squeeze Betsy's arm.

"Listen, there's somebody out front," she whispered.

They heard a knock at the door. They held their breaths as they heard Dr. Randell's footsteps going to answer.

"Why, Calvin, where on earth did you come from," the doctor said in a voice loud enough for the girls to plainly hear.

"It's Calvin," Elvira shrieked.

She jumped out of bed and rushed for the door in her nightgown.

"Oh, Betsy, he's here," she cried as she threw open the door. She was about to rush down the stairs when she suddenly realized that she was "not decent." She slammed the door shut as abruptly as she had opened it.

"Oh, my goodness gracious, Calvin's come all the way from North Carolina, and I'm not dressed. Oh, Betsy, where are my clothes? Please, Betsy, help me."

Betsy got out of bed and managed to get several petticoats and a dress on Elvira.

"Now you get dressed too and come on downstairs, I want you to meet him," Elvira called as she rushed from the room.

Betsy got dressed, but at a more leisurely pace. Frankly, she was puzzled over Elvira's reaction. She went down to the Randell's front room and found Elvira, Elvira's parents and her own mother gathered around a young man she guessed to be Calvin Sander. Calvin was red faced and perspiring, obviously uncomfortable with so much attention. By his side an adoring Elvira was holding tight to his hand and pleading with her father.

"Oh, please, Poppa, can we?"

An officious Doctor Randell noisily cleared his throat. "But, Elvira, honey, it takes time to make arrangements for a wedding," he said.

"We'll wait," Elvira offered. "Calvin can stay for a few weeks can't you, Calvin?"

"Well, I reckon, but Momma said for me to be sure to be home by Christmas."

"Oh my," Victoria wailed, "if you get married you won't be here for Christmas!" She burst into tears.

"Now, now, Dear," Doctor Randell said trying to soothe his wife. "Children do leave home. We have to expect it."

Elvira took her father's words as a sign that he expected to give in and allow her to get married. She jumped up and down in the floor in a frenzy of glee.

"Oh, he's going to let us, Calvin. He's going to let us get married."

Throwing caution to the wind, she threw her arms about Calvin's neck and kissed him boldly. The adults were mildly shocked.

"Ahem," Doctor Randell began, "you get control of yourself, young Lady. Nothing has been decided."

"But, Poppa, I can't let him go back to North Carolina all alone. You've got to let us get married."

From her place just inside the door, Betsy watched these demonstrations with something akin to amazement. In her estimation, Calvin was a near copy of Josh Gardner. For the life of her, she could not imagine such intense feelings as Elvira was showing. Not even Esther had acted so giddy.

Elvira suddenly caught sight of Betsy. With a startled Calvin in tow, she started in her direction.

"Calvin, Honey, this is my new friend Betsy Bell. Betsy this is Calvin, isn't he a darling?"

Calvin and Betsy eyed each other with cautious embarrassment. "Howdy, Betsy," Calvin said.

"Hello, Calvin," Betsy returned. Again, she wondered just what it was that Elvira saw in this most ordinary fellow. After a time, things settled down, and soon the grown-ups went back to bed. Elvira called Betsy aside and whispered in her ear. She intended to stay up a while longer so she could talk to Calvin. If Betsy wished, she could go back to bed.

Betsy undressed for the second time that night. As she climbed back into bed, she was trying to understand Elvira's behavior. In the time Betsy had known her, Elvira had seemed especially mature and of a most serious nature. Now all at once, she was acting worse than... than Richard William.

Betsy wondered if Elvira knew what boys did to girls after they were married. Probably not, since she seemed so intent on entering the relationship. Now she wondered if she ought to be the one to tell her. She felt almost certain that Elvira would never believe such a preposterous story. She would never have believed it herself, had she heard it from anyone except her own sister. Still with Elvira so bent on getting married, she probably did have an obligation. She felt certain that Elvira's mother would be no better than her own in such a crisis. She made up her mind that she would have a heart-to-heart talk with Elvira as soon as she came to bed. She turned to get more comfortable. From somewhere in the house, she heard the clock strike eleven, and closed her eyes for the moment. When she opened them, there was sunlight streaming into the room. Thinking that Poppa would be angry because she had lain in bed so long, she sat up quickly. Then she saw Elvira sleeping beside her and realized where she was.

Elvira slept soundly with a look of deep contentment on her face. It was still hard for Betsy to accept the way city people laid in bed until full daylight. But even at the Randell's she had never lain abed so late. Her fears were confirmed when she heard the clock strike six.

Sounds from the kitchen downstairs told her the slaves were fixing breakfast.

"Betsy, Elvira?" Betsy's mother, Lucy, was calling them. "Breakfast is ready."

Elvira merely turned in her sleep, and Betsy heard her murmur something. It sounded like she was saying Calvin's name. Betsy shook her by the shoulder.

"Elvira, you've got to wake up. It's time for breakfast."

Elvira opened her eyes and looked at Betsy. "What did you say?" she asked.

"They are calling us to breakfast."

"Oh," Elvira sat up and rubbed her eyes with her fist. Suddenly she looked at Betsy. "I didn't dream it, did I?"

As though she suddenly remembered something, Elvira jumped out of bed and turned down the covers. There was a spot of red about the size of a cherry on the bed sheet. As Elvira turned, Betsy saw a similar spot on the back of her gown. Betsy was immediately concerned. She had been present when Esther had started to have her periods, but the spots didn't look the same.

"Are you bleeding?" she asked.

Elvira now turned so that she could see the spot on her gown. "Looks like it," she said. There was a look on her face that seemed to be equal parts embarrassment and pride.

"I'll tell your mother," Betsy said as she started for the door.

Elvira hissed, "Don't you dare!"

Betsy stopped in her tracks. "But won't you need a granny rag?"

"I don't need anything. And don't you say a word about any of this."

"But, but..." Betsy sputtered now in utter confusion, "you are bleeding."

"Shut up," Elvira pleaded. "It's not what you think."

"Well, what is it?" Betsy asked.

"Look, Betsy, do you know where babies come from?"

"Of course, I do," Betsy said with some pride. "Esther told me."

64

"Well, last night, I let Calvin take certain liberties. Now father is going to have to let us get married. But of course, I don't aim to tell him unless I have to."

The effect on Betsy would not have been more dramatic had Elvira confessed to the murder of her parents. Her eyes went wide, and her face turned pale.

"You mean you let him put his seed inside you?" Her voice was a bare hoarse whisper.

Elvira laughed harshly. Betsy's lack of approval and support had suddenly made her afraid. Last night her course had seemed so clear and right. Now she wasn't so sure.

"Is that what they call it in the country?" she asked.

"What do you call it?" Betsy asked.

"Why... why...," Elvira sputtered. She really had no word to describe what she had done, or at least no word she wanted to use in front of Betsy. Her defiance quickly crumbled, and her eyes took on a mute appeal.

"Please, Betsy, please don't tell anyone. I did it because I love him so."

Betsy rushed forward and took Elvira in her arms. Looking at the spot on the bed, she asked, "How are we going to keep your mother from knowing?"

"I don't know," Elvira confessed.

"Pull the cover up for now," Betsy told her. "We'll think of something."

They went down the stairs together. That morning she was prepared to hate Calvin Sander forever. Calvin was already at the table. As the girls entered the room, he had eyes only for Elvira. He got up hastily so he could pull back her chair. Betsy had to concede that Calvin's conduct of the previous night was somewhat ameliorated by the fact that he so openly adored Elvira.

During the day, Betsy had further cause to revise her opinion of Calvin. The similarities between him and Josh were more superficial than real. He had a keen sense of humor, and once he started to feel more at home with Betsy, he was a great talker.

But the girls had other things to worry about. They took the sheet off the bed and somehow managed to wash the spot out in cold water. Then they hung it over the bed post to dry. By mid-afternoon, they were able to remake the bed and hoped that no one would be any the wiser.

When the younger children got home from school they gathered around Calvin. All seemed to talk at once as they told him of the indignity, they had suffered at the hands of ol' Mister Heever. Later Calvin agreed with Elvira and Betsy that there ought to be some way to repay Mr. Heever for being so mean to little children.

"I never heard of anyone being so stingy over a few apples," Calvin observed. "What I ought to do is let him get acquainted with Bull Whacker."

"What's a bull whacker?" Betsy asked.

Calvin looked at Elvira. "Don't folks here in Tennessee know what a bull whacker is?" he asked.

"I never heard anybody talk about it," Elvira told him.

"I never heard of it," Betsy said.

"Wait a minute and I'll show you," Calvin said.

He went to his saddle bags and searched through his belongings. He returned with a ball of string wrapped around a small wooden peg and handed it to Betsy. Betsy unwound some of the string and after the first foot, found it stiff and kind of tacky.

"That's the resin," Calvin explained.

"What do you do with it?" Betsy asked.

"I use it to scare niggers," Calvin told her.

"I don't see nothing here that would scare anybody." Betsy responded.

Again, Calvin looked at Elvira. "Do you think we could slip out tonight and go over to ol' man Heever's? Then I could show you how it works."

"I don't know," Elvira answered. "Daddy would skin me alive if he caught us doing something like that to one of our neighbors."

Suddenly she had an inspiration. "I know, tomorrow night Betsy and me are invited to a Halloween Party. I'd decided not to go because you were here, but if you'd go with us, we'd walk right past Mr. Heever's."

Halloween turned out to be a near perfect Autumn Day. All the leaves had turned, but the sun was warm enough for shirt sleeves by mid-day. Lucy Bell had intended to start for home that day, but Betsy persuaded her to stay over one more day so she could go to the party.

By the time Elvira, Betsy and Calvin left the house there was a chill in the air so that each welcomed a light wrap. The party was lively with lots of food and square dancing. Betsy was a skilled dancer and was much in demand as a partner.

They managed to slip away just before ten o'clock. A few minutes later they stood in front of the Heever house. There was a full moon, but its light had to filter through high flying clouds. Only the vaguest outline of the house could be seen among the shadows cast by the trees. There was no light, indicating that Mr. Heever had already gone to bed. The three young people stood near the gate whispering, giggling and shivering in delightful anticipation of moderate danger.

Calvin took the bull whacker out of his pocket and unwound some twenty feet of string. He coiled the string in one hand and held the wooden peg in the other.

"One of us has to sneak up to the house and stick this peg under one of the boards on the side of the house. It does better if it's up pretty high. Then we need a place where we can hide."

All three surveyed the area around the house. A rail fence ran around a yard that contained many large trees. On the side nearest the Randell place heavy shrubbery had been planted just inside the fence.

"That'll be fine," Calvin observed. "You and Elvira go hunker down while I go and wedge this peg under a board."

"No let me do it," Betsy pleaded. "I want to be sure I know how it works."

"Well, all right," Calvin agreed, "but be careful. Now make

sure you wedge it tight. Elvira and me will be over behind them bushes. Once you've got the peg in place you have to let out this string so it will reach over to where we'll be hiding."

At home Betsy had sometimes played "Settler and Indians." Unlike most children, she always wanted to be one of the Indians. In that role, she had become quite skilled at moving quietly and unobtrusively, so that she was often able to catch the "settlers" by surprise. Now she slipped through the yard gate and all but disappeared in front of Calvin and Elvira's eyes. They had barely reached the shrubbery and settled down in anticipation of stealing a kiss or two when Betsy slipped in beside them holding the end of the string.

"Boy, you did that slicker'n an Injun," Calvin said admiringly. "Did you get it stuck good and tight?"

"I shoved it as far up under the board as it would go," Betsy whispered.

Calvin pulled the string tight and tested it with little jerks. When he was satisfied that the peg was firmly anchored, he wrapped a length of the string around his left hand and pulled it tight.

"Well here goes," he whispered.

Reaching up to grasp the rosined string between the thumb and forefinger of his right hand, he drew the finger downward toward his left hand. Over beside the house, Betsy heard a faint noise like a woodpecker pecking on the shingles of a roof from far away. She looked at Calvin as if to say, 'is that all it does.'

Sensing her question, he whispered, "It sounds a heap louder inside."

He stroked the string again and waited. The house remained dark and still.

"He's just now come awake. He's lying in the bed listening and wondering what it was that caused him to wake up." Calvin whispered.

He waited for a full minute before stroking the string again. There was still no response from the house.

"He's still lying there wondering what in thunderation could be making such a racket," Calvin explained.

Again, he waited. Reaching up to grasp the string again, he said, "This time he'll jump up and light a candle."

Calvin proved to be a true prophet. No sooner had the rat-a-tat ceased when Betsy saw a candle in the window. The three held their sides in glee as they watched the light move though the house.

"He's checking every room trying to find out what could be making all that noise," Calvin chortled.

Eventually, Mr. Heever opened the front door and stepped out on his front step. Holding the candle high as he peered out into the night, he came around the house side of the house peering in every direction. Finding the yard empty, he went back inside.

"We'll give him time to get back in bed," Calvin whispered.

The light was soon extinguished. Calvin waited a bit longer then stroked the string. Now he repeated the act until Mr. Heever must have thought that a war party of savages was beating on the side of the house with tomahawks. Watching closely, Betsy made out a dim form at the window of the bedroom.

"He's looking out the window," she whispered to Calvin.

"I know," he answered.

The figure disappeared, and Calvin continued to pull on the string. For a time, it seemed that Heever had decided to ignore the assault on his senses. Then, suddenly, Betsy saw a pale figure sneaking furtively along the side of the house. She punched Calvin on the arm and pointed. He quickly unwound the string and allowed to to go slack. The three watched in fascinated terror as Heever moved about the yard like a silent shadow. He circled the trees and seemed to poke everywhere for the source of the tormenting noise. For some reason, he never thought to look among the shrubbery. Betsy and her companions held their breaths as they waited, fully expecting to be discovered and pelted with stones like the younger children. But soon Heever gave up and went back inside.

Calvin now explained his strategy to the admiring girls. "I let the string go slack so it would lie on the ground. If I'd kept it tight, he'd a been sure to run into it."

They gave Heever time to get back into bed then Calvin resumed his concert. Betsy now realized that by varying the pressure of his fingers, and the rapidity and length of the jerks, he was able to make a variety of pitches and sounds. As he gave the cord a final yank, that must have made Heever think that the house was falling in, the front door flew open and suddenly Heever was on his front step armed with a gun of ancient vintage. Pointing the gun straight up in the air, he pulled the trigger. A long streak of fire spurted from the barrel of the gun and the report echoed through the community. For the space of perhaps a full minute there was no reaction, then suddenly lights came on in every house in the neighborhood. People poured into the street with candles set behind the protective globes of lanterns. All came running toward the Heever house. One person came so close to where Betsy and her friends were hiding, that they had to remain very still to avoid notice.

"Mr. Heever, what on earth is the matter?" someone was asked.

"I don't know," they heard him answer. "Somebody is beating on the side of my house."

At first everyone crowded inside and there were lights at every window.

"Do it now," Betsy suggested.

"Naw, if they don't hear nothing or see nothing, they'll think ol' man Heever is crazy as a bed bug," Calvin giggled.

But as Calvin finished speaking, people started to pour out of the house.

"Now everybody spread out and search every inch of ground," someone shouted.

"It's time for us to get out of here," Calvin whispered. "Damn, I sure hate to lose that bull whacker. It was the best one I ever made."

"Wait here. I'll get it," Betsy whispered.

"Hey, there ain't no way on God's green earth you can get near that house without them seeing you," Calvin protested.

Betsy paid no attention. Crawling along the fence, she was lost to Calvin and Elvira's sight before she had gone six feet. When they next saw her, she was out on the street, strolling along like she had come out for a breath of fresh air. She approached the gate.

"What's all the excitement about?" she asked one of the neighbors searching in that area.

"Old man Heever says somebody has been beating on the side of his house," the neighbor explained. "Youngsters in the neighborhood playing a Halloween prank, I'd figure."

"Oh, do they have any idea who's doing it?" she asked. Then, as Calvin and Elvira watched in open-mouthed admiration, Betsy crossed the yard and went directly to the side of the house. She seemed to be looking for signs of blows on the weatherboarding. If anyone saw her pull the peg from under the board, they gave no indication.

Then, pretending to be examining the ground, she gathered up string until she came to the hiding place.

"I guess we all agree that there is nothing back here," she called loud enough for all to hear. At the same time, she was motioning for Calvin and Elvira to get to their feet. When they understood her strategy, they both stood up.

"If there's been any children in this yard, they have all gone home by now," Calvin said aloud.

"Do you suppose Mr. Heever's just hearing things?" Elvira asked as they passed through a group of neighbors.

The idea caught on quickly.

"I'd bet he's been drinking," someone said.

Slowly, but surely, the three moved among the searchers, but always in the general direction of the gate. Within five minutes they were out on the street. They were almost home before they burst into wild, insane laughter.

Early the following morning, Lucy and Betsy loaded their belongings into the surrey. Victoria had packed enough food into their basket to last for several days. Dean harnessed the horses and hitched them to the surrey. As Betsy searched through the house for anything that might have been forgotten, Calvin slipped up beside her.

"Betsy, did you give me back that bull whacker last night?"

She looked at him with wide eyed innocence. "I'm sure I did, Calvin, when we were still in the yard at Mr. Heevers."

"Darn, then I must have dropped it. I sure hate to lose that bugger."

"Can't you whittle out another one?"

"Oh, sure, but I'd never get another one that sounded as good. Man, I could almost make it play a tune."

"I'm terribly sorry, Calvin."

Lucy interrupted any further discussion. "Hurry, child, we simply must get started."

"I'm coming Momma."

The goodbyes were hasty and tearful. It was almost sunup, and they simply had to be on their way. Since Elvira would probably get married and move to North Carolina, Betsy knew that this farewell would be forever. As they drove briskly through the town Lucy chatted gaily about details of the visit. Betsy pretended to listen, but already her mind was far away. Slipping her hand inside a pocket of her cloak, her fingers came into contact with smooth wood wrapped in string. She smiled brightly at her mother.

"Yes, Momma," she murmured at some comment her mother had made.

Then she had a thought. "Do you think Doctor Randell will let Elvira and Calvin get married?"

Lucy smiled knowingly, "Oh, I think it's quite likely."

Now Betsy was thinking that things were turning out well for everyone. Calvin and Elvira were getting married, and Betsy had the marvelous bull whacker. She had no idea what she was going to do with it, or what had made her want it so much to steal it.

8

HOME AGAIN

By the time the surrey reached Goodletsville, it was obvious that they were behind schedule. Dean urged the horses to the utmost to make up for the late start, but instead of gaining, they lost even more time. Just beyond Goodletsville a piece of harness broke. Dean was able to fix it with leather from a box that John Bell always kept under a seat for just such purposes, but a critical half hour was lost. When they got back on the road, they made good time for perhaps an hour. Then the front wheel of the surrey started to wobble. After an examination, Dean told them the trouble seemed to be a loose axle nut. Because of the weight of the surrey, he was not able to lift the wheel high enough to fix it. He had to unhitch the team and search a nearby woods for timbers he could use to as levers to lift the wheel free enough off the ground before the nut could be tighten. By the time they were moving again more than an hour had been lost. A steep winding road led up out of the great Basin of Middle Tennessee to the top of the Highland Rim, and the horses had to be rested several times before reaching the top. As they came to level ground, the sun was about to set. It was obvious that they could not reach home before well after night had fallen.

Lucy was worried. Although there would be a full moon, it was still dangerous to drive at night without an out rider and lantern.

Acquaintances in Springfield would be glad to put them up for the night, but she knew

that John would be worried. Dean cracked the whip, and they passed through Greenbrier in deep twilight at a fast trot. They cleared the town and drove toward Springfield. Suddenly they saw mounted riders waiting in the road ahead. This was cause for alarm. Any horseman along the road was a potential outlaw. Having been brought up on stories about the crimes of the Harp Brothers, Betsy was frightened. Dean reined the horses to a stop and stood up in the surrey. He was a giant of a man and prepared to defend his charges with his life.

One of the housemen called out, "Dean, Momma, is that you?"

Betsy heaved a sigh of relief. The voice was that of her older brother, Zadok.

"Yes," Lucy cried, "is that you Zadok?"

"Yes, Momma, it's me and John Jr."

The reunion was joyous.

"How did you all come to be way out here?" Betsy asked.

"Where have you all been?" John Jr. asked, "Poppa has been terribly worried. He was expecting you home last night."

"Oh, Dear," Lucy said.

The story that unfolded soon made it clear why the family had been worried. Three days before, the bodies of a middle-aged woman, a young girl and a Negro male had been found on the road leading up out of the Great Basin. It was the same road that Lucy and Betsy had traveled only hours before. All evidence pointed to rape and robbery, and the blame was laid to one of the outlaw bands that sometimes roamed the roads. The bodies had been stripped of all clothing and possessions and had been mutilated beyond recognition. Word had spread and citizens deputized to hunt down the outlaws. John Bell heard about the incident but had not worried at first. But when Lucy failed to get home on Friday night, he began to worry in earnest. Taking the older boys with him, he had ridden into Springfield to make inquiries. Although the outlaws had mutilated their victims to foil recognition, both women had been too heavy to be Lucy or Betsy. Still, since his wife, daughter and Dean remained unaccounted for, John Bell sent his sons out on the road with instructions to ride as far as Nashville, if necessary, and call on the Randell's to learn the whereabouts of their mother and sister. Now greatly relieved, the boys escorted the surrey into Springfield where John had made arrangements for them to stay with friends.

John Bell was not in town when the surrey arrived. The outlaws had been captured, and he had ridden hard to reach the posse, hoping to be able to question the outlaws about his own family before they were hanged.

The two boys were bedded down in the stable, and Betsy was given a small room next to the one occupied by her mother. She awoke in the night to hear her father and mother talking. Later she learned that her father had reached the posse too late to question the outlaws and had not known the fate of his family until he had arrived back in Springfield late in the night.

The family got home shortly after noon on Monday. Betsy learned that school had started that very day. It was necessary to get things ready for her and Richard William to attend school the following day. She had little time for relaxing.

That night, while lying in bed and facing the prospect of attending school in the morning, she now allowed herself to think about her new teacher. She sensed that there was some dark mystery about him and wondered about the things she had seen in her vision. What had been in the letter to make him so angry? She could remember his exact words: "It's all your fault. You have to show them how clever you really are. Remember, Lad, from now on you are a proper gentleman and a most devout Christian."

That was the image of the man that intrigued her. What had he been if he had not been a Christian before that time?

Everyone she knew professed deep religious convictions and

mouthed Christian piety to excess. All her life she had been exposed to hell fire and brimstone. It was impossible for her not to fear it. God's eternal vengeance was as real to her as the sunrise. However, there were times when she found this image of Christianity to be repulsive. Of course, she never dared admit it even to herself.

Could Richard be different in some way from the sanctimonious Christians that Betsy had known all her life? Yet Richard professed the same beliefs and piety of the community. When called on to lead people in prayer, he used the same unctuous language as his neighbors--although she had noted that his prayers seemed to be shorter than most.

Was Richard leading a pretense? She speculated on that possibility with both fear and hope. With these thoughts in her mind, sleep finally claimed her. As she dozed off, she knew that in Richard Powell she would find someone more understanding and less intolerable to her deepest feelings—someone who would be a kindred spirit.

Betsy's arrival in school the following day caused something of a sensation. News of the murder of the travelers had spread through the community along with the fact that John Bell was worried over the possibility that Betsy and her mother might have been the victims. For her fellow students the two events had become interwoven.

Her schoolmates crowded around her asking questions.

"How were those two poor women murdered, and what did the killers look like?"

Despite Betsy's protests that she knew nothing about the murders, the questions continued until Richard Powell called the school to order.

"Well, Miss Betsy, did you have a pleasant trip?" Richard asked as he opened the Bible for the morning devotional.

"Yes, Sir," she answered meekly.

"Would you like to tell us about it?"

"We just went to visit a friend of Momma's. Somebody she knew in North Carolina," Betsy explained.

"Why won't she tell us nothing about them poor folks that got killed," her friend Tenny Porter complained.

"Perhaps she doesn't know anything about that," Richard said. "I believe that happened two days before Miss Betsy and her mother started home. Is that true, Miss Betsy?"

"Yes, Sir," Betsy said without looking up.

"So, you see Miss Betsy knows no more that we do, Miss Tenny. Now shall we read the twenty third Psalm?"

As Richard read, Betsy studied him from beneath her eyebrows. He read well, but she could tell that his reading was perfunctory.

Suddenly, out of nowhere, Betsy experienced another vision. She was suddenly looking down on a path that ran through a dark wood. She tried to brush the vision away so she could continue her study of Richard Powell's face, but it continued to intrude. It was a place she knew well. It was on her father's land, and the path ran up from the Red River. During the past summer, she had walked the path with Zadok.

She was now looking down on the very spot where Zadok had pointed out stones that marked an old Indian grave. According to Zadok, the grave had been there when the very first whites settled the area. Now she saw her father coming along the path. While she watched, he stopped and looked about, as though checking his bearings.

Then he stepped off the path and pushed aside some of the leaves with the toe of his shoe until he had uncovered the stones. Then he bent down and moved several stones about. Some he pulled to one side, others he carried out to the path and carefully stacked in a neat windrow. At last, he uncovered a large flat rock. He pulled at it, but it would not bulge. Looking about he found a large stick and using a second rock as a fulcrum, he pried up the stone. As the stone was turned up on edge, Betsy could see a grinning skull lying in a cavity lined with stones. The skull frightened neither Betsy nor her father.

77

Her father reached into the cavity and picked up the skull. As he lifted it the mandible fell away. He stood for perhaps a minute examining the remaining part of the skull then he casually cast it away. As the skull rolled to its rest among some dry leaves, Betsy could hear her school mates giggling.

"Miss Betsy, are you alright?" Richard Powell asked, and she could feel his strong hand on her shoulder.

She shook her head, more to clear her head than to provide an answer to the question. The vision was gone, and she was in the schoolhouse sitting on her bench. She gave an embarrassed little laugh.

"I was..." She could think of no way to explain what had happened to her. "I'm all right," she said.

Richard took his hand from her shoulder and walked to the front of the room. He looked at her questioningly.

"Madam Darce acted like that when she went into a trance." Richard thought to himself, remembering his time back in the theater.

That night John Bell verified the accuracy of Betsy's vision. While holding his usual pronouncements at the supper table, he turned to John Jr.

"Son, there is a little matter I would like for you to take care of tomorrow. I've noticed that the spring house needs work. I would like to lay a stone floor and line the water way with stone. Today I was back in the woods and passed by the old Indian grave. I selected some stones that appear to be ideal for our purpose. First thing in the morning, hitch old Jack to the sled, take two slaves and haul the stones down to the spring house."

Betsy heard her father's plan without looking up. Finding that her visions were accurate no longer surprised her.

Before the week was out, school had settled into a routine. There were still a few boys who had not finished with their farm work, and Richard was assured that he would have two or three additional students. One of these was Josh Gardner who showed up on Thursday. He bought a lunch basket and a speller that had been passed down by an older brother.

During recess period, Josh paid no attention to the girls, but when Richard called the school to order, Josh sat on a bench directly behind Betsy. While hearing recitations, Richard made a critical evaluation of the new student. On the whole, he seemed well behaved and well mannered, but Richard was soon convinced that he was not especially bright. For Betsy to marry him would be like hitching a racehorse to a mule.

Beyond the novelty of school, the rest of the week was uneventful. Each night at the supper table, Betsy and Richard William would be questioned about what they had learned that day. Their answers were as noncommittal as possible.

Josh paid his usual visit on Sunday. Betsy had come to enjoy the prestige of "keeping company," so she made an honest effort to entertain him. She remembered that her father had told her that the question of eventual marriage was one she would decide. She now decided that she could keep company until she was fifteen and then marry whomsoever she chose.

About an hour before sunset, Josh declared that he had to get home to help with the milking. After he was gone, Betsy went up to her room. There was still an hour of full light left, but she lay down across her bed.

She thought again about her most recent vision. Up until now all her visions had come without warning and without will. Now she wondered if she could make it happen. Since her visit to Nashville, she had heard nothing from Elvira. She wondered if she and Calvin had gotten married. She shut everything out of her mind, except Elvira and deliberately set out to conjure up a vision.

At first nothing happened. Then she thought she saw a faint

image of a forest. She concentrated, and slowly the forms took substance.

Wherever she was, the trees were enormous, and there was thick underbrush. But she was looking down on a well-traveled road. She knew that there was something disturbing about the scene, and by looking closer, she saw several men hidden behind trees. They were well armed, and she knew that they were waiting for someone. Thoroughly frightened, Betsy tried to close out the scene, but once began she could not avoid seeing the vision through to the end. She closed her eyes, but it made no difference.

Calvin and Elvira rode into view. Both were on horseback. Elvira rode sidesaddle and Calvin led a pack horse that carried two large trunks on its back. They were laughing, and Betsy knew that they had gotten married. Betsy tried to call out a warning, but she could not make a sound. There was a sudden volley of shot. Calvin fell from his saddle, dead before he hit the ground. Betsy realized that he had not even had time to be afraid. Then three men leaped from behind the trees where they had been hiding. One caught the bridle of Elvira's horse. Another started to pull her from the saddle. For as long as she would live, Betsy would remember the look of stark terror on Elvira's face. Then, mercifully, the vision was gone.

Betsy turned over on her side and drew herself into the fetal position. Her entire body trembled, but her eyes remained dry. She had no doubt, but that what she had just witnessed was God's way of punishing Elvira and Calvin for their premarital transgression.

9

SPECIAL LESSONS

R ichard Powell knew nothing about the theories of education in vogue at the time. As a consequence, he made an exceptional teacher. Most teachers thought that the only way a child could learn was through repetition. Education itself was thought to be an accumulation of factual materials stored in memory. Schools were apt to be noisy places as the children chanted their exercises in unison. That which was repeated often enough supposedly became chiseled into the marble of the brain and could never be forgotten. Preachers proved their devotion and scholarship by committing the Bible to memory, and a politician proved his fitness for office by reciting the Constitution and Declaration of Independence. Richard appealed to logic and taught his charges how to figure things out for themselves. At the time, that was a dangerous doctrine. Had those in the community known what was going on in their school, there might have been trouble.

But few in the community were fit to judge an educational program and most people were more than content when their child proved that he could read a newspaper and the Bible and was able to sign his name.

Richard's greatest handicap was a lack of printed material. Textbooks were expensive and hard to come by. Most homes had a Bible. Many of his students had learned to read from it, recognizing words like "Ezekiel" before they learned more simple words like "cat." He learned that two or three homes in the area had a copy of *Pilgrims' Progress*, and one had a collection of religious tracts. There were a couple of subscriptions to a biweekly newspaper published in Springfield.

Most people agreed with Brother Thomas Gunn who held that reading for pleasure was a form of idleness. Books that did not impart factual knowledge or improve morals were considered objectionable. The few textbooks stocked at the general store were heavily moralistic. The readers of the day were little more than religious tracts. The arithmetic text had exercises built around the calculations of Honest Tom, and the geography book spoke of the heathen "who knew not God."

Richard was perfectly aware. of the pitfalls that awaited a teacher who tried to take his students beyond the litany of religious dogma, but he wanted to try. He began to amass a small library of printed matter, riding as far as Springfield in search of some book he might buy or borrow.

As the short year progressed his students began to respond to his approach, and he wondered if teaching might be his calling. He was highly popular in the community. He was invited into homes, fed like a king, and several marriageable females had obviously set their caps at him.

Still, he was lonely. The Richard who was invited into homes was the man the community wanted him to be. He was compelled to keep his real nature hidden. He had no one to confide in, no one to laugh with, and no one who would accept him as he really was.

The one person who intrigued him was Betsy. Despite her age, Betsy was starting to fill out as a woman and was easily one of the most intelligent people he had even known. While other students poured for hours over a multiplication table, or a few lines of poetry he had asked them to memorize, Betsy would glare at it for a few minutes then turn and stare out the window, or, somewhat disturbing, she would watch his every move from beneath her heavy brows. Yet, when he called on her, her recitation was perfect. He remembered that once long ago, when his parents had traveled with a theatrical company, he had known a man who was billed as "Waldo," the man with a perfect memory. Waldo could quickly scan a newspaper then quote it word for word from memory. Betsy had some of the same talent. But he sensed that she was a deeply troubled soul. Almost from the first week of school she had been distracted and withdrawn.

Late in November the weather turned much colder. Richard now found it impossible to sit and read in his unheated bedroom. His landlady kept a roaring fire in her front room and all her guests were invited to spend their evenings before it. But the talk was loud and the laughter boisterous. Richard found the noise distracting.

It was also necessary to keep a good fire burning in the schoolhouse. He decided that he would be less disturbed if he stayed at the schoolhouse until he was ready for bed. He bought a candlestick and a supply of candles. Then as soon as school was dismissed, he would pull his chair up in front of the fire, select a book from his growing collection and read for as long as he liked.

In the community things moved at their usual pace. At a community meeting held in the schoolhouse, John Bell was appointed as a member of a delegation to go to Nashville to visit with General Andrew Jackson about the recent increase in crimes being committed on innocent travelers.

On the Friday that John Bell left with the delegation, Betsy brought Richard a note. It had been folded and sealed with sealing wax. "Professor Powell" was written on the outside in a woman's handwriting.

He had no opportunity to read the contents until school had been dismissed for the day. He then pulled his chair up to the fire, took the note from his pocket and read: "Dear Professor Powell, I feel that I must talk to you in private. I am deeply worried about Betsy and believe that you may be the only one who can help her. I will be able to receive you at any time within the next week. Betsy does not know of the contents of this letter. Please do not let her know of my concern. Sincerely, Lucy Bell."

Richard carefully burned the note in the fire then sat for a time by the fire in deep thought.

It was a most unusual letter, and only great distress could have caused Lucy Bell to write it. He realized that she had asked for him to call during a time that coincided with John Bell's absence which implied that she wanted to keep the matter from him as well as Betsy. Should such a thing become known in the community, it would have reflected badly on Lucy Bell's reputation. After reflection he prepared his reply: "Dear Madam, having received your letter, I will call at your house at nine o'clock on Wednesday evening. Respectfully, Richard Powell."

He sent his reply home with Betsy on Monday afternoon. On Wednesday morning Betsy arrived at school with a valise of clothing. In answer to his question, she told him that her mother had given her permission to go spend the night with Tenny Porter.

At the appointed hour he rode up the drive to the Bell place noting that the only light coming from the Bell house was from the front room. Lucy answered his knock, and he was ushered into the front room.

Forsaking the usual amenities, Lucy got straight to the point. Holding up a letter, she said:

"Professor Powell, this letter came just over a week ago. It's from my childhood friend, Victoria Trump."

"The lady you and Betsy visited when you went to Nashville?" Richard asked.

"Yes. Victoria married a doctor Randell and recently moved to Nashville. They had a daughter, Elvira, who was just a few years older than Betsy. Although the two girls had never seen each other before our visit, they became close friends. While we were there, Elvira's fiancé, a boy named Calvin Sander, came from North Carolina. Calvin and Elvira wanted permission to get married so Elvira could go back to North Carolina with

Calvin. The matter was not settled until after Betsy and I left Nashville, but Victoria had confided in me that Dr. Randell was inclined to grant his permission."

"Did they get married?" Richard asked.

"Yes. But neither Betsy nor I had any way of knowing this until this letter arrived."

"So, you think Betsy already knew this?"

Lucy held up her hand as though to prevent further interruption.

"The letter came on a Saturday," she continued. "Mr. Bell brought it from the Post Office in Adams. He laid it there on the table. He found me out in the yard and mentioned that there was a letter for me on the table. I had not heard from Victoria since leaving Nashville, so I hurried in and found Betsy standing beside the table staring at the letter. She was pale as a sheet, and I will never forget the look on her face. I asked her what on earth was the matter. She turned to me and said, `Momma, please don't read it, it's awful.' I picked up the letter and noticed that the seal was not broken. I said something like, 'Oh how nice, it's from the Randells. Betsy was almost hysterical and said, 'Please, Momma, please don't read it.' `Oh don't be silly, child,' I said, 'of course I'm going to read it.' You know, Professor Powell, I thought Betsy might be upset because Doctor Randell had refused to allow Elvira and Calvin to get married."

"So that was what the bad news was all about?" Richard asked.

"No," Lucy shook her head emphatically, "they did get married. But while on their way to North Carolina they were ambushed by outlaws. Calvin was killed and Elvira is missing. They feel certain that she is dead too, but at the time this letter was written, no body had been recovered."

"Good heavens!" Richard exclaimed.

"This was one reason Mr. Bell has gone to confer with General Jackson. Of course. we are all very upset over Elvira, but Professor Powell, how could Betsy have known what was in the letter before I opened it?"

"Are you sure she did know?"

"I am almost positive. In fact, this is not the first incident where she seemed to have foreknowledge."

Lucy now recounted the matter of the dress material, and her conversations with Nanny.

"According to Nanny," Lucy continued, "she was asking about visions."

"And what do you want me to do about it, Mrs. Bell?" Richard asked.

"See if you can draw her out. Get her to talk about it. When I try, she just draws deeper into her shell."

"Then why would she talk to me?" Richard asked.

"She's very taken with you. I think she might trust you."

"But how could I manage it? It couldn't be done during school hours, and I have little contact with your daughter outside of school."

Lucy stared into the fire and without moving her eyes, she spoke: "Professor Powell, could you instruct Betsy in Latin?"

"I'm not sure. I took two years of it when I was in school. It was hardly my best subject, but I suppose I know about as much as the average person with my background."

"Would you agree that Betsy is an exceptional student?"

"Certainly, she is the fastest learner I have ever known."

"Perhaps you might suggest to Mr. Bell that due to Betsy's exceptional abilities, she might profit from special lessons in Latin."

"Do you think Mr. Bell would agree to that?"

"Mr. Bell is aware that some of the ancient Biblical manuscripts were written in Latin. He had often expressed the wish that he understood the language. You could suggest that Betsy be kept after school for special lessons. That would give you the opportunity to get to know her better, and perhaps talk to her about the things that are troubling her."

"I suppose that might work," Richard admitted. "But I'm not sure I could teach her enough to satisfy your husband's expectations."

"Bearing in mind that Mr. Bell knows nothing about Latin, I would not think he would be very critical of Betsy's accomplishments, even if they are scant."

Richard left the Bell house worried, not because he felt inadequate to teach Latin, but rather because he found the prospects of spending afternoons alone with Betsy altogether too pleasing and enticing.

The next day he rummaged through his belongings and found his Latin texts. Then he sat down and started to brush up on Latin grammar.

By the end of the Christmas holidays, everything had been arranged. He had discussed the matter with John Bell and found him enthusiastic over having a member of his household versed in the classical language, which he incorrectly believed to have been the language spoken by Christ. His only reservation was over having such knowledge imparted to a female.

"Why not Richard William?" he had suggested.

"Richard William is not ready yet," Richard pointed out. "Besides I'm not sure he has Miss Betsy's capacity for learning."

In the end it was agreed that Betsy would remain after school for two afternoons a week. Bell insisted that Richard accept an extra five dollars a month for his trouble. It was a princely sum to Richard's way of thinking.

The lessons went through the month of January with Betsy showing her usual ability to learn with little or no effort. She learned enough Latin to impress her father. But Richard had to confess that he'd made no headway in getting to the root of Betsy's depression. She continued to go through her daily routine without enthusiasm or pleasure.

As the weeks went by, he started to share Lucy Bell's concerns. Then, realizing that he might he putting his own future in jeopardy he decided to do something drastic.

On a Tuesday afternoon he dismissed school, and once he and Betsy were alone, he sent her to the slate mounted on the wall to write out an exercise in Latin verbs.

As she stood there, waiting for him to read out the list of verbs, a voice spoke out of the air.

"Miss Betsy," the voice asked, "why are you always such a sad little mouse?"

The ruse worked. Betsy was instantly alert.

"Who said that?" she asked.

"Who said what?" Richard asked.

"You must have heard it. Somebody asked me why I'm always such a sad little mouse."

"I didn't hear anything," Richard said.

"Well, I sure did," Betsy said. She moved back to the slate eyeing him suspiciously.

Richard read a list of verbs, and Betsy wrote them on the slate. When she had finished, she turned to face him expecting instruction on how to proceed with the assignment.

Again, the voice spoke: "Won't you even answer my question?"

This time she caught the slightest movement of lips--the flaw that had caused his father to reject him as a possible professional ventriloquist.

Now, acting with the directness he had seen from her on that day she had come down to the gate to offer him his mother's dollar, she put her slate pencil on a bench and came to stand directly in front of him.

"How did you do that?" she asked.

"Do what?" Richard asked, continuing to play the innocent.

"I know it was you, but I don't know how you did it."

Sensing that now was the moment to strike, Richard laid aside his Latin grammar.

"How about making a swap?" he suggested.

Her eyes narrowed as though sensing a trap, and he feared she might draw back into the shell that had surrounded her for so long.

But for the moment curiosity was stronger than caution.

"What kind of a swap?" she asked.

"I'll tell you about the voice if you'll tell me what it is that's bothering you."

"Ain't nothing bothering me," she declared.

"Then I didn't hear any voice," he told her.

It was a standoff. Betsy went back to the board, and Richard read off more verbs. When they were finished it was dark, and Richard walked her home.

That situation lasted for a week. He knew that Betsy wanted to confide in him but was still afraid. However, Richard thought that he might be making some progress with her.

Over time, Betsy's grief and shock over Elvira's fate had begun to wear thin. Now her curiosity over a voice that seemed to come out of nowhere and to have no human source had forced her mind out of its depression and into other channels. She began to enjoy their afternoon sessions, and her curiosity about the real Richard surfaced once more.

One afternoon after completing an exercise, she laid the book aside and looked at him directly.

"What was in that letter that made you so mad?" she asked.

Richard was flabbergasted. The memory of that letter still had a sting to it, and there was no doubt of what Betsy was talking about.

"What do you know about a letter?" he asked.

"I saw you reading it. You crumpled it up and threw it across the room."

"But that happened in Louisville. That's more than a hundred miles from here."

"I never knew where it was," she admitted. Then she went on to describe the room in detail.

"So that's it," Richard said in a matter-of-fact way, "you have visions. "What was it you saw that day here in the classroom?"

"Just Poppa. He was taking some rocks from an old Indian grave. He opened the grave and found a skull, but he threw that away."

"But that's not what's been troubling you, is it? How did you know what was in your mother's letter?"

"How did you know about that?"

"I can't tell you."

"Momma told you about it in that note she had me bring to you the other day, didn't she? I wondered why Momma would be writing to you."

She nodded her head indicating her satisfaction of figuring out how Richard had known about her mother's letter.

"So, how did you know about it?" Richard repeated.

Betsy still hesitated. Then she opened up to Richard.

"One afternoon, I had this vision," she said. "I saw those men kill Calvin, and they were about to do something awful to Elvira."

Betsy bit her lip and her chin trembled. "Oh, God, Richard, Elvira saw them kill Calvin and when they came toward her, she knew what was going to happen, and she was so awful scared."

Suddenly she was crying uncontrollably. Richard took her in his arms and held her as a child, whispering soothing things in her ear.

Much to his relief, she soon regained control.

"I'll be all right," she told him.

He released her, and he was surprisingly shaken. He had acted as an adult acted to reassure a fearful or unhappy child. But the girl he had held was not like any child he had ever known. There was an intensity about her that radiated from every pore.

"I think we can dismiss for the afternoon," he said.

She looked at him puzzled then nodded her head and started to gather her things. As she drew her cloak about her shoulders, she stopped and looked at Richard.

"Why does God have to be so mean and hateful?"

"What are you talking about?" he asked.

"Well, before Elvira and Calvin got married, Elvira let Calvin plant his seed inside of her, but why did God have to punish them that way?"

"Is that what's been making you so sad?" he asked. "Have you been thinking that Calvin and Elvira were punished for their sins?"

"But why else would such an awful thing happen to them?"

"Oh, Betsy," he moaned in genuine distress, "what have these preachers done to you?"

This time he took her by the shoulders and looked her straight in the eye.

"Listen, child, if you never learn anything else from Richard Powell, learn this. We human beings are made of flesh and bone. We all do things the preachers would call sin. We live in a world with wicked men, and sometimes the good suffer and even die at their hands. But, Betsy, God has nothing to do with that. What happened to Calvin and Elvira was not because of something they had done. The fault lies with those who harmed them. Even the Bible says that it rains on the just and the unjust. What happened to Elvira could have happened to Thomas Gunn, to your father or mother, and to you or me. But if it did, it would not be because God is punishing us for our sins."

He abruptly stopped. The look on her face was intense, but one of pure trust.

He released her. "Come on. I'll walk you home," he said.

He wondered what Lucy Bell would have thought had she had known how her request of Richard Powell had led to this intensity between Betsy and him.

10

THE ENCOUNTER

When John Bell returned to Adams, his stature in the community increased to a degree even higher than previously. He had spent two nights in the Hermitage and had been cloistered with General Jackson for several hours. The General had promised to take his suggestions up with members of the Assembly. General Jackson was a famous and popular hero on the Tennessee frontier. Any man who had spoken to him or merely shaken his hand was something of a hero by association.

John Bell's neighbors suggested he ought to think about standing for the State Assembly himself, but the press of farm work forced him to wait until his land was further along in the process of development. Then there would be plenty of time for him to consider public office.

Astride his favorite mare, John Bell now attended the work of his plantation and visited every corner of his land to supervise the various projects assigned to his sons and his slaves. One afternoon while passing a field of new ground not yet put to the plow, he noticed something dark over near the woods. He reigned in the mare and watched closely until he was sure that he saw it move. Thinking that it was some neighbor's lost dog, he rode toward it, intending to coax it to follow him home so he could send word through the community for the owner to come and claim it.

But as he drew near, he realized that it was a most peculiar dog, if indeed it was a dog. And if it were a wild animal, it was a most peculiar creature. Instead of fleeing into the forest, the creature defiantly stood its ground and glared at John Bell with malevolent eyes. John Bell had never seen anything like it. If a mere look could convey hate that was the essence of the look the creature bestowed on John Bell.

As the horse drew near, the creature let out a low guttural growl. Despite his commanding self-assurance, John Bell was afraid. He raised his rifle intending to kill the evil thing, but as he pulled the trigger, the beast made a sudden movement, and the horse shied causing him to miss. While he was reloading his powder into the barrel, the beast continued to glare at him. When he reached for the ball, the creature suddenly turned and ran into the forest. The movement was so sudden that, to John, the creature seemed to disappear.

That night at the supper table, John related the experience to his family.

"It reminded me of a beast out of Hell. It was something filled with hate. It was a manifestation of the Devil. I got the impression that it possessed intelligence and that all its hate was directed personally toward me."

A spirited conversation followed, and all the boys made guesses as to what kind of animal their father could have seen.

Betsy took no part in the conversation. She had her own problems to ponder. She sat at the table with downcast eyes, hearing but taking no part in the talk going around the table.

Finally, after the topic of the creature was exhausted, her father turned his attention, as usual, to the question-and-answer session over what his children had been doing during the day. After the boys made their reports, John Bell turned his attention to Betsy.

"Well, Elizabeth, how is our Latin scholar doing?"

"All right, Poppa."

"Can you speak the tongue yet?" he asked.

Betsy shriveled. The thing she dreaded most about her

father's nightly sessions was the possibility of being called on to recite.

"A little," she answered. She would have denied having any significant knowledge, but she was afraid that a disclaimer of progress would reflect badly on Richard Powell as a teacher.

"Oh," her father beamed. "Perhaps you would say something for the benefit of us all?"

"Mica, mica, parva stella," she said.

"Which means?" her father asked in a near state of ecstasy.

"It just means 'twinkle, twinkle, little star.'" Betsy said.

"That's very good, Elizabeth. Mother, boys, you've just heard words spoken that would have been understood by our Lord and Savior, Jesus Christ."

Betsy slipped further down in her chair. She recognized her father's error but could not bring herself to contradict him.

As soon as supper was over, she quickly withdrew and went to her room. There she was transformed. No longer the meek little child, she threw herself on her bed. Closing her eyes, she gave herself over to her reverie.

Just as she was able to recall every word on a printed page, she was now able to recreate every detail of those precious moments when Richard had consoled her in his arms. In all her life there had been nothing comparable. Affection was not expressed through physical contact in the Bell family, and she never imagined that she would welcome it.

But beyond the comfort, Richard's arms had stirred something deep inside her that she had no name for. She reveled in the bliss of perfect memory. By that ancient alchemy that exists between men and women, she knew that the contact had affected Richard as much as it had her.

Now it occurred to her that he had wanted to plant his seed inside her. Much to her surprise, the thought did not repel her. In fact, she was intrigued by the idea of having his children and allowing him the pleasure of her body. She knew that when the time came, she would find a way to allow him the privilege.

She remembered that he had not been perturbed over her visions.

"So, you have visions," was the way he had put it in a matter-of-fact way, just as if it was something many people had experienced. He had evidently known about visions before she had told him about hers. He had said nothing about visions being witchcraft, nothing about sin, no hell and no damnation. He had simply said, "So, you have visions."

Somehow his casual approach outweighed all of Brother Gunn's thundering condemnation. And Richard's ideas that God did not punish sinners in awful and vengeful ways seemed entirely reasonable. If a man jumped out of a tree, should he accuse God of dashing him against the ground?

She still felt terrible about what had happened to Elvira, but somehow it was reassuring to know that she had not been punished for loving Calvin.

Suddenly she sat upright in bed.

"Well, of all the sneaky tricks?" she said aloud.

She had told him all about her visions, but she had learned nothing at all about "the voice." Setting her lips firmly, she resolved to confront him with his obligation to swap confidences.

"Yes," she thought to herself, "Richard Powell and I are going to have a lot to do with one another." She lay back in the bed and smiled with great contentment, and at no time in her thoughts did Josh Gardner enter her calculations.

During the following week, word about her father's encounter with the strange beast had spread throughout the community. It caused considerable excitement. Betsy heard the story being told at school. According to that version, the beast stood on its hind legs, whirled round and around, and had disappeared in a puff of blue smoke. On Sunday, she heard a different version at church. This time the beast had changed into a black devil in human form except for a forked tail and horns on its head. Then it had swirled upward and disappeared in a cloudless sky.

Her father tried to correct the exaggerations with little

success. In the days that followed, she heard even wilder accounts.

"Give folks a little help, and their imagination will do the rest," Richard told her when she talked about the matter with him.

She thought about that. She had just learned a valuable lesson. People were gullible. She decided to try a little test of her own.

"Did anybody see that lady down in the orchard?" she asked that night at the supper table.

"What Lady?" John Jr. asked.

"In the orchard."

"Do you mean our orchard?" Zadok asked.

"What's this?" her father wanted to know.

"When I got home this afternoon, I took a walk down in the orchard," Betsy embellished. "When I got down to the old sweet apple tree, I saw somebody down by the back fence. Their back was to me, and before I could call out, she turned, and I saw it was a woman. She looked right at me. I`d never seen her before, and she looked like she was terribly angry. For a moment, I thought she was going to throw something at me."

"Why, what do you mean?" John Bell reacted, "How dare somebody take such an attitude when you were on our own property?"

"What did she look like?" Zadok asked.

"She was tall and skinny," Betsy said. "She had on a bonnet, but her hair fell from under it. I think it was black, or at any rate it was very dark. Her cheeks were hollow, and she had on a gray shawl. I think her dress was dark brown".

"And you'd never seen her before?"

"No, never."

"Well, what happened?"

"Well, like I said, I first thought she was going to throw something at me, but instead she said something ugly and then she screamed and ran into the locust grove."

The discussion at the table was prolonged as John Bell and

his sons speculated over the possible identity of the woman in the orchard, her purpose for being there, the reason for her anger, and where she might have gone.

By that time Betsy had all but been forgotten and took no part in the continuing discussion. Instead, she sat listening with growing astonishment.

"They will believe anything I want them to," she was thinking.

The next day Richard William told the story in school, and before the day was out, it was the sole topic of conversation among the students. Some of her friends came up to her with questions. Betsy made no effort to further embellish the story.

"I guess it was just some crazy old woman who was wandering through the community," she offered.

Richard was soon aware of the story being discussed by his students and watched Betsy with mounting concern. When school was dismissed, Betsy remained sitting on her bench waiting for her Latin lesson. Richard stood at the schoolhouse door until the last child was out of sight then he turned to Betsy.

"All right, Betsy," he said. "What are you up to?"

His unconscious use of her first name without the title, 'Miss,' was indicative of a change in their relationship.

"What do you mean?" She looked up at him with an unwavering gaze.

"I don't believe there ever was a woman in the orchard," he said.

"Why not?"

"To me it sounds like an unlikely story."

She shrugged her shoulders. "You're right, there never was a woman, but after everybody made up such lies over Poppa's black dog, I decided to tell my little fib to see what they would make of it."

Richard stared dumfounded for what seemed like minutes. Betsy met his gaze steadily.

Finally, Richard looked away. "I'm not sure I approve of this," he said.

"You never told me how you made the voice," Betsy now said changing the focus of the conversation.

"What are you talking about?" Richard responded.

"You remember. When you wanted me to tell you about my visions, you offered to swap. You'd tell me how you made the voice speak if I'd tell me about by visions."

"As I recall, you rejected that offer," Richard replied. "Later you voluntarily told me about your visions," he concluded smugly.

She stared at him with a level gaze. He felt himself being drawn into something deep and unknown. Without breaking her gaze, she stood up and crossed to where he was sitting. Taking his face in her hands she kissed him on the mouth. Then she stepped back. He was flabbergasted.

"My, God, Betsy," he said after managing to find his voice, "do you know what would happen to me if anyone found out about this?"

"No one is going to find out," Betsy said. "You know me and you belong to each other. Now, I trusted you with my secret, and seems like you could trust me with yours."

He ran his fingers across his lips. "But you are just a mere child," he protested.

"I won't always be. Now tell me how you make that voice."

He continued to stare at her in amazement. "Why the little imp is taking control," he thought to himself. He marveled over the child before him that was no longer a shy innocent girl but now a forceful manipulating woman. And now Richard realized that he had no choice but to do her bidding.

"Have you ever heard of ventriloquism?" he asked her.

11

DEAN

Betsy Bell's story about the lady in the orchard had the expected results. Speculation was even wilder than it had been over John Bell's black dog. A few days after she had told the story, a group of men got together to scour the woods in search of the mysterious woman. When they failed to find her, the rumors got even wilder. Betsy could hardly believe the stories she was hearing. In her afternoon sessions with Richard, she would repeat the wildest of the tales with glee.

"I'd say you have stirred up a pretty kettle of fish," he admitted.

Within the span of a week, Richard had heard at least a dozen versions of Betsy's story, including one that the person in the orchard was a small child instead of a woman.

It was during this period that he first heard the word "witch" associated with the Bell family. He cautioned Betsy against taking the prank too far, but he made no effort to set the story straight. He had made up his mind, right or wrong, that he had cast his lot with Betsy Bell.

In the meantime, the school term was drawing to a close. In those weeks preceding the end of school, Betsy learned very little Latin, but she mastered ventriloquism as easily as she had mastered every other subject. By the time school was out, she had learned everything he could teach her, and now was starting to experiment on her own.

In a moment of introspection, Richard thought that his father would have been ecstatic if he could have found a prodigy like Betsy to train as a ventriloquist in the theater.

The voice Betsy projected sounded nothing like her own and had a quality that was hard to classify as either male or female. In later years those who heard it could never agree as to whether the Bell Witch was male or female.

During this same period, Betsy was learning details about Richard's past life, and she was utterly fascinated. But Richard was growing increasingly apprehensive. More and more he was putting his fate into Betsy's hands. He wanted to confide in her, but she was only a mere child, and he could not be certain that she would not at some point unwittingly reveal some damaging detail that would bring the wrath of the community down on his head.

He tried to caution her about the consequences of public exposure both for himself and for her. Betsy refused to be alarmed.

"I'm not aiming to tell anybody," she protested.

"Are you saying that you won't practice ventriloquism?" he asked.

"Well, if I do, I sure don't aim to let on it was me that made the voice," she said.

"But just remember how quickly you caught on when I spoke in front of you," he reminded her. "Don't you think other people could catch on to you just as easily?"

She grinned impishly. "But you are not as good as I am," she said, "then too I'm a lot smarter than they are." She waved her arm to indicate he wide world beyond the school room.

"You are terribly conceited," he accused.

"It's not conceit when it's true," she said. "Besides you like me the way I am."

"Does that matter?" he asked.

"Of course, it does. I aim to grow up and marry you."

"What do you plan to do about Josh?" he asked finally

putting into words the question that had been on both their minds.

"I haven't thought it all out yet," she admitted.

"Sooner or later, we are going to have to deal with that," Richard said. "In his own way Josh is quite fond of you."

"I know," she said soberly.

Lucy Bell had not spoken privately to Richard since the night he had called at her house. She had noticed changes in Betsy since she had started her Latin lessons. Obviously what Richard was doing was working. She was pleased with the results, but curious about how they had been accomplished.

One afternoon after Betsy arrived home from school, Lucy had Dean bring the surrey around on the pretext of going to Adams for some sewing materials.

En route, she directed Dean to stop at the schoolhouse door. She found Richard there getting ready to go to his boarding house for supper.

She invited Richard to ride with her to Adams.

Richard hesitated. He was certain that Lucy intended to question him about Betsy. Still there was no gracious way he could refuse, and he climbed into the surrey.

Lucy got straight to the point, "I've been anxious to know what you've found out about Betsy?" she said as soon as the surrey was back on the road.

Richard pondered the question. While Betsy had not asked him to keep things secret, he was sure that she implied such a condition. Still, he owed a debt to Lucy Bell. Without her arrangements, he and Betsy would still be merely student and teacher. It also occurred to him that a time might come when Lucy Bell's understanding might be terribly important. He decided to take her into his confidence.

"Betsy knew what was in that letter because she was a witness to Calvin and Elvira's encounter with the outlaws," he told her.

Lucy was thoroughly confused. "But how could she? She hasn't been off the farm."

"Mrs. Bell, Betsy sees things happening in other places. According to what she tells me, she's had a number of these visions."

"Oh, My Lord!" Lucy exclaimed.

"Most of her visions have been rather innocuous," Richard continued, "but the one about Elvira was most traumatic and caused her to be deeply depressed. Then somehow she got the notion that her visions were connected with witchcraft. But it seems that bringing it all out in the open and talking about it has helped."

"But what should we do?" Lucy asked.

"Do? We do nothing," Richard said emphatically.

"But aren't such powers evil?" Lucy asked.

"Certainly not," Richard said. "Betsy's gift is probably more common than you might suppose. Since most people think of it as evil, many who have the experience never reveal it. I once knew a Madam Darce who had visions quite frequently. She lived to have children, grandchildren and great grandchildren. She was a kindly soul and one of my closest friends."

"But how is such a thing possible?" Lucy asked.

"I don't know," Richard admitted. "But once we've learned enough about the working of the human mind, we will probably find that the answer is quite simple. Some years back I became good friends with a magician. But before I got to know him, I went to see one of his performances. During that performance he made a horse disappear from the stage. I left the theater that night convinced that the magician was in league with the devil. Later he showed me how he did it. It was so simple that I felt like a fool."

"But how did he do it?" Lucy asked.

"With a trap door to the basement," Richard explained. "Just before the horse disappeared, it was momentarily hidden from the view of the audience with a silk curtain. Then the magician stepped on a small lever and a spring mechanism with a counterbalance lowered the horse into the basement. When the horse's weight was removed, the door came back into place, so that when the magician removed the curtain, it seemed to the audience that a horse had vanished into thin air."

"Are you saying that Betsy's visions are some kind of trickery?"

"Not at all. I am saying that your daughter has some kind of special sensitivity that ordinary mortals living in these times cannot understand. She did not ask for the gift and does not understand how it works herself. But there is nothing we can or should do about it."

"Oh, dear," Lucy sighed.

The surrey was fast approaching the village of Adams.

"There is one other thing that I think you ought to know," Richard told her.

"Yes?" Lucy asked.

"I have fallen in love with Betsy."

"Yes, I suppose I knew that would happen," Lucy said. "You do realize that Betsy is too young to marry yet awhile?"

"Yes, but I am willing to wait until she's older."

"Then there's the troublesome matter of Josh Gardner. He has every right to feel that Betsy is waiting for him."

"I know," Richard said, "but Betsy doesn't seem to think that is a problem."

"It was Mister Bell who favored the match," Lucy continued. "At the time I had reservations but felt that perhaps Josh was the best Betsy could hope for. Now that all of this has come up, I am just as certain that Josh could never cope with it... but I have one thing to ask."

"What is that?" Richard asked.

"I don't want Josh hurt unnecessarily."

"I'll do my best to see that that doesn't happen," Richard promised.

As soon as Lucy Bell returned from Adams, Dean took the surrey to the carriage shed and tended to the horses. By nightfall he was finished with his chores. For a time, he sat on a box just outside the stable door savoring the quiet and his own inactivity. He had been born into slavery and could conceive of no other way of life.

Like many born to slavery, Dean had learned to find pleasure in mundane things like the natural noises in the quiet of the night and relaxing after a tiring day of work. Dean considered the songs of the crickets and bullfrogs to be the sweetest music ever sung.

He could neither read nor write, but he possessed some powers that whites neither suspected nor comprehended. Without formal learning to clutter up his mind, his memory was prodigious. Shapes, colors, scents and sounds could be recalled in exact detail months after the encounter.

The stars sparkled brightly in the moonless sky, and no breeze stirred from any direction. But Dean knew that it would rain tomorrow. He had no explanation for this knowledge, but he was as certain of it as he was of the coming sunrise.

He acknowledged the great splendor of the vast number of stars coursing through the night sky. Dean had no name for the individual stars and constellations, but an astronomer would have been amazed by his knowledge of their movements. It was the same with the moon. Lying abed, he would watch the moon through the window of his cabin, noting every phase and variation. In the face of the moon, he saw shapes and symbols and felt a response to its subtle forces.

Dean rarely spoke of his abilities. Just as the printed page was a hopeless riddle to him, so his perceptive powers would have been a mystery to white people.

He understood that the demonstration of such powers and knowledge was apt to be looked on as witchcraft or voodoo. He had never forgotten his mother's account and warning of being punished for the exercise of similar powers.

Sitting by the door of the stable, Dean was aware of the

scents of the stable. He inhaled deeply and without conscious thought identified the earthy scent of horses and cattle mingled with musty hay and rich manure. To Dean it was a pleasant aroma

He stretched his great arms and yawned with deep satisfaction. Now he detected the smells of his mother's kitchen. That reminded him of how hungry he was. He left the box and went toward the kitchen. There in its usual place he found a large tin plate piled high with the victuals his mother always set aside for him. He took the plate outside and hunkered down in deep shadows with his back against a large tree. He ate slowly, savoring each flavor of the different foods.

The area around the house was totally dark except for pools where candlelight spilled through the windows. No white man would have seen the movement in the deepest shadows. Even to Dean it was more something sensed than seen. He paused with a morsel of food halfway to his mouth and remained perfectly still, his eyes fastened on the spot where he had sensed movement. A shadow only a fraction darker than its surroundings changed shape. Now he was positive that there was a presence in the darkness. He allowed air to flow over the scent cells in his nostrils and considered the composition of the aromas. Faintly, faintly, faintly came a scent of soap--not the lye soap that was issued to the slaves, but a more refined soap his mother made for the main house. Whoever was responsible for the presence was white, not Negro. Sensing more than seeing, he knew that the shadow was now moving in his direction, and as it passed on the opposite side of the tree from where he was sitting, he heard a soft swish--the sound made by a woman's skirt. It passed without ever being aware of his presence, and soon he knew that it had passed around the corner of the house. He turned his attention to his plate and finished his food.

Several years ago, Dean had taken himself a woman, a slave belonging to the Reverend Thomas Gunn. Now with his stomach full, he recognized another kind of hunger. He followed the drive to the road and turned in the direction of the Gunn farm. As soon as he was beyond the last outbuilding, he raised his voice in a mournful wail: "Yea o, yea o, yea o o o o o o. Yea o, yea o, yea o, yea o o o o o o."

The sounds he made were neither words nor song but rather a rhythm that rose and fell in pitch and volume as the voice moved up and down the scale. Across the countryside and beyond the Red River, blacks in their cabins paused to listen and then nodded. Dean was on his way to see his woman. However, as he drew near the Gunn place, he fell silent and moved as unobtrusively as a shadow.

The mating of blacks always posed a vexing question for those whites who professed high moral character. Nowhere along Red River would any white person have argued passionately that the Negro had a soul. Still the form of the Negro was similar to the white man, and masters would have been repulsed for the mating between slaves to be arranged like that for domestic animals. Yet a slave was property of value, and the progeny of slaves increased the property and wealth of the white owner. And a slave child sired by such a specimen as Dean had special value.

The institution of slavery did not encourage slave marriages or the maintaining of slaves in a family unit. The wise course was for the master to sleep soundly and not concern himself with what went on in the slave quarters. As long as Dean was discrete no one would interfere with his mating. Nevertheless, if he were caught, he would be punished.

When the pregnancy of a female slave started to show, there would be rebukes, prayers and the wringing of hands. But once the child was born, the master would quietly add the child to his list of tangible assets with a clear conscious while protesting that he had been unaware of and disproving of the union that produced the child.

Tonight, Dean went quietly to the usual cabin and quietly pushed open the door that had been left unlatched for him. When he left the cabin, the stars told him that it was getting on toward morning. But there was plenty of time to walk back to his own cabin so he could be on hand for the morning chores.

He did not repeat the rhythmic scale that he had sung while on his way to see his woman. Instead, he was contemplative. "Who was it," he asked himself, "who had moved so stealthy around the main house?" He was certain that he knew the answer.

For some reason when whites wanted to discuss something personal, they always seemed to believe that Negros in their presence were struck deaf.

Earlier in the day while driving Miss Lucy and Richard Powell in the surrey, Dean appeared to be absorbed in his driving. But he had heard every word that had passed between Professor Powell and Miss Lucy. He had no trouble believing that Miss Betsy was possessed of visions. In his lifetime he had known slaves who claimed such magic power. Had not his own mother once been a voodoo woman? It was his mother who had always told him that Miss Betsy was one of the "old ones." A woman who could call up visions would have no trouble in moving through the dark of night like a will-o-the-wisp.

To Dean the gulf between the races was deep and wide. But he also recognized that in the cult of magic there was a bond that transcended race. Those possessed of the power commanded all who considered themselves as true believers.

As Dean walked toward the Bell plantation the moon started to push out over the horizon. He paused to examine it carefully for an omen. It was plain as day. Tonight, the face of the moon was the face of Betsy Bell. In her was the power, and Dean knew that he would be eternally cast in the role of her servant and protector.

12

NOISES

Two weeks after Richard and Lucy had talked, the school term ended. But before the end of the term arrived, Richard and Betsy had a quarrel. Betsy learned about the meeting between Richard and her mother when Lucy inadvertently let it slip that she had seen Richard the previous day. Betsy was immediately suspicious, and Lucy knew immediately that she had made a mistake by letting it slip.

"Oh, and what did you talk about?" Betsy asked her.

"You," Lucy admitted.

"What about me?"

"Oh, you know--how you are doing in school, and in your Latin lessons."

Lucy's discomfort heightened Betsy`s suspicions, but she pressed the matter no further.

The following afternoon during her Latin lesson, Betsy challenged Richard.

"What's this you have been telling my mother?"

The question caught Richard by surprise, and he tried to deny having had any conversation with her mother. Betsy was furious.

"Don't you dare lie to me, Richard Powell!"

Caught in his own lie, Richard made a bad mess of things and finally admitted that he had told Betsy's mother about her visions. By that time Betsy was crying with rage.

"I'll never tell you anything again as long as I live," she wailed. "Now, Momma thinks I'm a witch."

"No, she doesn't," Richard said positively.

"How do you know what she thinks?" Betsy asked.

By now Richard was beginning to regain his composure and explained his reasons for confiding in Lucy. Betsy was only partly mollified.

"You still had to right to tell about that unless I told you you could," she finally concluded.

Relations between them remained strained until school was dismissed for the year.

As the children disappeared down the road at the end of that final day of school, Richard realized that once again he was among the unemployed. John Bell had assured him that he would be welcome back to teach the following year, but that was possibly seven months away. He had saved enough money to carry him through the summer, but even so, he would be starting out the following term in the same situation that he had the last--dead broke. He decided that he would find a job for the summer. It took less than a day for him to find out that there were no employment opportunities in Adams. He thought about going to Natchez as originally planned, but he did not want to be so far away from Betsy.

Then John Bell suggested that he call on one of his friends in Springfield. John Bell's friend owned a tobacco warehouse. Locally, it was called a "loose leaf floor." It turned out that Bell's friend, a Mr. Crosswy, needed a clerk to handle his correspondence and keep his books. The seven months that Richard had to spare was ideal for the situation. The salary would be $45 a month. That added to what Richard had made teaching meant that he no longer had any immediate financial worries. But still, he did worry. If he was going to marry Betsy, he wanted to have something to offer. He suspected that John Bell would bestow a generous dowry when the time came, but he was determined not to be put into a position of having it said that he had married for money.

He worked diligently, and in the meantime, he kept his eyes and ears open. Leaving Adams had presented problems. By the time he was ready to leave, Betsy had forgiven him to the extent that she was willing to beg him not to go so far away. When he insisted that he must, she had grown sullen and angry. It was then that he realized that for all her intelligence and adult ways, Betsy could still be very childish.

"If you leave me, I just might decide to marry Josh," she threatened.

"Perhaps Josh is better suited for a person of your age," Richard conceded.

"But I don't want to marry him," she stormed.

"Then you can wait for me. I won't be gone forever."

"I don't want you to go. Don't you understand? I need you."

"You did very well before I came along."

"No, I didn't. I was turning into a witch."

"No, you weren't. There's no such thing as a witch."

"It talks about them in the Bible. Brother Gunn has preached about them."

"Brother Gunn is a silly old man who doesn't know what he's talking about."

"Please, Richard, don't leave me all alone."

"It's because of you that I'm going," he explained.

She had cried and threatened, but much to her surprise, she found that Richard could be very stubborn once he had made up his mind. The best she could get from him was a promise to visit her during the summer.

Left to her own devices, Betsy found the summer boring. Josh still came every Sunday. It was no more entertaining than before. For the rest of the week, Betsy spent a lot of time in her room.

One Sunday when John Bell had invited many guests to dinner after church, Betsy espied Esther and Bennett coming up the drive with a spare horse tied behind the buggy. She went to meet them and learned that the animal was a three-year-old mare named Fanny.

According to Esther, Fanny was the colt of a fine saddle mare that belonged to Bennett's father. But not until after dinner did Betsy learn that the horse was intended for her as a present. All her brothers and sisters had pooled their funds to buy the animal in the hope that the gift would help Betsy get over her depression.

For a while, the gift seemed to work as intended. Betsy squealed in delight. Finding a side saddle in the stable, she spent the rest of the afternoon riding up and down the road. Poor Josh was totally neglected. But it did not seem to make much difference to him. Betsy's preoccupation left him free to join in the conversation of the men folk.

The thrill of having her own horse lasted for a full week then the novelty wore off. Fanny was turned out to pasture, and Betsy returned to her room to lie on the bed, stare at the ceiling and miss Richard.

One afternoon she felt so sorry for herself that she started to cry. She got off the bed and went to look for a handkerchief. While rummaging through a drawer, she came upon the bull whacker she had stolen from Calvin.

She held the peg and string in her hand, remembering the night the three of them had tormented poor Mr. Heever.

"They were so alive then," she thought, "how can they be dead?"

She put the bull whacker back in the drawer and went to stare out her window. She felt very strange and totally alone. In such a mood, she would ordinarily have resolved to talk things over with Richard the following day, but he was far away, and they had not parted on good terms.

She supposed she might end up marrying Josh after all. The thought plunged her into dark depression. She went back to the drawer and again took out the bull whacker. Without looking at it, she went to her wardrobe and searched among her clothes until she found a hooded cape. The cape belonged to Esther but had not been used by anyone for the past two winters. It was dark blue and, at night, appeared totally black. She thrust the bull whacker into a pocket of the cape.

Closing the wardrobe door, she left the room and descended the stairs. From the hallway she went out into the yard and walked around the house. Anyone seeing her would have thought that she was out for a breath of fresh air, but, in reality, she was examining the house and grounds in great detail.

That night at the supper table, Betsy pleaded a headache and excused herself as soon as she finished eating. Those at the table heard her climb the stairs and seconds later walking about in her room. Soon the slave women cleared away the dishes from the table, and John Bell opened his Bible and began the family devotional.

It was Richard William who first mentioned the noise.

"Poppa, somebody is knocking on the wall."

His father gave him a look of rebuke for having interrupted his reading. Richard William quailed under that look, and his father resumed his reading. He got through several verses before the rapping became loud enough to disturb his concentration. He glared at the boys, thinking that one of them was responsible for the disturbance. Each in turn swore his innocence.

By Sunday news about the strange knocking at the Bell house had spread throughout the congregation. John was besieged with questions and tried to play down the incident.

"Most likely a squirrel or maybe a rat," he told those who asked about the noise.

Nearby Betsy listened with a smile of satisfaction tugging at the corner of her mouth. Deep in his own mind John Bell was not so certain about his explanation. Although he and the boys had searched for the source of the noise that night and even more thoroughly in the daylight of the following day, they had found nothing to explain it. The house had been built of logs, later covered over on the inside with weatherboarding and plaster. The logs would have prevented any small animal from getting between the walls, and they had found no opening that would admit a squirrel or rat. A vexing question crossed his mind: Was there a possible connection between the noise and his encounter with the strange beast, or with Betsy's encounter with the woman in the orchard? His good sense told him the thought was preposterous, but he was not able to lay it aside. He was, after all, a man who believed in the supernatural.

Next Sunday, Brother Gunn preached about 'The Wiles of the Prince of Darkness.' Brother Gunn's Satan was very real and exceedingly active. According to Brother Gunn, Satan walked up and down the earth without ceasing in search of souls he might lead astray. For John Bell, the sermon was discomfiting.

No one was invited to dinner that Sunday. At the table John held family council. All were admonished about loose talk.

"Matters more properly handled in the family should not be discussed with the neighbors."

One by one, he swore each member of the family to secrecy.

For the next few days, Betsy was content to let matters rest. No one suspected the disturbances had anything to do with her. In that anonymity she felt elation and great power.

"Perhaps," she thought, "I really am a witch."

She considered the possibility and no longer found it so frightening. All alone she had created a sensation in the community that had everyone talking. Zadok reported that everyone he saw at the law office was questioning him about the matter, and the other Bell children confessed that it was all but impossible to avoid discussions about the strange happenings. Betsy listened to these reports with mock alarm as if mortified by the family's growing notoriety.

At about this time Betsy appeared to renew her interest in horseback riding. One morning she had Dean saddle Fanny and bring her to the front door. She left the house with no clear idea as to her destination, but a short time later turned the horse into the woodland path that led to the old Indian grave. By this time the path was so overgrown that she eventually had to dismount and lead Fanny. After walking for half a mile, she came upon some of the stones that her father had removed from the grave and still beside the path. John Jr. had hauled some of the stones away, but others were still where John Bell had left them.

Betsy tied Fanny to a small tree and stepped off the pathway. She immediately encountered the gaping grave and the stone slab her father had pried away. Nearby lay the jawbone that had dropped from the skull when her father had lifted it out of the grave. Recalling the details of her vision, she moved away from the grave and soon found the skull itself. She left both pieces where she had found them and returned to the open grave. Moving aside a few leaves, she found other bones in the shallow depression. She selected a large straight bone and returned to where Fanny was hitched to the tree. When she got home, she hid the bone in her wardrobe.

Betsy awoke in the middle of the night. The house was perfectly dark. Faintly she could hear the regular breathing sounds that indicated all were sound asleep. She slipped out of the bed and wrapped herself in Esther's dark cape. She stepped out into the hallway. The hallway was pitch dark, and she had to feel her way along the wall until she came to the door that opened into the room of her younger brothers. The unlatched door opened easily, and she slipped into the room a little surprised at how quietly she was able to move. She moved slowly in the direction of the boys' deep breathing until her legs came into contact with the bed. Groping about with her hand, she found the quilt that the boys used for cover and pulled on it.

Richard William stirred and tried to hold on to the cover.

"Joe E., stop hogging all the cover," he protested in a sleepy, groggy voice.

Joe E. continued to sleep, and now Richard William tried to pull the receding cover back over his shoulders. He was no match for his sister, and a moment later the quilt came free of the bed.

"Momma," Richard William called, "Joe E. is taking all the cover."

Betsy dropped the quilt on the floor and moved out the door. As she passed the top of the stairs, she could see candlelight in the room downstairs where her parents slept and knew that they had been aroused by Richard William's call.

She moved quickly to her own room and replaced the cape in the wardrobe. Then hesitating only a second, she slapped herself hard on the cheek. The blow made a loud clap, and she let out a scream. She repeated the blow on the other side of her face and let out another scream. Hearing her mother and father on the stairs, she rushed to the door. She flung it open as if in a near state of hysteria.

13

DISCOVERED

As Betsy came into the hallway, her mother had just reached the top of the stairs. Betsy ran into her arms.

"It was in my room," she cried hysterically. "It was right there in my room."

Lucy was utterly confused. "What was in your room, child?"

"I don't know, but it pulled my hair and slapped me in the face."

Bearing a lighted candle, her father pushed by the two women. He first looked in the boys' room. Both were now wide awake and sat up in their bed with eyes that looked much like the eyes of an owls. They were thoroughly frightened. The quilt lay on the floor at the foot of their bed. But there was no indication of another presence in the room. He turned down the hall and looked in Betsy's room. It was empty. As he returned to the women, the two young boys were also out in the hallway. Both were talking at once, but soon John Bell learned that something very strong had pulled the cover off the bed.

"I thought it was Joe E.," Richard William explained.

"I was asleep," Joe E. protested.

"Neither of the boys would have pulled the cover over the foot of the bed," John Bell observed. "It must have been something else."

"But what?" Lucy asked.

"I don't know," John Bell admitted.

For her part, Betsy swore that she had neither seen nor heard anything, but that she had felt her hair being pulled with a force that lifted her from the bed and felt the sting of the blows on her cheeks.

John held the candle close to her face, and he and Lucy examined the cheek. They agreed that the cheek seemed red and possibly there was the imprint of a hand, but in the poor light they could not be sure.

"It has to be some intruder," John concluded, "but what on earth was he after and what became of him?"

By this time the older boys were awake, and Nanny had come from her room over the kitchen to see what was causing all the commotion. It took a good hour for things to settle down. During that time John Bell admonished all to be certain that they said nothing of what had happened outside the family.

"We don't want the neighborhood stirred up and a lot of wild talk going through the community," he reminded everyone.

But when he returned to bed, he was a much-worried man. All his life he had been able to control his own affairs. Now, suddenly, he was faced with a situation he did not understand and seemed powerless to control. Once again, he wondered about a possible connection between this and all the recent strange events and whether there was possibly some supernatural force at work.

For her part, Lucy Bell was also worried. She kept remembering her conversation with Richard and his conviction that Betsy had visions. Was it possible that Betsy was behind all this? But the child had seemed genuinely frightened. She wished that Richard was near so that she could discuss the matter with him.

In her room, Betsy now slept soundly. When Richard left Adams, Betsy had tried to make him promise to write to her. He had refused.

"God, Betsy, that would be most improper as long as you are

supposed to have an understanding with Josh Gardner. Your father would be justly offended."

She had begged and pleaded, but once more she found that once Richard made up his mind, it was all but impossible to change it. The most she could get from him was a promise to visit the family during the summer.

He had been gone for over a month, and the promised visit had not materialized.

At last Betsy decided on her own solution. She had willed the vision when she saw Elvira and Calvin's encounter with the outlaws, but it had been such a traumatic experience that she was reluctant to try it again. But now in her impatience with Richard she decided to use her power to pay him a visit. She waited until an afternoon when she was alone in her room and certain that she would not be interrupted. Lying on her bed, she stared hard at a spot on the ceiling, and thought about Richard.

As with her vision of Elvira, the first images were faint and indistinguishable, but soon the view became sharper and at last perfectly clear. She was inside an office with a large stand-up desk set in front of a large window. Two large ledgers lay open on the slanted top of the desk. At the very top the desk became flat and there was an ink stand and an earthen jar holding a few goose quills. Several sheets of foolscap lay beside the ledgers, and they were covered with a jumble of figures. A door to the left opened and Richard entered the room. He selected a goose quill from the jar and picked up a small knife that lay beside it. He was soon absorbed as he carefully trimmed the end of the quill. Again, the door opened, and this time a young lady about Richard's own age entered the room. She had long dark hair and a pretty face.

"Richard, father wants you to come to supper tonight."

"What time?" Richard asked.

"He usually dines at nine, but he wants to discuss the Assembly seat. He's talked with several of the businessmen about town and has encouraging news. Perhaps you could come at seven."

"Your father's most kind. Tell him I accept his kind invitation. Will you and Martin be there?"

"I think so. If not, we will see you on Sunday."

The woman left the room, and Richard turned to the ledgers. He picked up a piece of foolscap and was soon busy entering figures into the ledger as the scene faded.

When it was completely gone, Betsy remained on the bed. She lay very still. She was terribly frightened. In a way, the vision had been as traumatic as the one about Elvira. There was no way she could know the meaning of what she had seen, only that there was a very attractive woman who seemed to be interested in Richard.

The night that followed was not the kind of night that Betsy would have selected. First and foremost, the moon was much too bright. Since the days she had played Settler and Indians, she had known the importance of waiting for a dark night to undertake any kind of clandestine movement. But knowing that Richard was having supper with a woman she now considered her rival made her reckless. She took Esther's dark cape from the wardrobe and the bull whacker from its drawer. The family had retired, so she had no trouble slipping down the stairs. Once outside, she pushed the peg firmly up under the weather boarding and ran the string to a large pear tree some fifteen yards from the house.

The action of the bull whacker brought quick reaction. A light appeared in the window of the front room and soon her father and brothers were in the yard determined to find the source of the strange noise. Recalling Calvin's strategy, she allowed the string to go slack. Her father and the boys examined the side of the house in detail, but the poor light kept them from finding the bull whacker. Satisfied that there was nothing unusual about the wall, they spread out to search the yard. Now Betsy was worried. In the bright moonlight, she would discover her behind the tree. She was about to drop her cape and pretend that she had come down from her room to help with the search, when she happened to look behind her. There, close enough to reach out and touch her on the shoulder was the bulk of a man. She almost screamed before she realized that it was Dean. He touched a finger to his lips, signaling her to remain quiet. At the same moment, she saw his mighty right arm swing as he hurled a stone in a great arc up over the house. A second later Betsy heard the rock hit and then go rolling down the steep-pitched roof before it finally fell to the ground behind the house. Upon hearing the clatter John Bell and the boys stopped in their tracks and turned and ran to the back of the house, hoping that at last they would find something that would explain the sounds they had heard in the house.

Dean took Betsy by the wrist pulling her along as he quickly crossed the remaining yard to shelter in the woods that stood between the house and the spring. Without pause and without explanation, he led her in a circuitous route that eventually brought them out behind the stable. By this time John and the boys had decided that whatever they heard land in the backyard was no longer there and had moved back to the north side of the house, still determined to find whatever, or whoever was responsible for the strange noise.

Now Dean motioned Betsy to follow. Moving quickly from shadow to shadow, he brought her to the south side of the house. From there she easily slipped through the front door. A moment later she had quietly climbed the stairs and taken refuge in her own bed. She realized that she had taken a foolish chance and had come within a hair's breadth of being discovered.

But the close call brought on a feeling of exhilaration. She felt as though she was intoxicated.

Why on earth, she wondered, had Dean gone to so much trouble to keep her from being discovered? Had they caught him, they would surely have beaten him and possibly sold him at the slave auction.

As soon as she finished her breakfast the following morning, she left the house and went out to the stable in search of Dean. She found him in the harness room cleaning and oiling several pieces of harness. She stood in the doorway watching until he sensed her presence and turned.

"Mawning, Miss Betsy," he fawned with a wide grin that exposed a set of perfect teeth.

"You know, don't you?" she said in the direct way that was becoming more and more a part of her mannerism.

"Know what, Miss Betsy?" he asked appearing puzzled.

"What I was doing last night."

"Yessum, you was pranking with dis here bull whacker."

As he spoke, he drew the peg wrapped in its string from his pocket and offered it to Betsy. She stared at the thing a moment then waved it away.

"What do you know about bull whackers?" she asked.

"I seed `em over in North Carolina foe Massa cross de mountains," Dean told her. "White folks use `em to scare niggers."

"Do you know how to use one?"

"Yessum, I knows."

"Why did you help me get away last night?"

"Youse a voodoo lady. Dean a voodoo man."

Now Betsy had a new idea.

"Suppose I let you keep the bull whacker," she said to Dean, "would you use it whenever I wanted you to?"

Dean flashed his wide grin, and Betsy knew that she had gained a valuable ally.

14

CALL FOR HELP

The arrangement between Betsy and Dean was simple and uncomplicated. When Betsy wanted Dean to use the bull whacker, she would place a lighted candle in the window of her room that opened to the rear of the house. Seeing the candle from his cabin, Dean would slip out into the night and a few minutes later the strange noise would be heard throughout the house.

Now the noises occurred while she was present with the family. Suspicions that might have resulted because of a pattern of her absence were now averted.

During the days that followed, noises were heard almost nightly. No sooner would the family be abed than the knocking- -which was the way John Bell described the noise--would start.

There were other demonstrations. Cover would be jerked from the boys' bed, and Betsy would be assailed by some invisible force that pulled her hair and slapped her cheeks. John Bell now accepted the supernatural origin of all the demonstrations and made no further attempts to find the source. Had Betsy known her father better, she would have realized that this was an ominous sign.

Since John Bell had prohibited his family from talking about the frequent and strange phenomena happening in his home, the community had not learned about it. Normalcy now reigned in the community, especially since those earlier happenings that had held the community's interest had now died down and were forgotten.

Richard visited the family in May without realizing that anything out of the ordinary was going on. Richard had missed Betsy greatly, but it was a need to confer with John Bell that finally brought him back to Adams. He wanted to let John Bell know that he would not be available to teach school that fall.

As it happened, the county had a vacant seat in the state assembly, and Richard's employer, Tom Crosswy, wanted him to stand for it. For a person of Richard's background and nature, this was heady stuff. At last, he would be a person of influence. If his efforts were successful, he would become the state senator for Robertson County. At Tom Crosswy's urging, a number of local businessmen had agreed to support Richard's candidacy. The salary was modest--the theory being that only men of substance should run for public office--but Richard saw the office as a way of opening doors that would make it possible for him to support a family. The election would be held in the fall, and if elected, Richard would not be available to teach the school. He felt it only fair to give notice so John Bell could find another teacher.

He left Springfield late on a Saturday afternoon and did not arrive in Adams until very late that night. Rather than disturb the Bells, or his old landlady, he decided to spend the remainder of the night in the schoolhouse.

The schoolhouse door had no latch. He pushed it open and rummaged about in the dark until he found one of the candles that he had brought the previous winter. He lit it and stood looking about the room, savoring the sights and smells that in five months had become so familiar.

His eyes were drawn to the bench where Betsy always sat. He went over to examine it and found a bit of blue ribbon that she sometimes used to tie back her hair. He picked it up, pressed it to his cheeks then carefully put it into his pocket.

It was May, but there was a night chill in the air. He went out to the wood pile and gathered some small sticks of wood.

Back inside he built a small fire. The knowledge that he was so close to Betsy made him very lonely. He stretched out in front of the fire on the rough puncheon floor and watched the flames.

"Oh, Betsy," he thought, "Why can't you see me in your vision and come to me now."

In her own bed, Betsy awoke from a dream. She had been in the schoolhouse with Richard. They had been lying on the floor together, and the evidence of his desire was in his eyes.

"You want to plant your seed inside of me," she had told him.

His eyes had been like flames, and he nodded his head in the affirmative.

"I don't think I would mind at all," she had told him.

Then as he pulled her into his arms, she had awakened. The dream was one that she had dreamed before. She had not suspected that Richard was so close to her now.

She saw Richard the next morning at the church. As the Bell family surrey pulled into the churchyard, she saw him standing in a crowd of people. Their eyes met, but there was no opportunity for them to talk. Josh Gardner was already hovering by her side, and everyone at the church wanted to talk to Richard.

The day continued to be an exercise in frustration. Betsy's father assumed that Richard had returned to renew his acquaintances in the community, so he invited many of the parishioners to dinner.

Richard's news about standing for the State Assembly meant that John would have to go to the trouble of finding a new teacher, but nevertheless he was thrilled with Richard's decision and promised his wholehearted support.

It was Lucy that kept the day from being a total frustration for Betsy. After the guests had finished dinner, she called Betsy into the house and sent for Richard. Once Betsy and Richard were together in one of the downstairs bedrooms, Lucy discretely withdrew and closed the door behind her. But even this brief interlude failed to live up to their expectations. The moment they were alone, Betsy rushed into Richard's arms and hugged him with furious intensity, and before he could explain about his decision to stand for the Assembly and how he expected that to eventually make it possible for them to get married, Betsy stepped back from the embrace and demanded.

"Who was she?"

"What on earth are you talking about?" he asked.

"That woman I saw in your office. The one whose father wanted you to come for dinner."

Richard realized that she had seen him in one of her visions but had a hard time remembering the incident. But at last, he was able to assure her that she had seen the daughter of his employer--a lady who was happily married.

Lucy's return interrupted any further conversation, and by mid-afternoon Richard left to return to Springfield without having a chance to explain his plans to Betsy.

On Monday night, John Bell announced that it would be necessary to find a new teacher for the school since Richard was going to stand for the Assembly seat.

Shortly after retiring to her room, Betsy was angry and very frightened. She lit her candle and placed it in the rear window, and later Dean put on a most spectacular display. Although John Bell had enjoined the family from discussing the happenings of the past few weeks, he was now about to break his own rule. He was fully convinced that the events that plagued his family had a supernatural origin. Since the supernatural belonged in the realm of the Devil, relief could come only by Divine intervention. All his life, John Bell had counted himself among the righteous, but now he wondered if he might be punished for some sin he had unknowingly committed.

Beset by increasing self-doubt, John Bell decided that he must discuss the matter with the Reverend Thomas Gunn. The next day Bell hitched his horse at the Gunn gate and knocked at the door.

In addition to his ministry, Thomas Gunn operated a small plantation with the help of three slave families. That morning he was out supervising the preparation of a field he intended to

125

plant in tobacco. Mrs. Gunn directed John to the field, where he found the Reverend leaning against a wagon watching his slaves work with plow, harrow, and drag to pulverize the soil and smooth it down in order to receive the tender tobacco plants. For the next half hour, the two men discussed crops, weather and current events, but eventually John Bell got around to explaining the reason for his visit.

Thomas Gunn was dumbfounded. He had preached on the sin of witchcraft many times and certainly believed in the supernatural, but he had never expected to encounter it in his own congregation.

"Are you sure that there are no natural causes for these noises?" he asked.

John recounted the efforts he and his boys had made to find the source of the noises.

"Have you seen any manifestation of this spirit?" the Preacher asked.

"No, nothing visible," John answered.

"Has the spirit made any effort to communicate with you or with anyone in the family?"

"No, all that has happened so far are the noises, the pulling of bed covers and some physical abuse of Betsy."

"In what way has Miss Betsy been abused?"

John explained.

"Brother John, have you prayed about this?"

"Many times, but as of yet my prayers have not been answered."

"Have you tried speaking to the spirit, perhaps to learn why it has seen fit to visit your family?"

"No, I haven't tried that."

Before John Bell took his leave, Thomas Gunn had suggested that he and Mrs. Gunn spend the following night at the Bell house to see if he could make contact with the spirit. He admonished John to be of good cheer.

"The Lord will not abandon his children," Reverend Gunn assured him.

John Bell hurried home to inform the family of the impending visit. For the first time since he had decided that the demonstrations had a supernatural origin, he had hope of relief. The announcement that the Reverend and Mrs. Gunn would be guests for the night, and that they were coming for the express purpose of determining the nature of the recent happenings aroused only mild interest at the table. The exception was Betsy. Having indulged herself in pranks over the past few weeks, she was starting to become bored. As each new manifestation became common place, the family became resigned so that each event aroused less and less excitement.

That very morning, she had awakened physically exhausted, and had thought about dropping the whole business, at least for the time being. Now she was to have a new audience and a new challenge. Her pulse quickened. The Gunn's arrived just as the family was about to sit down for supper. They assured everyone that they had eaten before leaving home, but on John Bell's urging they allowed themselves to be seated at the table and then to partake of the meal. During supper, the conversation was about the most recent events that had disturbed the household. Brother Gunn also told stories about what he called strange manifestations of spirits in other times and places. According to him, so-called ghosts were, in reality, disturbed spirits of the deceased who had been unable to break their bonds with their past life.

"I am told that it is sometimes possible to communicate with the disembodied spirit. If this is possible, we may be able to learn the reason for their restless condition and perhaps find a way of putting their anxieties to rest."

Across the table Betsy sat demurely. But she heard every word with fascination and amusement. Eventually the conversation got around to the physical abuse she had suffered at the hands of the spirit. Brother Gunn questioned her about the details.

"Your father tells me that the spirit often pulls your hair," he prompted.

Betsy nodded without looking at the Reverend.

"And slaps you on the cheeks," he continued.

Again, she nodded.

"When it pulls your hair, does it pull hard?"

"Yes," Betsy said in a near whisper that prompted her father to urge

"Speak up, child. Brother Gunn is here to help us."

"And when it slaps your cheeks, do the blows sting?" Brother Gunn asked.

Betsy nodded emphatically.

"Do you ever see anything?"

"Not since I saw that lady out in the orchard."

"Does it ever try to speak to you?"

All through this conversation, Betsy appeared to be the soul of reluctance and modesty. But her mind had been racing, and now she had an inspiration.

"Only once," she whispered.

This was news to the family. Interest perked up.

"You never mentioned this," her father said.

"I know," she answered, "I was afraid you might be disturbed." Again, her voice was barely audible. "It was hard to understand. I don't think it spoke English very good."

"What language would it speak?" her father asked.

"Did you understand any of it at all?" the Preacher interrupted.

"I thought I recognized the word `Gardner,'" Betsy said.

"Do you mean a person who works in a garden?" The Reverend asked.

"I thought maybe it was a name," Betsy countered shyly.

"Could it possibly have something to do with the Gardner family--Josh Gardner, perhaps?"

"I don't know, maybe," Betsy conceded.

Supper was followed by a family devotional. While Betsy yawned, John Bell read a long chapter from the scriptures. Brother Gunn then led the family in prayer. It was a long and rambling harangue that reminded God of the family's many Christian virtues--of John Bell's support of many righteous causes, of Lucy's administrations in the community, and even of Betsy's maidenly modesty.

The Reverend then took God to task for allowing a disembodied spirit to haunt and torment "this righteous family." He ended with a plea that the Heavenly Father allow "this cup to pass" and that the household might continue in peace and righteousness of the Lord.

The prayer was elegant and interspersed with flowery phrases. Betsy recalled that the slaves called Thomas Gunn "old sugar mouth" and fought to suppress a giggle.

When the family devotional was over, all retired to bed. The younger boys had once more been dispossessed and the Gunn's occupied the room across the hall from Betsy. In her own room, Betsy took Esther's cape from the closet and put her lighted candle in the window. Across the hall, Thomas Gunn assured his nervous wife that it was most likely that they would spend a quiet and restful night.

"If there were a spirit, our prayers may have already sent it on its way to Limbo, the place between heaven and hell where the spirits await final judgment."

He lay down beside his wife and pulled the covers up snugly about his shoulders. Then he closed his eyes and released a long sigh. As he drifted into sleep, his wife elbowed him in the ribs.

"Thomas, what's making that racket?"

He awoke fully and lifted his head to listen. At first, he heard nothing. Then he detected a gentle rasping that seemed to come from under the bed.

"It's likely a rat," he assured his wife.

"It sounds like it's gnawing on the leg of the bed," his wife said.

Upon first entering the room, Thomas had made certain to latch the door. Now it suddenly burst open and before he could react, the covers were snatched off the bed. Both he and his wife lay exposed in their nightgowns. Mrs. Gunn screamed, and Thomas bolted upright. He was thoroughly frightened, but he proved to have more courage than the spirit had expected.

In a loud voice, he demanded, "Who are you, and what do you want of these good people?"

"The room was suddenly filled with wild insane laughter and suddenly words poured forth that were a strange mixture of Latin and nonsensical phrases. The only word that was remotely decipherable was the single word "Gardner."

At the same time there was a scream from across the hall and the distinct sound of an open palm striking human flesh. The entire household was aroused. Everyone gathered in the upstairs hallway. Betsy appeared to be on the verge of hysteria and there was a babble of voices as everyone tried to talk at once.

Little by little the story came out. Thomas and Mrs. Gunn told how they had first heard the rasping noise.

"Thomas told me it was just a rat, but I knew I had never heard a rat make that kind of noise," Mrs. Gunn told Lucy.

Thomas related how the door had burst open and the covers had been snatched off the bed. Betsy sobbed out a tale of being pulled from the bed by the hair of her head and slapped on both cheeks. Both Thomas and Betsy agreed that the spirit had spoken in an unintelligible voice.

"But I distinctly heard the word "Gardner," the Reverend said, "though I know not in what context the word was used."

"I thought I heard it say, 'you must never marry Josh Gardner,'" Betsy said.

The two men took the candle and went to examine the guest room. The bed covers were piled on the floor at the foot of the bed, just as they had been on the previous occasion when the two young boys occupied the room. They then turned their attention on the door latch. It was intact.

"I made sure that it was fastened," the Reverend said. "Mrs. Gunn can assure you of that."

"There is no way the latch could be lifted from outside the room," John said.

"Except by supernatural power," Thomas concluded.

"When we had the first disturbance, I thought perhaps there

had been an intruder," John said. "But an intruder would have had to break that latch to get in this room tonight."

The men joined the women in the hall.

"I'm certain that what happened here tonight was beyond human ability," Thomas Gunn told the women. "But at the same time, I had the feeling that I was dealing with something that had powers of reason."

"Then what on earth can we do?" Lucy Bell asked.

"We must pray for guidance and deliverance," Gunn told her. Then he turned to John. "Brother John, I do question the wisdom of remaining silent about your troubles. The people of this community are your Christian brothers. You must allow them to help you bear this burden. Their prayers can be a great source of strength and comfort. I must ask you to allow me to lay this matter before the congregation next Sunday."

"But I hate to burden others with a family problem," John Bell protested.

"Brother John, the church is your family," the Reverend reminded him.

The discussion lasted well past midnight, but at last exhaustion overcame excitement, and all agreed to return to bed to try to get some rest. As the last candle was snuffed out, the house became still. As everyone dozed off, the sound of soft laughter seemed to penetrate every corner of the house.

15

THE WITCH GETS A NAME

The Oak Grove congregation assembled for worship the following Sunday never suspecting anything out of the ordinary. Two and a half hours later they filed out of the church completely stunned by the thing they had just heard from Reverend Gunn. John Bell was a pillar of the community, and a man who, in many eyes, was as solid as the Rock of Gibraltar. Now they had learned his house was haunted.

Had the story involved a lesser person, they might have laughed it off as some prank to gain attention, but with Brother John, that was not possible. And the source of this astonishing news was none other than their own Reverend Gunn. Even more amazing, the good Reverend had been present when the Witch had demonstrated its power.

The good people of the Adams community were honest and uncomplicated people. A fair percentage of them could neither read nor write, and a few could not sign their names. But, to a man, they believed every word spoken in the Bible, and the Bible spoke about witches.

Thomas Gunn was the man they looked to for guidance, not only about getting into the next world, but also about the conduct of their affairs in this life. From long experience, they knew that he would never lie, and they never considered the possibility that he could be mistaken. Thus, the Bell Witch made its public debut through the highest authority the community could imagine. Two men, whom they trusted, said that the Bell house was haunted, and that settled the matter.

During the discussion neither Thomas Gunn nor John Bell had used the word "witch." But it was a word that sprang automatically into the consciousness of the community. In those days, "witch" was a catch-all word applied broadly to any person or spirit versed in the supernatural. It could apply to man or woman who practiced black magic or, just as well, to those disembodied spirits unable to make the transition to limbo.

Before night fell on that Sunday, people on both sides of the Red River were speaking of the "Bell Witch" as though its existence was an established fact.

Although John Bell's neighbors were superstitious and often unlearned, they were not without courage. That night several families assembled at the Bell home and announced that they had come to lend moral support and, if possible, to persuade the Witch to haunt elsewhere.

No one in the group knew what to expect, or if there was any risk involved, but they all knew that a neighbor was in trouble, and that was all that mattered. As the night descended, Betsy went up to her room to light her candle and placed it in her rear window. At eight the visitors left the front room and took chairs in the dining room. They insisted that the Bell family go to bed.

Reluctantly John and Lucy went to the front room where their bed was located and bolted the door. Both undressed and put on long nightgowns. John was first in bed, and as he stretched out, his feet came into contact with something under the cover.

"What in the world do you have here in the bed?" He asked his wife.

"I don't have anything in the bed," Lucy answered. "What are you talking about?"

"Well, I feel something," he said as he got out of bed and threw back the cover.

At first neither recognized the thing that lay on the bed linens. Lucy picked up the candle and brought it closer.

"It looks like a bone," she said, "but how on earth did it get here?"

A chill wet through John Bell's body. Without further examination, he knew that the bone would prove to be human. Both got dressed again.

Among their visitors that night was Doctor Hopson, the family physician. He was summoned to the front room.

"It's a femur," he pronounced. "That's the large bone here in the thigh."

He touched his own thigh to give emphasis to his explanation.

"I'm quite certain that it's human," the doctor continued. "But I would say that it's very old. I'd guess it was taken from a grave where it has lain for many years. How did it get here?"

As though to answer the good doctor's question, there was a loud rasping sound that vibrated through the entire house. (Someone later described it as sounding like a bow being drawn over the strings of a witch's fiddle). With it came soft laughter that echoed from the hallway.

Suddenly from upstairs the guests heard Betsy screaming. She came running down the steps as though pursued by devils. She ran to her mother's arms.

"Momma, it told me I could never marry Josh Gardner," she sobbed. "It said that terrible things would happen if I did."

Doctor Hopson examined Betsy and noted that both cheeks were red and slightly puffed. He thought he was able to make out the imprint of a human hand.

All the guests were convinced that they had witnessed a supernatural manifestation.

A more erudite man possessed of a more logical mind might have raised some critical questions about what had been witnessed that night. Why, for example, had a disembodied spirit left the imprint of a living hand on Betsy's cheeks? Why could it not have been quite easy for someone to have placed the bone in the bed much earlier in the day? Why would it not have been easy to ascribe a human origin to the rasping and noises that could have been easily accomplished under cover of the pitch darkness that normally reigned in the house at night? If, according to the wisdom of the day, witches worked for universal evil, then why would a witch warn Betsy away from the evil of an impending marriage? Certainly, marriage is a concern of the living, not the dead.

Betsy knew that a man like Richard would be asking such questions. Given Richard's knowledge of Betsy's visions, skills and imagination, he would have caught on immediately to what was going on tonight. But for the moment, Richard was in Springfield with friends planning his campaign to become the county's state senator. Therefore, the Witch was left to sew its seeds of superstition unchallenged.

Early the following morning the delegation of neighbors left the Bell house absolutely certain that a witch was troubling the Bell family. There was much concern for poor sweet Betsy who seemed to be the particular object of the Witch's wrath.

Betsy did not get out of bed that morning until all the guests had left. All the excitement was taking a lot of her energy. She decided to go riding as soon as she finished breakfast. She had Dean saddle Fanny, and she rode out along the road with no thought as to a destination. A mile from the house, she decided to go visit Esther.

Lucy watched Betsy ride away. Recent events had left her deeply troubled. Her concern had less to do with the fact that the house seemed to be haunted, than it did with the effect on both John and Betsy. So far, the spirit had not shown any intent to do anyone any real harm. The rapping and rasping sounded a lot like the noise she had heard back in North Carolina when pranksters tried to scare folks with a bull whacker.

The attacks on Betsy were probably painful but did not inflict any real damage. She decided to go upstairs and see if she could find anything the men had missed on the night of the Gunn's visit. In dim candlelight, things could easily be overlooked.

At first, she found nothing out of the ordinary. Betsy's room had its usual austere neatness (in contrast to the usual disorder of the boys' room). The spirit had left no physical sign of its presence. She was about to go back down the stairs when she noticed something in a corner of the hallway. Even in the light of morning, deep shadows made the outline indistinct. She prodded the object with the toe of her shoe. It rattled across the floor and came to rest in better light. It was a knife. Lucy picked it up. It was old and worn, but familiar. It was the knife that Nanny used in the kitchen to scrape the grease and grime off pots and pans. The blade had been ground down from years of whetting and scrapping until it was not much thicker than a sheet of paper. Intending to return the knife to the kitchen, Lucy started back down the stairs. As she passed the boys' room, the door caught her attention. The door had been made from rough boards shortly after the family had moved into the house. Four boards had been tightly fitted onto a Z frame. In time the boards had dried and warped leaving narrow slits between one board and another. On impulse, Lucy pushed the blade of the knife through one of the cracks. Looking on the inside of the door, she saw that the blade penetrated by several inches. It now occurred to her that by moving the knife upwards, the door latch could be lifted. Thoughts reeled through her mind. That could easily explain how the door had been opened the night the Gunn's had slept in the room. If the knife had been used to open the door, it meant that the door could have been opened by a human hand, not by a spirit. So, if a human hand had opened the door, it likely followed that the rest of the noises and disturbances could have had a human origin. But who? Nanny? The knife was from the kitchen. But Nanny would never strike Betsy. Lucy knew that for all her gruffness, Nanny was truly fond of Betsy.

Lucy recalled Richard telling her that Betsy had visions. Richard considered such an ability to be rare but not impossible. But Lucy still associated such gifts with dark powers. Still, if Betsy had unlatched the door, who had slapped Betsy? Her questions led her round and round without providing an answer. She went down the steps, wishing she could talk to Richard, but she could think of no way a meeting could be arranged.

The day that Lucy found the knife was also the day that Josh Gardner first learned that the spirit had mentioned him by name. A cold chill ran down his spine. Nevertheless, he swore that it was going to take more than some silly old witch to make him give up Betsy, and he knew he could count on the support of friends and community in support of his resolve.

The community had now reached a firm decision. Various neighbors took turns in coming to the Bell house to sit with the ghost. They came expecting strange things to happen, and the witch rarely disappointed them. By now every person in the area knew that the witch was warning Betsy not to marry Josh Gardner.

There were differences of opinion as to whether Betsy and Josh should go through with their marriage. Some people contended that since witches were of the devil, it would be wrong for Betsy to heed the devil`s advice and break off with Josh. Others urged John Bell to have Betsy and Josh break off their understanding. No decision was reached for the time being.

That spring, Betsy began riding more often. Almost every day she would have Fanny saddled and ride over to visit one of her girlfriends. Frequently she would stop by the general store. Wherever she went, people would gather to express their sympathy and tell her what a brave girl she was.

Locally, Betsy had become something of a celebrity. Now stories about the Bell Witch were being heard beyond the immediate community.

Richard heard about the stories in Springfield, but the story was so outlandish that he considered it nonsense, thinking that the unsophisticated people of the Adams community were blowing things up out of proportion. But the stories persisted. He started to worry. He guessed that Betsy was behind the haunting, but being terribly pressed for time, he allowed himself to do nothing for the time being.

All during this period, Betsy practiced her ventriloquism. Her best opportunities were while out riding alone. Her commands to the horse were relayed through what she had come to call "the Voice." By this time the Voice could sing church hymns without Betsy's moving her lips. Still, she wondered just how good she really was. Richard had praised her, but she found it hard to believe that such a simple thing could really fool anybody. What she needed was an opportunity to try out the voice without subjecting herself to risk.

On a Sunday morning in June, John Bell awoke with a strange feeling. He got out of bed and was getting dressed. He noticed that he was having trouble fastening buttons. When Lucy awoke, he told her that he wished only a few biscuits and coffee for breakfast. When he spoke, he found that his tongue seemed abnormally thick, and he had difficulty forming the words.

Lucy noticed at once. "Why are you talking like that?" she asked.

John pointed to his lips. "My tongue," he mumbled, "it feels like it's swollen."

Lucy took him over to the window where there was good light and insisted that he allow her to examine his tongue. She could see nothing amiss, and shortly after eating his breakfast, John admitted that the strange feeling had gone away.

They went to church as usual, and Josh came home with them for his weekly visit with Betsy. That afternoon while Betsy and Josh occupied the front room, the rest of the family went to sit in the front yard where it was cooler. According to John Bell's rules, some member of the family was always supposed to chaperon Betsy and Josh, but over time, enforcement had grown lax.

Betsy and Josh were pretty much alone in the house. Betsy wondered if Josh ever thought about stealing a kiss from her. But Josh was totally absorbed with other things. Stealing kisses never crossed his mind. Now he was talking about the coming year's tobacco crop. This year he hoped to earn enough money to buy his own slave. For something like the tenth time he told her how it had rained at just the right time to give his newly transplanted tobacco a good start toward growing.

Betsy yawned. Her opinion of Josh's intelligence was certainly biased. He was smart enough about things he was interested in, but romance and witchcraft were not his best subjects. Betsy saw him as a dumb clod as he droned on. Now as Josh started talking about how his mule had gone lame in the right foreleg, it occurred to Betsy that it might be a good time to practice her ventriloquism.

She cast a cautious glance around the room to make sure that everyone else was outside, and as Josh continued to express his concern over his mule, a voice spoke out of thin air.

"Betsy Bell."

Betsy looked up, feigning wide-eyed alarm.

Josh was merely puzzled. He looked at Betsy, noting her alarm. He then looked about the room trying to locate the source of the voice.

Up until that very moment, Josh had had no direct contact with the Witch. He had heard the stories circulating in the community, but, as of yet, the reality of the witch had not hit home.

"Betsy Bell," the voice called again.

"Is that the thing you've been hearing?" Josh asked.

Betsy nodded.

"Betsy, I'm calling you," the voice persisted.

"Yes," Betsy answered aloud. "I hear you."

"So, you are still seeing Josh Gardner, even in spite of all my warnings," the voice accused.

"Yes," Betsy said meekly.

"You know you two can never marry," the voice continued. "I have warned you. If you marry, there will be great calamity."

By this time Josh was on his feet groping about in the air as though he expected to catch hold of the spirit. He was braver than Betsy had expected, but as he lunged about the room, he made such a comical sight that Betsy had a hard time containing her laughter.

On the other hand, the voice laughed wildly at Josh as he lunged and groped around the room. When Josh's actions brought him close to Betsy's chair she yielded to temptation and put out her foot. Josh tripped and came crashing down to the floor.

Betsy jumped from her seat and ran out to the yard. "Momma," she called, "it was the spirit. It spoke to me as plain as day. Josh heard it too. It says we can never get married."

"Oh, dear," Lucy sighed, "it never bothered us during the day before.

There was great commotion in the yard. Josh confirmed Betsy's story. The Witch had spoken and had physically thrown him to the floor. It was the first time that someone other than Betsy had heard the witch and had suffered its abuse.

A thorough search was made through the house, and when nothing was found, John Bell went to the stable and had Dean saddle his mare. He rode off down the road. Now that the spirit was speaking, he was anxious to take the news to Reverend Thomas Gunn.

Thomas Gunn was very excited.

"Now that we have established communication," he told John, "We should be able to find out what keeps the spirit from passing on to Limbo."

He made preparations to return home with John Bell. He was most anxious to have a talk with the spirit.

"Who knows what mysteries we may uncover by talking to someone who has already experienced death," the Reverend Gunn conjectured.

16

THE WITCH'S STORY

The fact that the Witch was speaking ran like wildfire through the community. Although Josh had been completely fooled, Betsy still lacked confidence in her ability to fool anyone else. That night, Thomas Gunn waited in vain for the spirit to make a manifestation. Betsy put the spirit to rest and rested easy herself. Now that another person was attesting to the presence of the spirit, her own story had been confirmed, and there was no reason to take needless chances in the ultimate fulfillment of her goal to break off her engagement to Josh and marry Richard Powell.

Although the Reverend Gunn came to sit with the Bell family every night for more than two weeks, nothing happened. This would be remembered as the longest period of inactivity between the time the spirit had first manifested itself and its final performance some years later. Even Josh was spared a performance during this period.

The inactivity was frustrating to Brother Gunn. Now that the spirit was speaking, he was most anxious to engage it in conversation. Each night he would arrive with the scheduled visitors. Then the elder Bells would be persuaded to go to bed and get their rest. The visitors would gather in the dining room where Thomas Gunn would stand and challenge the spirit.

141

"I call on the spirit that has troubled this good family to speak up and identify itself."

All would wait patiently, some with wide eyed apprehension, but nothing happened.

During this period Betsy often came down from her room to sit with the visitors. Everyone assumed that she was staying with the group in hopes that the spirit would not assail her in the midst of so many.

During these long night vigils, Betsy would allow herself to doze with her head resting on the table. Although she slept at times, she missed little that was said about the table. Believing that she was deeply asleep, the guests talked freely. Betsy especially enjoyed their expressions of sympathy.

"Isn't it awful for such a sweet pretty child to have such vexation."

"But she's so brave about it. I've never heard a word of complaint."

"And such a modest young lady. She sits so quietly and never interrupts her elders."

"I wish my own were half as polite."

By the end of the second week, some of the visitors began to express skepticism.

"This is the second time I've set up all night, and I've yet to see or hear anything out of the ordinary."

"Reverend, are you sure this house is haunted?"

By the following Sunday night, the doubters were in a majority, and Brother Gunn was stung by their skepticism. His appeals to the spirit to reveal itself began to carry a note of desperation.

Betsy sat quietly, as she often did, among the visitors at the table. She was becoming concerned over the expressions of doubt about the existence of the Witch. She knew that the success of her plans depended upon the community's belief in the Witch. Despite the Witch's manifestation around Josh,

Betsy now realized that that would not be enough evidence to sustain the community's belief in the Witch. Belief in the Witch would have to be reinforced by a more dramatic manifestation in the presence of a larger number of witnesses.

Betsy excused herself and went to her room to get a pillow. When she returned to reassume her seat at the table, a candle burned brightly in the window of her room. She placed the pillow on the table and laid her head to rest upon it. Heaving a sigh, she appeared to drop off to sleep within the minute.

The conversation around the table droned on for about five minutes when the assembled visitors heard a series of light taps, no louder than a set of fingers drumming on the table. Conversation ceased immediately. Each man cast a fearful look at his neighbor. Skepticism evaporated.

Thomas Gunn arose immediately from his chair. "Spirit, I call you. Speak. Tell us why you torment these good people."

The tapping stopped, and the only sound in the room was Betsy's deep breathing and what might have been a rat gnawing on the leg of the table.

"Speak, Spirit, speak." Thomas Gunn challenged.

Suddenly the very walls seemed to tremble and there was a noise as though the whole house was shuddering.

"Who is this sugar-mouthed preacher who disturbs my rest?"

The question came out of thin air, and every man at the table thought it came from a different direction. No skeptics remained in the room. Brave men trembled in the presence of the spirit. Later some of those men swore that they had seen a shimmering over the table. Others claimed that a cold chill cut through them.

No man was more frightened than Thomas Gunn, but his calling as the spiritual leader of the people gave him courage.

"Who are you?" Thomas shouted. "Why do you bother these good people?"

"I am a spirit departed," the voice answered. "Once I was at rest. He who disturbed me must suffer his transgression. Those who would bring disaster must be stopped from further pursuit of their folly."

"Who were you in this life?" Reverend Gunn persisted.

"In another time I was chief among my people. When I passed away, my people laid me to rest with great honor. Yet for the sake of a stone, my rest was broken, and my bones scattered. I shall not rest until all have been returned to the grave. Now I have spoken. Preacher, you need not call me, I shall not return until I am ready."

For the space of a full minute, there was absolute silence in the room. When it became apparent that the spirit had finished, everyone began talking at once. The resulting babble was indecipherable. Each person in the room had heard the spirit's words, but no one professed to understand their meaning. After some heated discussion, Thomas Gunn decided to awaken the Bells.

"Maybe John will know the meaning," Thomas explained.

Betsy's parents were summoned, and once dressed they joined their guests at the table. There was renewed confusion as each guest tried to be the one to tell what had happened.

Eventually John and Lucy got the gist of the story.

"I thought it might have some meaning to you, John," the Reverend Gunn explained.

John shook his head. "I know of nothing that would explain it," he said.

"'I am a spirit departed,'" the Reverend Gunn quoted. "'Once I was at rest. He who disturbed me must suffer his transgression.'"

John Bell continued to shake his head. "I've certainly disturbed no spirits," he protested.

"'For the sake of a stone, my rest was broken, and my bones were scattered,'" the Reverend continued quoting. He spoke slowly and deliberately as though trying to fit the pieces into a puzzle.

"'For the sake of a stone,'" he began repeating the sentences once more.

"Could it possibly refer to the Indian grave?" Lucy asked.

"What Indian grave?" John asked impatiently, and Betsy now realized that her father had forgotten about his disturbing the old grave.

"You know," Lucy clarified, "the one back in the woods where you got the stones to pave the spring house floor."

"Aw, surely not," John protested.

"That Witch said something about being an Indian," one of the guests blurted out.

"Yes, yes," Thomas Gunn agreed. "Let me see if I can remember it: 'In another time, I was chief among my people. When I passed away, my people laid me to rest with great honor. Yet for the sake of a stone, my rest was broken, and my bones scattered. I shall not rest until all have returned to the grave.'"

"See, I told you," Another man said. "Once, that spirit was an Indian chief."

"But it was only an Indian grave and very old," John protested, now recalling the incident.

"Did you open it?" Thomas Gunn asked.

"I picked out some rocks that were suited for paving the springhouse," John admitted.

"Did you expose any bones?" Thomas asked.

"I suppose I did. Yes, there was a skeleton. There was this big rock, bigger than all the rest. I pried it up, and there were bones under the rock."

"What did you do with them?"

"I remember picking up the skull. The lower jawbone fell away. I believe I cast it aside."

"Oh, God!" Lucy gasped. "The bone in the bed. Don't you remember? Doctor Hopson said it was a human leg bone and that it was very old and looked as though it had lain in the grave a long time, and we didn't know how it got here."

Now the Reverend Thomas Gunn made a pronouncement: "Tomorrow we will all see that the bones are reburied and that the grave is restored. That should lay the spirit to rest."

Early the following morning a party of men carrying the

bone that had been found in John Bell's bed left the Bell house long before Betsy was out of bed.

Betsy awoke well rested and satisfied with her accomplishment of the previous evening. The Voice had performed far beyond her expectations. Everyone had been fooled.

"Richard would have been proud of me," she thought.

It was after noon when the men returned from the woods. All were in good spirits, but none more so than John Bell himself.

"The skeleton has been returned, and the grave fully restored," Thomas Gunn told Lucy Bell. "Now you should have no more visits from the spirit world."

The men were escorted down to the spring house to taste the drippings from the Bell still, and afterwards they gathered at the dining room table for a late afternoon dinner.

Betsy helped her mother and Nanny serve the late diner. She was aware of the general trend of the conversation. Everyone shared Thomas Gunn's opinion that the community was finally rid of its troublesome spirit.

The following day John Bell felt that a celebration was in order, and he sent out invitations to all his neighbors. The Bell family would host a barbecue at the Bell farm on Sunday afternoon. Everyone was invited.

Farm work came to a standstill. Every slave was needed to get ready for the great event. John even sent a rider to Springfield to invite Richard Powell, reminding him that this would be an opportunity for him to contact a large bloc of voters.

No one was more excited than Betsy. Each day she kept busy helping with the many chores. Each night she lay in bed thinking how she would handle the spirit's next appearance. More than anything, she wanted Richard to be proud of how well she had mastered her lessons.

On Sunday morning final preparations for the celebration were well in hand as pigs roasted on the spits. John Bell decided to forego the Sunday morning service to oversee the final preparations, but he made sure that Lucy and the children attended church. He felt better than he had for months. There had been no disturbances for almost a week. Apparently, the restoration of the Indian grave had laid the spirit to rest. Once more he looked to the future with confidence. There would be no further need for the community's nightly vigils in his home. His neighbors could return to the routine of their daily lives.

Betsy also wanted to stay home that Sunday hoping to surreptitiously catch a few minutes alone with Richard Powell when he arrived. But her father insisted she accompany the rest of the family to church.

At nine in the morning, Dean drove the surrey around to the door, and all the family except John climbed aboard. In the churchyard, Josh commandeered Betsy and followed her inside to the family pew. Services were routine. Brother Gunn preached about the Prodigal Son. It was a sermon he had delivered many times, and Betsy could have repeated it from memory. She turned her mind to other thoughts. The service dragged on, and Betsy could only think about getting home to see Richard before the crowd got too big.

In addition to inviting the Oak Grove congregation, her father had also sent a special invitation to the congregation of the Drake's Pond Baptist Church to attend the barbecue. Her father was on the Board of Deacons of that congregation, and its minister, Brother Sugg Fort, was almost as close a friend as Brother Thomas Gunn.

Now, out of boredom, Betsy consciously called up a vision of the Drake's Pond Baptist Church service on the off chance that there might be something more interesting going on there. There wasn't. Brother Sugg's sermon was about the Twenty-third Psalm, and again it was something Betsy had heard plenty of times before.

When the services finally ended, Dean collected the family to drive them home. Dean sensed Betsy's urgency to get home, but speed was out of the question. Traffic clogged the road as invited guests converged on the Bell plantation. When the surrey pulled into the drive, a large crowd had already gathered. As the surrey neared the house, Betsy spotted Richard. A crowd of people were gathered around him talking and asking questions. Betsy was frustrated knowing there would be no opportunity to have a private word with Richard, much less any show of affection.

17

THE SPIRIT CONFOUNDS
THE PREACHERS

The afternoon wore on slowly, and Betsy's frustration grew more pronounced. She had barely spoken to Richard. Wherever he went, well-meaning neighbors followed talking to him about politics and his candidacy for state senator. Since General Jackson's victory over the British in New Orleans just over a year ago most men were fervently patriotic and keenly interested in politics. There was not a man in the yard that afternoon who would have not given his eyeteeth to hold a political office. Lacking that, the next best thing was to be on a first name basis with an elected official, and in this case a potential politician like Richard was one of their own.

Richard had been highly respected as Professor Powell, but now that he was aspiring to run for elected office, his fame and reputation were enhanced more than ever.

In Springfield, Richard had allowed himself to be persuaded to run for office with great reluctance. Memories of past rejections made him cautious and very apprehensive about being put into a position that would attract so much public attention. Even now he lived in dread of being pointed out as that "actor fellow" and having his dreams dashed around him.

Nevertheless, the thought of being an elected senator was as appealing to Richard as it was to any man. Winning such an election was the ultimate measure of public acceptance. Attaining such high office and esteem could likely protect him from his past. On the frontier, men with shady pasts had often redeemed themselves through heroic deeds and service. General Andrew Jackson was a good case in point. The General had married a woman still married to her first husband. There had been scandal and extreme criticism over the General's sinful impropriety, but his success as an Indian fighter and defender of New Orleans against the British, had erased all public memory of his past indiscretions, and he was now a living frontier hero. Most of the men on the frontier, including those of Spingfield and Adams, would have followed General Jackson through flood and fire had the need arisen.

Richard had allowed himself to be persuaded to run for office, and as time passed, and there had been no exposure of his past, he had started to enjoy the approbation. Of course, his real opinions on many topics had to be concealed behind a facade of banality, and now his campaign smile was almost a permanent fixture on his face.

That afternoon Betsy watched his performance in the yard with ill-concealed disgust. She recognized the falseness of it all, and she inwardly scorned at the hypocrisy emanating from this political candidate.

Finally, she turned away, sending a deliberate signal of contempt to Richard. She grabbed a reluctant Josh Gardner by the arm and took him to the front room of the house where, for over an hour, she listened attentively while Josh chattered on about crops and weather.

Richard understood the signal Betsy had given him. His emotions were mixed. He knew that he should make a determined effort to have a few words in private with Betsy. But that was simply too risky. In the presence of so many people, he could not risk searching out an intimate moment with Betsy. The people around him were gullible but not totally unobservant. In addition, he could not risk offending a bloc of voters by abruptly turning away and leaving them for no good reason.

Richard continued smiling at those self-important men who continued to shower him with the benefit of their opinions. Most of their conversations focused on roads, postal deliveries, Indian and outlaw dangers, and other civic concerns that their local representative to the state legislature should be sure aware of.

Now as Richard talked and smiled to those around him, he began to pick up on the recent activities surrounding the "Bell Witch." He noted that some people were now referring to the Witch as "Old Kate." He ultimately picked up enough tidbits of conversations to figure out why some people applied that new name to the Witch.

Richard learned that among the neighbors of the Bell family was a family by the name of Batts. Old man Batts was an invalid. Of necessity his wife, Kate, had assumed the role as head of the family. Evidently Kate Batts had never been pretty. She was outspoken. "Apt to give a neighbor a good piece of her mind," as someone put it.

Years of bearing the weight of caring for her family and doing the heavy farm chores had taken their toll. Kate Batts grew old before her time, and she became even more irascible and sharp-tongued with her neighbors. She had become a local character. Some of her neighbors simply laughed at her antics, while others who had felt the wrath of her temper and the bite of her sharp tongue came to resent her. Eventually everyone avoided her, and she was isolated from the community.

In those days, it was easy for people to believe that an ugly, old, bad-tempered woman living in isolation from everyone was a likely candidate for witch hood. Some people did not hesitate to characterize her with that description. When the trouble with the Bell family began, some people believed that Kate Batts could have been the cause, and even when subsequent developments disproved Kate Batts' involvement beyond any doubt, the name nevertheless stuck, and people were apt to call the spirit haunting the Bell home "Old Kate," as well as "The Witch."

That afternoon, as Richard continued conversing with

several people, he learned the latest story (along with the attendant embellishments) about the manifestation of the Witch among the visitors in the Bell home, and how the following day the men had gone to restore the tomb of the Indian chief.

Richard had no trouble believing that Betsy had been the source of these manifestations. Betsy was extremely skilled in her ventriloquism, and that, coupled with the gullibility of folks in the community, made it easy for her to pull off the things he was now hearing about the Witch. Richard was concerned and somewhat fearful. He was not concerned about the effect of her pranks on the rest of the Bell family or on the community in general as much as he was concerned for Betsy's welfare. He figured she was getting into deep water. More to the point, he was concerned about Betsy's motivations for her continued actions and the possibility that she had been doing these things purely for childish entertainment. He resolved that he must talk to Betsy alone before leaving Adams.

In the house, Betsy continued to listen to Josh, giving every indication that she was interested in the usual prattle that came out of Josh's mouth. She encouraged him with an innocent smile, and occasionally she would contribute a "really?" or an "is that so?" in response to what Josh said.

Betsy knew she was being hypocritical with Josh, just as Richard was playing the hypocrite with the neighbors in the yard. She resented everything happening today, and she knew just as well that Richard was miserable in the role he was being forced to play as candidate Richard Powell. By turning away from him and leaving his presence, she had hurt him, and she was sorry for it. She had to do something to get Richard's attention back on her and everyone else's attention off Richard. She firmed up the half-formed plan in her mind that would bring on the next appearance of the Witch. She knew Richard would not approve of her witchcraft, but she was determined to carry out her plan.

At around five o'clock several families announced that they had to "get on home" to do the milking. As they were saying their farewells, Betsy suddenly cut Josh off in the middle of a sentence.

"I'm going out in the yard," she said.

There was a fair-sized crowd still in the yard. Those who had slaves did not need to worry about milking or other evening chores. They would linger on and possibly stay for a bite of supper in the evening.

Now, the crowd was gathered into three groups. The women sat around the long makeshift table. Some of the men were still gathered around Richard, and others were talking with John Bell. John was seated in his favorite rocking chair that had been moved out to the yard for the occasion.

The group around John Bell included the two preachers, Brother Thomas Gunn and Brother Sugg Fort. Everyone was jolly and content after the generous feast and the ongoing congenial conversation in the shade of the Bell house. Laughter broke out over some tale as Betsy approached the men. She sat on the grass to one side of her father's rocking chair.

Josh followed Betsy out into the yard and took up a seat in the grass, not so much positioning himself to be near Betsy, but rather to listen effectively to the conversation of the older men.

"Well, company's fine," John Bell was saying, "but it don't seem like Sunday. Missing services is an awful lot like missing dinner. Food feeds the belly, but praying and preaching nourishes the soul."

"Amen," Brother Fort intoned in a solemn voice usually reserved for the Sunday service.

"Yes, we had a right inspiring service today" Brother Thomas Gunn said, "It's a shame you were not able to attend."

"What did you preach about?" Brother Fort asked.

"I delivered a discourse on the Prodigal Son," Thomas Gunn said.

"And for the fourth time this year!" a loud, unworldly voice interjected out of nowhere.

The tenor of the gathering changed instantly. All conversation ceased. Those men halfway across the yard, who had been in animated conversation with Richard, now forgot Richard and looked in the direction of John Bell and the preachers.

Richard recognized the voice as Betsy's practiced ventriloquism, and, knowing this, he was not surprised by the voice. But he was utterly surprised by the fearful reactions of the people in the yard.

John Bell had risen two thirds out of his chair remaining there frozen with his hands still gripping the arms of the rocker. He seemed suspended in time and motion, then sank back into the chair.

Reverend Gunn remained seated but twisted his head about as he tried to determine where the voice was coming from. He glared at the air like a pugnacious hawk. Reverend Fort merely looked startled. Everyone remained rooted to their spots, mouths gaping and eyes bulging. They all waited agog over what was to come.

Richard recognized an element of comedy about the scene.

The Voice broke out into a wild uncontrolled laughter.

"The little vixen," Richard thought, "she's using the voice to keep from bursting out into laughter herself.

"We restored the grave," Brother Thomas finally found his voice. "We laid your bones to rest."

"You restored the grave and prayed to your Christian God," the Voice retorted. "Your God is not my God. Besides that, my rib is missing. How can I rest without my rib?"

"What do these good people have to do with missing ribs?" Thomas Gunn asked.

"Old Jack Bell was the one who opened my grave. He must pay for disturbing my rest. Besides that, this child has refused to obey me. She still allows the Gardner boy to call."

Suddenly, Betsy's body went hurdling across the yard as though propelled by an irresistible force. There was the sound of a slap. Betsy screamed in pain and landed on her hands and knees.

154

"Let me alone!" she cried.

Now even Richard stood with his mouth agape. "My God," he thought, "what an actor she is."

Even while Betsy was sobbing on her hands and knees, the Voice continued speaking as though nothing had happened.

"...and I will rise and go to my Father and will say to him, Father, I have sinned..."

The Voice was now imitating the voice of Thomas Gunn repeating the sermon that his congregation had heard from him that very morning. It was immediately apparent that the Witch was deriding the Reverend by raucously imitating his voice and repeating his sermon word for word in a mocking tone. As a result of the evidence provided by the Witch, everyone was certain that the Witch had been attending Reverend Gunn's Sunday services.

The mocking Voice was strange and forceful, but it was more comical that frightening.

Thomas Gunn's vanity was stung, and now he sought to restore his dignity in face of the Witch's derision. "Well, it is true that I have preached that sermon before, but the message is timeless. I am certain that my people can well profit from repetition of old truths."

Again, the Voice broke into laughter. "And is it also true that last week you spent your days in the tobacco patch and your nights trying to get me to talk to you, and you had no time to prepare a new sermon. For a lazy preacher it is easier to remind the people of old truths than to prepare a new sermon."

Now that the shock of the manifestation began to wear off, many now began to twitter over the comical image the Witch had called up about Thomas Gunn. A man who had always appeared erudite and officious to the crowd, sometimes to the point of putting on airs, was now getting a comeuppance from the Witch who seemed to know everything about the good Reverend, including his hidden weaknesses and peccadilloes.

One of the men near the preachers who was chuckling over the general amusement provoked by the Witch at the expense of

Brother Thomas now turned to Brother Fort and asked, "How about you, Brother Fort? Did you preach an old sermon too?"

The Voice interrupted. "Brother Fort preached on the Twenty-third Psalm today. It's a sermon he preached many times before he came into this area. But I dare say that his members will hear it again."

To everyone's amused amazement, the Voice went on to detail in a derisive manner the Drake Pond Services and even sang the closing hymn.

Later the story got out that the Witch had repeated both services word for word, and this was accepted as proof that the Witch had been in two places at once. Those few people who may have doubted the supernatural existence of the Witch before, now doubted no more.

After poking fun at Brother Fort, the Witch abruptly ended the show and said nothing else. When the Witch had attacked Betsy, Lucy Bell rushed over to her to attend to her and comfort her. Other women came over to assist Betsy surrounding her with a protective ring of women to thwart any further attacks from the Witch. With so many people around her, Betsy knew she could not safely continue her performance because it was possible that someone near her might realize the Voice was emanating from Betsy.

Finally, the women escorted a still-sobbing Betsy into the house, while everyone else continued talking animatedly about what had just happened in the yard. Of all the witnesses that day, perhaps only Brother Thomas and Brother Sugg were less animated than the rest of the crowd in voicing their opinions about the Witch's appearance today.

After an hour or so, things began to quiet down. A good number of guests departed for home. A few remained to have a little supper with the Bell family that night.

John Bell begged Richard Powell to stay overnight, but Richard politely refused saying he had to be back in Springfield early in the morning to attend to some pressing business, and a good portion of his travel would have to be at night.

Instead of riding a good portion of the night, Richard Powell stopped at the schoolhouse that night and stretched out on the floor. He needed some time and isolation to think about what he had witnessed today. Despite his foreknowledge of Betsy's skills, intelligence and imagination, he was nevertheless amazed over Betsy's performance. His own father could not have delivered a more convincing demonstration of ventriloquism, and he had never known an acrobat that could have duplicated Betsy's feat of hurling herself through the air as if propelled by some unknown force.

Why was Betsy doing all this? Why was she being so adamant about doing things to vex her family and fool her neighbors? What she had done today was beyond the need to protect herself and discourage an unwanted marriage. What kind of satisfaction was she looking for as a result of today's performance?

From his earliest experience with Betsy, he had recognized the strange mixture of child and adult within her. No doubt, part of what she was doing was out of childish petulance--a result of a bright child not having sufficient challenge. But Betsy was also a woman—a woman suppressed by a society that did not provide the outlets available to men. Women could not aspire to public attention. They could not seek the limelight. They could not seek recognition or approbation. They could not undertake the range of activity available to men. Women were universally cast in the roles of wives and mothers. Very few other choices were available to women much less to girls. To a woman as intelligent and imaginative as Betsy the environment in which she had been raised was stifling.

Part of what Betsy was doing was an attempt to break out of the day-to-day routine and find attention, even if she could not be acknowledged for it. Through the Voice, Betsy could vent long suppressed emotions. The Voice could say things that Betsy the child would never dare say. Through the Voice she was a tiger who dared poke fun at pompous men like Thomas Gunn and Sugg Fort. Through the Voice she could defy her father. Those who would have scorned her childish opinions trembled at the pronouncements of the Voice. The Voice bestowed an awesome power upon her.

Richard understood Betsy's motivations and in no way begrudged her power and desires. But he was still concerned about her. Things were moving too fast. She had a feeling of invincibility that was not justified. What would happen to her if anyone ever caught on to what she was doing? She would be excoriated by the community and probably beaten and cast out of her father's house. Everyone in the whole state would certainly characterize her as a witch.

Richard needed to talk to Betsy to tell her his concerns and get a promise from her to be more circumspect about her power and her use of it. He pondered over what he should say to her.

As he lay deep it thought, the door of the schoolhouse swung open. A figure came directly toward him in the pitch blackness.

18

STRANGERS CALL

Betsy crossed the room as quiet as a shadow. Although it was very dark, she avoided obstacles and seemed to know exactly where Richard was lying. When she reached his side, she sank down beside him. He took her into his arms and drew her close.

"Can you also see in the dark?" he asked.

"Not really," she giggled.

"How did you know I was here?"

"I saw you in my vision," she told him.

"That was quite a show you put on this afternoon."

"Was it really? Am I really good?"

"The best I ever saw. But I'm not sure just what you are trying to prove."

"Prove? I ain't trying to prove anything."

"Then why are you doing this to all these people?"

"I ain't hurt anybody. The only person who's been hurt is me. I've slapped the daylights out of my face, and this evening I skinned my knee. All them people came to see a show, and I gave them one."

"Betsy, you know it's not that simple."

"Why?"

"Do you know of any other girl of your age who dabbles in witchcraft?"

"No."

159

"So, you see how unusual all this is."

"Only because nobody else could get away with it. Besides, you don't think I'm a witch—you told me there is no such thing as witches."

It was much too dark for him to see her face, but he could well imagine the wicked little grin of triumph on her face.

"I'm not so sure about that now," he told her.

"Are you mad at me?" she asked.

"No. But I'm terribly worried."

"What about?"

"About you. Did you ever think what might happen if they catch you? And what'll happen if they don't catch you?"

"Well, I don't aim to get caught, and as for that other 'if,' I don't know what you're talking about."

"I'm not sure that I do either," he confessed. "But I just think you're carrying this too far."

Before she could contradict him, he continued. "Tell me one thing," he said. "You don't attend the Drake Pond services very much. How did you know that Sugg Fort never preached on the Twenty-third Psalm there before, but that he had used that sermon at another congregation?"

"I don't know," she said as though she had never considered the question before. "I did know, but I don't know how."

Lying close together and enjoying the warmth of each other's body, both fell silent. Soon Richard felt a passionate need. Terrified of losing control, he fought back the feeling. Betsy had sensed it.

"You know, I've dreamed about this," she said softly.

"What did you dream?"

"About us. Together like this. You wanting me, but before I let you, I always wake up."

"Oh," Richard replied.

"But this time, I won't wake up."

He ran his fingers through her hair. He was tempted but overcame the temptation.

"No, Betsy," he whispered. "We can't. Not yet."

"Why not?"

"You might get a baby, and you are much too young to become a mother."

"Esther says that it don't happen every time," she argued.

"Esther's right, but it might happen. We can't take the chance. But our time will come."

She nodded her head accepting his decision. She knew how much he had been tempted. She loved him even more intensely, knowing he had fought back his passion out of concern for her welfare. They continued to lie together for a while in each other's arms.

"Remember, I once told you that you might have to help me?" she finally asked.

"Help you with what?" he asked.

"Well, for one thing, if I'm always close by every time somebody hears the Voice, sooner or later somebody is going to put two and two together."

"Betsy, that's just what I've been talking about. You really need to consider putting an end to these pranks for good."

"But I can't stop now. Not until I get Josh to break off our understanding. I thought maybe the Voice would've scared him away by now, but it looks like it's not going to be that easy."

"In his own way Josh cares about you," Richard analyzed.

"Maybe so, but we have to think up something else to make him decide he don't want me."

"Why don't you just tell him you aren't in love with him?"

"I don't know. Everybody is so sure about me and Josh. Poppa would be so mad at me. I guess I want Josh to be the one to make the break so people won't hate me for fooling him for so long."

"And after Josh leaves, will you stop all these pranks?"

"If you want me to," she said.

"All right," Richard said, "how do you want me to help you?"

"I want you to be the Voice part of the time. Sometimes when I'm not near the house."

"Have you forgotten?" Richard countered. "I'm not especially good. You caught on in a minute."

"That won't matter now. Folks come expecting a ghost. They don't even think about any other explanation."

Betsy got back to her room only minutes before Nanny came into the dining room to put breakfast on the table. She dropped into bed and was soon sound asleep.

That same morning, John Bell awoke and realized that his earlier affliction was back. Recalling how the earlier attack had soon passed away, he got out of bed and tried to get dressed. This time the task proved impossible. His arms and legs simply refused to obey his wishes. He lay back on the bed and went into a spasm of shaking that awoke Lucy. When she realized that he could neither speak nor control his shaking, she went to the boys' bedroom and awoke John Junior to go for the doctor. The doctor came, sat by the bed for a time and prescribed medicine, but this time several days passed before John Bell was well enough to get out of bed.

On a Saturday afternoon in mid-July the family was sitting out in the yard when they saw a surrey coming down the road. There were five men in the surrey, all strangers. The surrey turned into the driveway and stopped near the house. John, still shaky from his recent illness, walked out to meet them. A few minutes later, Betsy learned that they had driven all the way from Nashville to investigate for themselves stories they had heard about the Witch.

It never occurred to John Bell to turn these curiosity seekers away. It was still frontier country, and the tradition of hospitality was deeply ingrained.

John introduced the men to the family and told them to make themselves at home. During the introductions Betsy made a mental note of each name, and during the conversation that followed paid careful attention to everything each guest revealed about himself. In the course of the conversation, she got the impression that while each man was careful not to express any doubt about the stories the family told, they were, in reality, skeptical about the Witch's existence.

That night Betsy sat in the dining room where the guests set up their vigil to await the appearance of the Witch. Betsy sat with them so quietly and shyly that the men soon forgot that she was there. But they did not ignore the Voice when it came. The Voice gave a most convincing performance. By skillfully weaving bits of personal information into its conversation, it left the guests convinced that the spirit was omniscient. The visitors were completely mystified.

No one realized that the spirit had revealed nothing that the guests had not told the family earlier in the afternoon. The men departed the following morning, but the family was soon to learn that they were only the first of many visitors to follow.

From that day on there was rarely a weekend that the Bell's did not have at least one stranger as a house guest. Some would stay a night, some several days and a few would linger for weeks. Yet each and every one was made welcome by the Bell family and encouraged to stay for as long as they liked. For the first time in his life, John Bell purchased a steer so his guests would have meat to eat.

By fall people were appearing at the door even in the middle of the week. The Voice never disappointed them, and the visitors left to spread the story further afield.

Betsy reveled in the attention the family was getting and went to great pains to make the spirit's demonstrations convincing. By the beginning of winter, she was using her power of vision to learn who was coming ahead of time. Thereafter, the Voice frequently greeted callers by name as they reached the door, before they could introduce themselves. And just as often the voice was able to reveal intimate details about the callers' personal lives. Not all of guests had unblemished pasts, and some guests found the Witch's foreknowledge of their pasts to be most discomforting. Nevertheless, the Witch continued to reveal secrets of guests with the utmost gusto.

In addition to strangers, neighbors continued to come each night to sit with the spirit while the family got their rest. Life at the Bell house took on a carnival atmosphere that Betsy found most exciting.

Over time, other things happened that Betsy had no part in. Her father had three more bouts of his illness, each causing him to be bedridden several days at a time. Lucy noticed that each successive illness was a bit more debilitating and that it took John longer to recover. By now his condition was obvious even on his best days. Word went through the community that "Old Kate" had put a curse on John Bell and was determined to give him no rest until she had laid him in his grave.

Betsy also had no control over Richard Powell's election to the state legislature. Although everyone was elated over this development, Betsy was disappointed knowing that Richard's attention would now be monopolized by his political duties.

Betsy also had nothing to do with Dean's run in with the Witch one night. Because of Dean's close association with the Bell family, his prestige in the slave community grew as the Witch's fame and prominence increased. All along Dean had taken great pleasure in telling stories about the Witch. Most of his stories were pure fabrications, but the other slaves listened to the stories with wide-eyed wonder.

"T'other night whenst I wuz going to Marssa Tom's house to see my womans," he began, "this big ol' black dawg come outten the woods jus ahead o'me. Thinks I to myself, dey's sump'n powerful 'cular bout dat dawg. Den I see he doan hab no head, and knows he had to be Ol' Kate."

"But, Dean," some slave would interrupt, "ifen dat dawg did'n hab no head, how he see where he wuz going?"

"Did'n need to see," Dean would reply. "Old Kate is a haint, cumb to de tree she walk right fru it."

"You see her walk fru de tree?"

"Shore did."

"Twarn't you scarit?"

"Naw, I just whistle dat dawg over and pat he on de head."

"I thought you sayed he ain't got no head."

"He ain't, but I pat where de head is sposed to be."

Dean's supposed familiarity with the spirit made him immune from challenge from most blacks. But the Porter family had a slave named Isaac who was as big as Dean and who often bragged that he wasn't scared of man, beast or witch. He told several fellow slaves that if he had been Dean, he would have grabbed hold of the Witch and squeezed out her innards.

Dean allowed as how that might take some doing, since he had once had hold of the witch and found it strong as an ox.

Taunt and countertaunt was passed between the two men until there came a night when Dean met Isaac while coming home from a visit to his woman. In the fight that followed, each came out about even. But when Dean got home, well after daylight, he was a sorry sight with bruises, scrapes and scratches. While Lucy doctored him, he told a tale about being buffeted by "dat Ol' Kate." Lucy refused to believe a word of it, but the story soon became a part of the Bell Witch lore.

Soon the family began to hear other stories. When Sid Turner's mule ran away and wrecked the plow, community wisdom concluded that the mule had surely been spooked by the Witch.

That was followed by an even more serious charge when the Boswell family's horse ran away, wrecked the surrey and killed little Cindy Boswell. That too was put down to the Witch's doing after a grieving and hysterical Mrs. Boswell swore that she had seen a ghostly apparition sitting on the back of the horse just before it bolted.

Incidents grew. Any inexplicable occurrence was ascribed to the Witch.

A cow went dry after the farmer saw a strange light hovering over his stable. A dog got rabies after chasing a stray cat out of the yard. A neighbor came down with chills after refusing food to a tramp passing by his house.

Then there was the time down on Red River when the witch chased Alec Murphey from his pasture to his house. One late afternoon when he had finished plowing, Alec led his mule to a field about a half mile from his house. He removed the harness back at the stable and led the animal by a check chain fastened to its bridle. At the pasture gate, he removed the bridle and allowed the mule to run free. By now it was twilight, and as Alec walked toward his house, he heard a noise close behind him. He glanced nervously over his shoulder but saw nothing. The sound persisted. After a few more steps he stopped to listen. The sound had also stopped, but as soon as he started again, the sound continued as before. He stopped suddenly and whirled around. The road behind him was empty. Once more he started walking, but this time much faster. The sound kept pace and stayed right on his heels. Soon he was running as though pursued by the hounds of hell, but the sound remained right behind him to his front door. When he got there, he threw the bridle aside and plunged into the house to the alarm of his wife and children.

Everyone he told the story to assure him that the Witch had followed him to his front door for whatever purpose witches have for their mischief. Alec himself never doubted that explanation until many years later when a similar thing happened. But this time he discovered that in gathering up the bridle over his arm, he had inadvertently dropped the check chain so that it dragged on the ground behind him. The sound made by the dragging chain was exactly the same as the sound he had heard on the night he had raced the Witch to his front door. Unfortunately, by that time the original story could never be retracted.

Other stories grew out of natural phenomena. Since it was relatively new country, the area around Adams had its quota of swampy woodland. Swamps were ideal for the formation of phosphorescent gases and fungi. Early settlers were perfectly familiar with these things and understood the causes, but in a climate of Witch hysteria, encounters with strange lights seen dimly through the trees on a dark night were likely to have a ghostly interpretation.

Stories were also told that were outright lies, told for whatever reason the teller thought appropriate. In more enlightened times these stories would have been recognized for what they were, but in those days even the thinnest lie was often accepted as gospel.

19

HAZELNUTS FROM HEAVEN

B ecause of his election to the Tennessee State Assembly, Richard knew that it would be impossible for him to return to Adams for Christmas. Instead, he made a special effort to arrange for an extended visit at Thanksgiving. Several weeks before he left, he wrote to John Bell to emphasize that he was coming for a rest and to renew his acquaintances with the family. On no account did he want to do any politicking. John respected Richard's wishes, but there was not much he could do about the house guests that were now constantly on hand.

School had reopened, and Betsy had begun what she intended to be her last year. Her teacher was an elderly gentleman who had been recommended by Thomas Gunn. Betsy considered him a terrible bore, and he was exceedingly nervous over teaching a young girl who was so obviously under the watchful eye of the spirit.

Josh had already withdrawn from school and now devoted himself entirely to farm work. He had managed to acquire a hundred acres of land, his own mule and plow, and a male slave. He continued to visit Betsy every Sunday afternoon. He was troubled by the spirit's attention to Betsy, but it had never occurred to him to discontinue his courtship. While he deeply sympathized with Betsy's apparent suffering, he was unable to associate that with his visits.

Betsy was in her room on Thanksgiving Eve when she

spotted Richard riding up the road toward the house. His long absence made her reckless. She tore down the steps and was standing beside the barn lot gate when he rode into the yard. John and Lucy were sitting beside the fire in the front room. As Betsy came down the steps it sounded as though the house was falling in.

"What on earth?" John mumbled. His voice had not returned to normal since his last illness.

He slowly got to his feet with the aid of a cane and made his way over to the front window. He could see Richard coming up the drive, but the barn lot gate was to the rear of the house, and he was not able to see Betsy.

"I see Professor Powell has arrived," he mumbled to Lucy, "but I see nothing to get Elizabeth so excited."

Lucy knew very well the reason for Betsy's excitement but merely said, "It will be nice to see Professor Powell."

Since his first illness John had been restless. Now instead of returning to his chair, he left the room to wander through the house. A few minutes later he called Lucy from the back door.

"Lucy, Elizabeth is out here at the barn lot gate pestering Professor Powell."

"Really?" Lucy replied.

"Maybe you should call her. Professor Powell has had a hard journey. He shouldn't be bothered by a child."

"I am sure that Professor Powell does not consider Betsy a child or a bother."

"She certainly is a child," John Bell contradicted. "She's only thirteen."

"I believe you were the one who decided that she was old enough to keep company," Lucy rejoined.

John caught the implication and was stunned. "But that was with the Gardner boy," he sputtered.

"Apparently Betsy has other ideas." Lucy answered.

John dropped into his chair and sat tapping his cane against the floor. He was grappling with this new idea that his wife had thrust upon him so abruptly.

"But what about the Gardner boy?" he protested.

"Well, you know how dead set the spirit is against their marriage."

"But they have an understanding."

"Do you really think that Josh could cope with all the complications caused by the spirit?"

"He's a good lad, a hard worker. Besides they have an understanding."

"But if a marriage can't work, don't you think it's better to find out about it now--before they are married?

"But what about the neighbors? What will they think? They all know that Betsy and Josh have an understanding."

"Betsy's happiness is more important than what the neighbors think."

"Well, when I was a young man, a girl who broke off an understanding was considered loose. Besides that, Professor Powell is so much older."

"Times have changed, John. One might think that of a girl who breaks her engagement, but hardly for a mere understanding. As for age, a young girl is apt to consider an older man more appealing. Now Professor Powell is well thought of--enough to be elected to the Legislature. He will make Betsy a fine husband and you a good son-in-law."

"I guess you're right," John admitted, still somewhat dazed over this new concept.

"Besides that," Lucy said, "if Betsy breaks off with Josh, perhaps we will have some peace around here from that dreadful spirit."

John gave his wife a quick hopeful look. The idea of Betsy and Professor Powell would take some getting used to, yet as he considered it, it did have much to recommend it, not the least of which was getting shed of the spirit.

"Well, I *did* say that the final decision as to whom Elizabeth marries will be hers." He was still mulling over these thoughts when Betsy and Richard came through the back door.

During the time that Richard had been taking care of his

horse, he and Betsy had made some plans. They had no idea that the objective of their schemes and plans had just been tacitly approved in a quiet conversation between Betsy's mother and father. Thus, Richard and Betsy were still determined to go through with the elaborate charade to force an end to the understanding between Josh and Betsy, thereby removing any obstacles that would prevent an eventual marriage between Richard and Betsy.

Their plan required Richard to take over the functions of the Voice on a night when Betsy was away from home, spending the night at her sister Esther's place. Losing a night with Richard was painful, yet it was necessary for the Voice to make an appearance when Betsy's absence was conspicuous. Richard was the source of the Witch's voice on that night, while Dean provided the usual background noises.

A connoisseur of ventriloquism would have considered Richard's rendition of the Voice a poor imitation of Betsy's, but, as Betsy had predicted, those who had appeared at the house were not critics. All came in anticipation of hearing the Witch, and the Witch they heard. Richard's performance was adequate. Any possible suspicions by those who may have pointed out a correlation between Betsy's constant presence and the appearance of the Witch's voice were laid permanently to rest.

Thanksgiving came and went, and Richard returned to Springfield to get ready for the coming session of the Assembly. At that time the capital of Tennessee was at Murfreesboro--a good thirty miles beyond Nashville. There would be no opportunities to return to Adams until after the session was over.

A few days after Richard left, Betsy's mother, Lucy, took to her bed with a strange illness. Betsy, who had been only moderately concerned over her father's illness, was beside herself with worry over her mother. Doctor Hopson came and frankly admitted that he did not have a diagnosis. The slaves whispered among themselves that Miss Lucy had also been hexed by the Witch. Lucy lost all appetite, and her condition grew steadily worse until she slipped into a semi-coma. Doctor Hopson called the family together and warned that they should be prepared to lose their mother. In those days it was not unusual for people to sometimes up and die for no apparent reason.

Betsy now slept in her mother's room. Betsy administered to her mother and constantly coaxed her mother to eat. Because of her upbringing, Betsy, like the rest of her siblings, found it difficult to express her feelings and love in words. No one in the family had ever been very good at it. Betsy struggled to find words--to no avail. But the Voice was eloquent. The Voice took over.

"You mustn't die, Luce," the Voice would plead, "your family needs you."

Lucy was too sick to care about living, but even through the haze of her semi-coma, the Voice registered. For the first time she was sure that the Voice belonged to Betsy. She understood that this was the only way Betsy had of telling her that she loved her. From that knowledge a spark was struck to kindle what Doctor Hopson called a "will to live." When Betsy brought a broth, she managed to swallow a few feeble sips.

"All right now, Luce, just take a few more spoons full," the Voice would encourage.

Later Doctor Hopson admitted that he did not know what had turned the tide for Lucy Bell. He was fairly sure that it was not his medicine.

In later years, Lucy Bell always said that the Voice had pulled her through. But at the present time, even after her recovery was certain, Lucy still found all food to be tasteless and ate for health rather than pleasure.

"You need to eat more, Luce," the Voice would plead. "You must eat to regain your strength."

"But nothing tastes good," Lucy would complain.

"What would you like to eat, Luce?" the Voice asked one day.

"Nothing," Lucy said wearily.

"There has to be something you would like."

"Maybe some hazelnuts," Lucy said with resignation.

Betsy looked at her mother and felt helpless. The hazelnut grew on wild bushes throughout the Adam's area. But the nuts had ripened and had already been harvested by squirrels and other animals, including humans. They were now out of season.

"We will see, Luce," the Voice promised.

Betsy went to see Dean.

"Momma is asking for hazelnuts," she told him.

"I 'spect dey's all gone by now, Miss Betsy," Dean told her.

Betsy stomped her foot.

"I don't care how far you have to go, or how long it takes!" she ordered.

Early the next morning while Betsy was sitting with her mother, she heard a timid tap on the door. She opened it to find a weary Dean standing red-eyed holding a double handful of hazelnuts. She never knew where he managed to find them. In effect, Dean's accomplishment had rivaled one of the labors of Hercules.

Lucy was still asleep, and Betsy stood holding the nuts considering them carefully. She decided that it would be nice to use them to surprise her mother.

Her mother's bed was covered with a canopy. Taking a white linen napkin, Betsy soon rigged up a small sack with an opening that could be made to open by pulling a string. She filled the sack with the nuts and pinned it to the underside of the canopy.

Later when Lucy was fully awake, the Voice asked, "Luce, do you think you could still eat some hazelnuts?"

Lucy knew that there were no hazelnuts at that time of year. She had mentioned them more to escape the Voice's insistence than from any real desire for the nuts.

Now she answered in the same spirit of resignation.

"If there were any available," she said.

"Then hold out your hands, Luce."

Lucy obeyed, more to please Betsy that anything else. Betsy drew the string, and a shower of hazelnuts poured onto the bed. When visitors asked where she got hazelnuts so late in the year, Lucy told them, "Well, the spirit told me to hold out my hand, and the nuts just rained down from heaven."

Thus, another feat was added to the amazing lore of the Witch.

20

GENERAL JACKSON
MAKES A REQUEST OF
SENATOR POWELL

U pon his return to Springfield after his Thanksgiving visit to the Bell home, Richard packed up his belonging and moved to Murfreesboro. He had already made arrangements for a room in a commercial boarding house a few blocks from the Courthouse where the General Assembly would meet. He arrived late one afternoon and spent the following day settling in. Several times that day, he had the feeling that Betsy was watching over his shoulder.

"Nothing puts a man on his best behavior like having a woman who has the gift of vision," he thought.

On his second day he left the room to take a walk about the town. It was slightly larger than Springfield and had several fine homes. It had been selected as the state capital because of its location near the geographic center of the state. Around the courthouse there was a flurry of activity in preparation for the Assembly to meet the following day. It had rained during the night, and a large freight wagon was mired directly in front of the courthouse. The driver was swearing at his mules as though profanity alone would lift the wagon out of the mire.

The streets were filled with lighter vehicles and many rode on horseback. Stores were crowded, and everyone seemed excited over the coming session of the Assembly. He shopped for a Christmas present for Betsy and settled on a woolen shawl.

The following morning, Richard was sworn in as the Senator from Robertson County. The Senate sat in the main courtroom, and he spent the next several days learning how the body functioned. Within two weeks, he had introduced two bills and had been appointed a member of a committee.

The Senate session was less formal than he had expected. While their colleagues continued their private conversations and wandered in and out of the room, men arose and spoke earnestly about one bill or another and seemed not the least bit distracted by all of the confusion. He soon realized that for individual members the gathering offered an excellent opportunity to buy, sell and make other business deals. It seemed to Richard that these matters commanded more individual attention than did the affairs of state. Land, horses, horse races, and women were major topics of conversation. Still, things seemed to get done. One of his bills passed both houses and was signed by the Governor.

Richard found the Assembly dull and boring, and he decided that he really wasn't interested in a political career. He wished Betsy were around to liven things up a bit.

A few days later, he took advantage of a recess to get a breath of fresh air. While walking through the hallway of the courthouse, he saw a small group of his fellow Senators gathered about a stranger. The man was very thin and stood a head higher than the tallest man in the group. The head was crowned with a mane of rusty red hair generously peppered with gray.

He was talking earnestly and giving emphasis to his words with short chopping motions of his hand. Although Richard had never seen the man before, he knew that he was looking at General Andrew Jackson. Jackson had been a popular hero on the frontier for many years, and his victory over the British at the Battle of New Orleans the previous year had given him national stature. He was now the senior commander of the United States Army.

Suddenly the group broke into hearty laughter and broke up as each man went his own way. Left alone, the General looked up and down the hallway. He saw Richard and started toward him with outstretched hand.

"I say, Sir, are you a member of this Assembly?"

Richard accepted a bony hand and looked into a pair of the bluest eyes he had ever seen with the exception of Betsy's.

"Yes, Sir," he answered. "I am the Senator from Robertson County."

"Oh, yes, Robertson County. And what might your name be?"

"Richard Powell."

General Jackson assumed that his own name was known and did not introduce himself.

"Well, Senator, it's good to meet you. Now there was something that I aimed to ask the first man I met from Robertson County, but it seems to have slipped my mind at the moment."

"Well, we raise a lot of tobacco up there, and the finest snuff tobacco, I might add."

"Yes, I'm somewhat familiar with the cultivation of dark tobacco. But no, there was something else."

"I'm not sure that I know what you may have heard about our county."

"Of course, you don't. Probably not important. But you will have to pass through Nashville on your return to Springfield. Correct?"

"Yes."

"Then by all means you must come visit me at the Hermitage. Just stop along the road and ask anyone the way. We can talk, and perhaps I shall remember what it was that I wanted to ask about your county."

The two men parted.

The following week Richard learned that while members

of the Senate seemed very casual about their responsibilities for the most part, they could, under the right circumstances, become deadly serious. He entered the chamber one morning to find small knots of men standing in the aisles talking in low voices. From the look on their faces, he realized that they were all in a somber mood. At that moment one of his fellow committee members left a group and started down the aisle. Richard started after him to find out what was going on.

"You haven't heard?" the man asked.

"Heard what?"

"Oh, that's right. You left the session early yesterday."

"Yes, I had an appointment."

"Well, it must have been shortly after you left. Senator Foxx challenged Senator Benton to a duel."

"What on earth for?"

"No one seems to know for sure. I've heard that Senator Benton made some statement in the privacy of his boarding house to the effect that Senator Foxx had introduced a bill solely to please one of his shady ladies. Anyway, just as yesterday's session was about to end, Senator Foxx crossed the room and slapped Senator Benton across the face with his glove. It was most dramatic. Of course, Senator Benton had no choice but to tell Foxx his seconds would call on him as soon as the matter could be arranged."

"I thought the Assembly made dueling illegal," Richard said."

His friend shrugged his shoulders and smiled benignly. "My dear Senator," he said, "you can't outlaw human nature."

"Couldn't the matter be forgotten if Senator Benton would apologize?" Richard asked.

"Certainly, but what man could live with the shame?"

"What will happen now?" Richard asked, still having trouble assimilating this strange development.

"Everything will be arranged quietly. One morning we will call the roll and either Senator Foxx or Senator Benton will fail to answer."

That day Richard watched in morbid fascination as the two Senators went about the routine of Senate business. Senator Foxx entered into spirited debate, and as Richard passed close to a group gathered around Senator Benton, he overheard enough to know that the Senator was bargaining for a racehorse. Watch as he might, Richard could detect no outward sign that either man was worried or concerned over the upcoming deadly appointment.

Upon returning to his boarding house that afternoon, he found a letter from Betsy. It recounted her mother's illness and recovery and the neighborhood gossip. It was the last sentence that reminded him that Betsy was not just an ordinary young lady.

"I think the shawl you bought me for Christmas is very pretty, I will wear it for you when you get home."

He shook his head in resignation. He had mailed the shawl along with a present for Lucy Bell the previous morning, and it could not have arrived yet.

Early in January a roll was called, and Senator Foxx failed to answer. Richard quickly looked about the room and saw Senator Benton entering through a door in the rear with his arm in a sling. Men exchanged knowing glances, and the business went on as usual.

The session ended in late January. As Richard prepared to return to Springfield, he remembered General Jackson's invitation. As he drew close to the city of Nashville, he stopped a wagoner and asked how he might get to General Jackson's place. The directions proved complicated. After making the first few turns, Richard stopped at a farmhouse to ask again. Once more he was given directions that were not easy to follow. Unlike the area around Springfield, this part of the country was where the Red Cedar grew lushly. Great gray-barked trees with twisted gnarled trunks lined the roadway.

Now he realized that Jackson's Hermitage was some distance up the Cumberland River from Nashville and quite a bit out of his way. But at last, he came to a lane that he had been told would lead him to General Jackson's house. At that time Jackson lived in a simple rather crude block house built of logs. A similar building for the accommodation of guests stood nearby. The elegant manorial structure that would embellish the Jackson estate in the future was still in the planning stages.

When Richard knocked on the door, a slave woman answered. He gave his name, but before he could explain that the General had asked him to call, the slave woman stood to one side to allow him to step through the door. Obviously, the policy at the Hermitage was to never turn away a caller.

He found himself in a large room encompassing the entire first floor. A great fireplace was burning at one end of the room and the floor was puncheon. But the furniture was elegant. Jackson had ordered it from a firm in Philadelphia, and now it looked strangely out of place in the crude cabin.

Richard stood in front of the fireplace absorbing heat into his chilled body. It had been a long ride on a cold day. The slave left the room, and a few minutes later he heard the sound of footsteps on the stairs.

The woman who appeared was fifty but looked older. Regardless of any desire he might have had to be kind, "fat" was the only way to describe her. She had black hair and deep dark eyes that carried a shadow of frequent pain. He recalled the many stories he had heard about the scandal that ended her first marriage. She had suffered more from the scandal than from the General's frequent absences.

But for the moment she had a smile of welcome on her face.

"Senator Powell, I am Rachel Jackson. Mr. Jackson had to go into Nashville this morning. I expect him back soon if you would care to wait."

She crossed to the fire and picked up a clay pipe from the mantel.

"Are you a family man, Senator Powell?" she asked as she filled the pipe with tobacco and packed it firmly into the bowl.

"No, Ma'am," he answered. "I have never married."

She took a pair of tongs from beside the fireplace, selected a live ember from the fire and used it to light the pipe.

"Don't put it off too long, Senator," she admonished as fragrant white smoke wreathed up over her head. "You are a young man now and have much to command your attention, but a time will come when family will be all you have. The General and I have always hoped for children, but the good Lord has seen fit to deny us. We have adopted children, and then there are my nieces and nephews. They are almost like our own. But a man needs sons to carry on his name."

"I hope to marry soon," Richard admitted.

"Well, a fine handsome man like you shouldn't have any trouble finding a good woman." She laughed heartily and gave him a mischievous glance, and suddenly Richard had a brief glimpse of the woman that Andrew Jackson had fallen in love with.

"Will you stay the night, Senator," she asked. "I know the General will want to talk to you about your impressions of the past session of the Assembly."

"I would be honored," he said.

"Then just make yourself at home while I go and see about dinner. Mr. Jackson said that I could expect him home for dinner."

Rachel Jackson did not stand on ceremony. As soon as the noon meal was ready, she beckoned Richard to the table with no intention of waiting for her husband.

"Sometimes Mr. Jackson gets tied up and is forgetful of time," she explained.

Yet they had barely sat down at the table when a slave came running into the house with the news that General Jackson was riding up the lane.

That afternoon the General took Richard on a tour of the farm. He took immense pride in each aspect of farm life. Richard realized that for all his ability as a commander of armies and a skilled politician, Andrew Jackson's heart was in the simple life of a farmer. The tour included a visit to the stables where the

General's famous racehorse, Truxton stood at stud. If Jackson had a weakness other than giving vent to his famous temper, it was for horse racing. His eyes glittered with excitement as he recounted stories of some of Truxton's more spectacular victories.

After supper, Richard and the General sat beside the fire in the great room. The General had an insatiable curiosity, and he plied Richard with questions, not only about the actions taken by the Assembly, but also about Richard's impressions of a score of personalities that had been involved in the last session.

He was especially curious about the duel between Senators Foxx and Benton. He asked innumerable questions, and when Richard had told everything he knew, the General shook his head sadly.

"Foxx had great talent. His death is such a terrible waste. Have you ever fought a duel, Senator Powell?" he finally asked.

"No, Sir," Richard admitted.

"Then don't. Those kinds of things have a way of haunting your nights. As you must know, I have fought my share of duels. The last was with as insolent a little coxcomb as ever walked the streets of Nashville. I was hot blooded in those days and could not rest until I had laid Charles Dickinson in his grave. I've since shed no tears over Dickinson. He got what he deserved. But I widowed a young wife and orphaned young children. When I got home after the duel, Mrs. Jackson met me at the door. She swore that she would leave me if I ever fought another duel. I have never doubted her love, but I know today that if I killed another man in a duel, I would come home to an empty house. I have had some bad dreams over men I've killed."

The General spent a few moments in reverie remembering those past duels. Then without warning he quickly changed the subject.

"Now I know what it was I wanted to ask you about Robertson County. I am told that there is a family in that county that has frequent visits from a ghost or spirit. Would you happen to know anything about that?"

Richard was mildly surprised at the General's interest. "I wonder if you might be referring to the Bell family?" he replied.

"Why, yes, I do believe that was the name."

"Last year I taught school in the Adams community," Richard explained. "The Bell children were enrolled in the school. I know the family quite well."

"Then you are the person I should talk to. Mrs. Jackson is devout, and I attend church with her whenever I happen to be home. I listen to the ministers and have a good deal of curiosity about the hereafter. I also hear their discourses on witches and spirits. I have some skepticism about that. I would be very much interested in witnessing such a phenomenon. Do you think it would be possible for me to visit the Bell family?"

"I think I could arrange for such a visit," Richard told him."

"And if I came, what would be my chances of actually witnessing a manifestation of this spirit?"

"I think I could almost guarantee it," Richard assured him.

21

THE DISTINGUISHED GUEST

The morning after Richard visited the Hermitage, Betsy awoke and was not sure whether she had seen Richard in a vision or a dream, but she was sure that he was on his way home. As was so often the case, she had been looking down on the scene from some vantage point high above. Her view had been of an extraordinarily large room. Richard and a stranger had been sitting in front of a large fireplace where a great bole of a hickory tree was being used as a backlog. It was so large in fact that Betsy wondered how many slaves had been required to place it on the large black andirons where it rested. Smaller sticks, no larger than a man's thigh, burned in front of the back log, and yellow flames roared as they seemed to leap up the chimney. The flames cast a yellow light that caused shadows to dance over the faces of the men before the fire. The stranger was an older man with reddish hair, liberally streaked with gray, and sharp chiseled features. There was something vaguely familiar about him that caused Betsy to feel that she ought to know who he was, although she was certain that she had never actually seen him before. He was questioning Richard about the recent session of the legislature. The vision faded away just as Richard started to tell about a duel fought between two of the senators. She did not know why, but she felt very sure that she would see the stranger again, just as she knew that Richard would now be home in a few days.

She was impatient with delay and a little put out with Richard for taking time out of his homeward journey to pay a social visit. There were several things she was anxious to tell him. Her father had again taken to his bed with what the community referred to as John Bell's terrible affliction. Doctor Hopson called it a nervous disorder. At any rate he had spells when his body shook so violently that once he had thrown off his shoes. People in the community said that John Bell's spells were caused by the Witch. Doctor Hopson dismissed such talk as the wagging of idle tongues. According to him the shaking was the natural progression of the nervous disorder.

Betsy's brother, Drewry Bell, figured among those who believed that the Witch was responsible for his father's disorder. Since Drewery lived across the river, he had not been exposed to the Witch's demonstrations. As a consequence, he found them disturbing whereas others who had experienced the manifestations of the Witch found them more innocuous and comical rather than disturbing.

Drewery started spending more of his time at his parents' home so he could be close by to help take care of his father. Dewery took his father's illness as proof of the Witch's evil power and intention. Dewery frequent railed against the Witch, and his angry outbursts against the spirit unnerved Betsy. If she had ever had any inclination to confess, she now firmly put it aside.

Dewry began talking about a man he had heard about over in Kentucky who claimed to be able to cast out spirits. He mentioned the matter to Lucy Bell and tried to persuade her to allow him to have the witch chaser rid the family of the spirit.

Lucy, knowing that Betsy was the origin of the voice, would not hear of such a thing, but Betsy was certain that Drewery had not given up on the idea.

By this time strangers from all over Tennessee and Kentucky were such frequent visitors at the house, and there was rarely any room for local people. For a time, Betsy enjoyed the excitement of having so many visitors, but now she began to tire of so much company. Despite all her efforts, nothing seemed to discourage Josh Gardner, and she was beginning to feel a little desperate. She hoped that Richard might have a suggestion. As she saw it, it was about time he took a hand in having Josh put aside.

Betsy had a good breakfast that morning and was about to leave the house to go riding when her mother called her to an empty bedroom. She went bounding into the room, thinking that her mother wanted her to take care of some errand while she was out riding. Instead, Lucy motioned her to a seat on the bed, and as she sat down, her mother firmly latched the door.

"Betsy, she began, "I've had a talk with your father."

Betsy stiffened visibly. The old dread of her father's disapproval was still deeply ingrained.

"What about?" She asked cautiously.

"About you and Richard."

Betsy looked up in surprise. She had never considered that her mother knew anything about what there was between her and Richard.

"What about me and Richard?"

"That you two want to get married."

Betsy wilted. Her father knew about her desire to marry Richard. This was the worst possible development she could imagine. She shuddered to think of the consequences her father had in store for her.

"Oh, Momma!" she sobbed.

"Now don't get so upset," Lucy soother her. "The news came as quite a shock to your father, but he's not totally opposed to the idea."

"He's not?" Betsy questioned incredulously, twisting her hands in her lap. She looked at her mother in disbelief. Was it possible that her ears were playing tricks on her?

"No,' her mother answered, "but we both think it's time to clear the air. It's only fair that you give up Josh and put an end to your understanding with him. Your father offered to go have a talk with Josh's parents, but I thought perhaps it would be better for you to handle it. Josh is a good boy, and I don't want him hurt unnecessarily. I suggest that you tell him that because of the spirit's opposition, it is impossible for you to consider eventual marriage any longer. Then after a respectable period of time, Richard can speak to your father. You are still much too young to marry, so Richard must be prepared to wait a few years longer."

"Yes, Momma," Betsy said meekly. Betsy was still in shock. It was simply too much to comprehend. She simply could not absorb the idea that something she had so fearfully dreaded was turning into good news. Hardly realizing what she was doing, Betsy walked mechanically out the door and mounted Fanny to begin her ride. While riding down the road the impact of the news finally hit fully. She struck the horse on the flank with her riding crop, and as the mare broke into a full gallop, she let out a whoop of glee and was off to tell Esther the good news.

Richard arrived the next day, and as soon as he told the family about General Jackson's wish to pay a visit, there was an immediate flurry of activity. John Bell, still shaky from his recent illness, insisted on leaving his bed to supervise the preparations. Assured of the General's welcome, Richard wrote a letter suggesting a convenient time for him to call.

Betsy rode with Richard to the post office to mail the letter, and it was then that he told him that her father had given her permission to break her understanding with Josh Gardner. Aglow with the good news, Richard, in turn, confided to Betsy that as soon as his term as state senator ended, he planned to end his political career. His term in the Senate had served its purpose. Through contacts made while in Murfreesboro, he had secured a position with a firm that made snuff from the dark tobacco grown in Robertson and adjoining counties. He would act as the company's Tennessee and Kentucky representative. In that capacity he would buy as much of the dark fired tobacco as the company needed. The company paid a generous commission, and if he worked reasonably hard, he could be assured of a good living—enough to support a wife and family. The trip to the post office was the happiest time the couple had spent together since they had known each other.

John Bell wanted to move himself and Lucy out of the front room so that General Jackson could have the most comfortable bed in the house. He gave up the idea only after Richard insisted that the General would not accept such treatment at the expense of his hosts.

"I was told to make you understand that General Jackson will not think of imposing on your hospitality," Richard told him. "He will bring his own tent to sleep in and his personal slave to tend his needs."

John Bell finally agreed to sleep in his own bed, but he insisted on providing the General's meals. He began making plans for a large barbeque.

The following Sunday, Betsy broke off her understanding with Josh.

"It's that wicked ol' Witch," she told him. "I know that because it's so opposed to us getting married, we could never have a peaceful moment together."

Betsy's rejection came as a surprise to Josh, but he experienced a feeling of relief. He had long harbored doubts about having a wife haunted by a spirit. Yet, he felt duty bound to protest.

"I'm not afraid of any spirit," he boasted.

"I know," Betsy said dryly. "But it ain't you it wales the daylights out of. I'm the one who gets slapped silly."

They continued talking into the afternoon, while Josh continued to voice his token resistance to kowtowing to the Witch. Finally, to put the issue fully to rest, Betsy allowed the Voice to enter the conversation, and together Betsy and the Witch persuaded Josh to take the escape being offered to him.

Josh was relieved. A month before, he had learned about some land across the Tennessee River being opened for settlement. Up until this very moment, his understanding with Betsy had made it impossible for him to consider taking advantage of it. On his way home that night, he was already making plans to move to West Tennessee.

On the road to Springfield, Andrew Jackson arose from his cot at daybreak and dressed in the semi-darkness. It was mid-February, but a spell of unseasonably warm weather had persisted for several days.

As he stepped outside his field tent, he found that he was the only one in the camp awake. He started to call his manservant, William, but since yesterday had been a long and tiresome day of travel, he decided to let his entourage continue sleeping for a while longer.

Despite having a heavy wagon in the caravan, they had made good time since leaving the Hermitage, and if they kept up the pace, they should arrive at the Bell farm by late afternoon.

To kill time, Jackson walked beyond the camp and down to the creek. It was called Carl's Creek, and he remembered that it was only a few miles south of Springfield. A gravel bar extended out into the creek, forming a narrow channel in the stream. He walked out onto the bar and saw large sycamore trees lining both banks of the creek. Tree branches hung out over the stream forming a canopy of leaves that shut out the sky and sun as the water flowed placidly along. An almost perfect silence was marred by the ripple of the water as it ran past the gravel bar.

In his occupation as a farmer and soldier, Jackson had spent much of his life out of doors. He firmly believed that life was never so full as when one was in a natural setting. He took a deep breath to savor the smells of the river.

Although his body was wracked with ailments, Jackson, at that moment, felt vibrantly alive. It occurred to him that before the night was over, he could well be in the presence of an entity that was not living. He was curious rather than afraid. Fear was something of which he knew little.

All his adult life Jackson had lived almost daily under the specter of sudden and violent death. He had killed Charles Dickinson in a duel, and even though Dickinson had a great reputation as the best shot in the West, Jackson had not been afraid of facing him, dueling pistols in hand. On the way to the dueling ground, Dickinson had demonstrated his skill to his friends by shooting the blooms off the flowers that grew along the road. As the two men faced each other, Jackson knew he was going to be shot, and the odds were that the wound would be fatal.

"Even if he puts a bullet through my brain, I shall not die until I've killed him," Jackson told his aide.

Jackson made no attempt to shoot first, and Dickson's bullet struck hard, missing the heart by inches. Jackson stood firm. Dickinson was heard to utter: "My God! How could I have missed him?" Then Jackson took slow and deliberate aim and killed his opponent.

Jackson had determined to visit the Bell Witch for a purpose beyond that of idle curiosity. It was a quest for his soul. His wife, Rachel, believed in the hereafter, and she was concerned for husband's immortal soul. For his wife's sake, Jackson wanted to believe, and he had listened to preachers, many of whom were good and intelligent men, who had no doubt about their belief in the hereafter.

Yet he had trouble believing what other men seemed to accept by simple faith. Could proof be substituted for faith? If spirits could return to speak to the living, would it not prove that there was a hereafter? Jackson knew he was going to Adams to find that proof. And if he did find proof, could there be salvation for a man who refused to believe by faith alone? Jackson shook his head, admitting to himself that he did not know the answer.

Jackson's thoughts were interrupted by a voice calling from

the camp. It was his manservant, William calling to the wagon driver: "Sam, Sam, you get up. It's done daylight, and Massa Jackson is done up and gone."

"I'm down here by the creek, William." the General called.

Thereafter things moved quickly. The General ate a substantial breakfast while the slaves took down the field tent and loaded it into the wagon along with camp provisions. By the time the sun was shining through the treetops, they were on the road. The General rode in his carriage and the baggage wagon followed along behind. He normally brought a wagon and field tent when he travelled. While he could expect hospitality at any house along the road, long experience had taught him that the quality of bed and board varied greatly from house to house. He found travel much more tolerable when he provided his own accommodations and would abandon them only when he was able to stay at the house of friends whose accommodations he was familiar with.

It was within an hour of sundown when the carriage made the turn onto the country road that would lead to the Bell place. Here the General stopped the carriage to wait for the wagon to catch up. Although the weather had been fair for the past week, roads were still muddy from winter rains and thaws. A short distance beyond the turn, the road ran through a patch of woodland. Here the trees had protected the road from drying winds, and the mud was even deeper. As soon as the wagon came up behind the carriage, the General gave the order, and the carriage led the way down the road. They soon came to a very deep mud hole. The carriage passed through easily, but when the General looked back, he saw that the wagon had mired in the mud and that the mules were helpless because the mire gave them no footing. He sent William back to tell Sam that they would go on to the Bell house and send back help to get the wagon out of the mire.

Hours before the General's arrival, John Bell had sent one of the slave children out to the road to watch for the General's carriage. Hogs had been on the spit since morning, and now a meal could be ready for serving on a half hours' notice. The surrey had been rolled out of the carriage shed and the floor swept clean. Since the weather was warm, the meal would be served in the shed, and the long table used for outdoor occasions had been set up there. In addition to Jackson, there were neighbors and the extended family to serve--ten house guests in all. The house guests were from all parts of Tennessee and Kentucky, and two of the guests claimed to be on intimate terms with General Jackson.

Just as the disc of the sun touched the rim of the horizon, a breathless and excited slave child came running around the corner of the house on a dead run.

"Him acoming, him acoming," he shouted with great pride. It was the high point of a slave child's life to be the bearer of important tidings.

Betsy was helping Nanny and her mother in the kitchen. Now she was taking corn bread out of a large iron skillet. The warm weather made it possible to have the kitchen door open, so Betsy was able to see the General's carriage as it came around the house and pulled to a stop at the stable lot gate. She paused momentarily to watch. A small army of slaves rushed forward competing to be the one to help with the horses and carriage. Despite his infirmity, John Bell was among those who rushed to greet General Jackson. He opened the carriage door and stepped back to allow the General to alight.

"General Jackson, welcome to my humble home," he said with great dignity.

Richard had reminded the General that John Bell had been a visitor to the Hermitage, and the General was too good a politician to miss the opportunity the situation offered.

"Ah, Squire Bell, it's certainly good to see you again."

The "again" had the exact effect the General had intended. John Bell beamed his pleasure, and the guests who were now crowding around for introductions were all the more impressed with their host.

After the guests were introduced, John escorted the General

about the grounds to meet neighbors and members of the family. As they approached the kitchen door to meet Lucy, they met Betsy coming out of the kitchen on her way to place a large platter of corn bread on the table. She passed her father and the General demurely with downcast eyes. The General was not fooled at Betsy's apparent modesty. He noticed the cat-like grace with which she moved, and as she passed, he sensed her intensity.

"There goes a witch if I ever saw one," he thought with amusement.

22

THE GENERAL GETS A
GLIMPSE OF THE FUTURE

A s soon as the introductions had been finished, John suggested that the men retire to the spring house to sample the latest run from his still. Jackson was agreeable but reminded John that his wagon was still mired in the mud back on the road.

"I'll send my most trustworthy slave to take care of it," Bell assured him.

He called Dean and explained the situation then he led the way down to the spring house with the General at his side and the rest of the guests following close behind.

Dean found the General's slave William and had him explain the situation with the mired wagon. He selected several young blacks from the slave quarters who were most susceptible to the powers of suggestion, and they all made their way down the road where Sam waited with the mired wagon.

Even before they left the Hermitage, Jackson's slaves, Sam and William, knew the reputation of the Bell house. Like most slaves they believed in ghosts and black magic and were deeply apprehensive about "trifling" with such matters. As Dean and William walked down the road to where Sam waited with the mired wagon, William expressed puzzlement.

"Ain't you got no mules?" he questioned.

"Course we got mules, man," Dean replied disdainfully.

William was still adamant. "No way is we going to get dat wagon out'en dat mud hole lessen we's got an extra team of good mules," he declared.

"Aint gonna need no mules," Dean declared.

"What you mean, man, we aint gonna need no mules," William exploded in disbelief. "Dat wagon is mired up to de axle."

"Miss Kate put de wagon inter de hole, Miss Kate get de wagon outen de hole," Dean said with the supreme confidence of one in league with the Devil himself.

Once more William started to protest, but there was a look in Dean's eye that warned that it might not be wise to challenge the Devil's disciple.

They soon got to the wagon guarded by a nervous Sam. The first thing Dean did was to examine the situation carefully. As William had explained, the wheels were sunk in mud up to the axles, but the real problem was the slippery footing that prevented the mules from exerting their power in the pull.

After he was certain that he knew what needed to be done, Dean ordered all the slaves to gather around and cautioned them not to be bothering the spirit with a lot of racket. Then he closed his eyes and pretended to be listening to inaudible instructions. By then it was twilight, and a chorus of night noises from the forest made those around Dean even more nervous.

Suddenly Dean began mumbling a voodoo chant. None of the slaves could understand the words, but all knew that the chant was one that voodoo priests and priestesses used to summon the spirits.

As suddenly as the chant began it ended, and Dean seemed to be listening to inaudible voices.

"Yes'sum." he said aloud. "Yes'sum, I hears," he continued, "Yes'sum, Miss Kate. "Yes'sum, I hears."

The other slaves were watching him with saucer-wide eyes. They heard nothing, but each would later swear that an unseen presence had talked to Dean. Dean now opened his eyes and glared banefully at those around him.

"Miss Kate says she de one who stop dis wagon all right," he told the frightened slaves. "She say she have to show dat fine General he too subject to the power ob de spirit."

A murmur of awe went through the assembled slaves.

"Now Miss Kate say she ready to let go ob de wagon, but she say dat I must do de drivin'."

Sam who was an expert driver, muttered his dissent. "Dem mules ain't nebber gonna pull dat wagon outen dat hole," he said.

"Miss Kate say she might push a little," Dean assured him, and he waded through the mud and climbed into the driver's seat. He spoke calmly to the mules and carefully gathered the reins into one hand.

"Whoa, now mules," he said softly as he picked up the whip with his free hand.

The mules shifted restlessly in anticipation of his command. He touched the lead mule softly on the flank with the tip of the whip.

"Easy now, easy now. Let's tighten up dem traces," he ordered.

The mules had been well trained, and now in Dean they recognized voice of a master. They leaned against their traces. The weight of two fifteen-hundred-pound mules against the traces caused the wagon to strain forward for perhaps as much as half an inch, but the effort was not sufficient to cause the hooves of the mules to slip in the mud. Dean cracked the whip and shouted, "Har, har," and the mules lunged against the traces. Suddenly the wagon was moving and never stopped until it was clear of the mud.

Richard arrived at the Bell farm just before the guests were called to the table. General Jackson greeted him warmly.

"It seems that your spirit has already produced a miracle," the General told him.

"Oh, and how was that?" Richard asked.

The General related the story of the rescue of the wagon as he had heard it from his manservant, William.

As soon as possible, Richard worked his way over to Betsy. "What have you been up too now?" he asked in a confidential tone.

"I don't know what you are talking about," she answered.

"I'm talking about miring the General's wagon in the mud," he said.

"Until it drove up here in the yard just a while ago, I didn't know the General had a wagon."

"The story I get is that ol' Kate caused the wagon to get stuck in the mud and nothing could move it until Kate decided to let it go."

"I swear," Betsy said with resignation, "Kate gets blamed for everything that happens."

After filling his plate, General Jackson took a seat beside John Bell.

"Well, Squire Bell, you are to be congratulated on a fine family. "I've met your good wife and fine sons, but that young lady yonder, does she happen to be one of your family?"

"Oh, do forgive me, General," Bell apologized. "That's my youngest daughter, Elizabeth."

He called Betsy over. "Elizabeth, this is General Jackson. You've heard us talk about his great victory over the British at New Orleans. And, General, Elizabeth just happens to be a Latin scholar."

"Oh, Poppa," Betsy said in a blushing voice barely audible. She made a deep curtsy then looked up to meet the General's eyes. He was standing very tall and smiling down on her. He was, she decided, the most impressive man she had ever met.

At the time of this visit to the Bell plantation in Adams, Jackson was nearly fifty years old, and he was convinced he did not have much longer to live. He was determined to devote what little time he had left to provide for the security and comfort of his wife, Rachel. He loved Rachel to the exclusion of everything else in this life. Even now Jackson was making ambitious plans for the construction of a stately mansion at the Hermitage where Rachel could live out her years in comfort and security.

But the years had not been kind to Rachel. Gossip mongers continued to rail against Rachel's impropriety for divorcing her first husband in order to marry Jackson. The gossips also took pleasure in pointing out Rachel's rough frontier manners, and they twittered over her habit of smoking a pipe like a man. As a result, Rachel was excluded from "refined" society. Over the years the rejections and malicious gossip had taken their toll on her. Despite Jackson's famous impetuosity and angry resolve to protect his wife from the malicious gossip mongers, nothing he did could stem the tide. To him Rachel was still the young dark-haired beauty he had met at her mother's house where her high spirits led her to rebel against the petty jealousies of her first husband.

Now Rachel had grown fat, and she had become a religious fanatic obsessed with the salvation of her husband's soul. Out of his deep concern for Rachel, Jackson wanted nothing so much this day in Adams as to encounter proof of an afterlife so that he could return to Rachel and comfort her with the news that the two of them would continue being together in the hereafter for all eternity.

Other women sensed Jackson's devotion to his wife. Because of society's shabby treatment of Rachel, Jackson never spoke ill of other women, even some women for whom there was no doubt about their lack of virtue. He considered all women to be ladies, yet any relation he had with other women was strictly platonic. There was never any breath of scandal that Jackson could in any way be unfaithful to his wife.

Now Jackson was anxious to fulfill his mission at the Bell house by talking to the famous spirit from beyond. But first he was required to partake in the standard amenities and congenial conversation of his host's home. After a substantial meal, the guests moved into the main dining room of the Bell house. This was the largest room in the house, but it was soon crowded with adults occupying all the chairs. Betsy brought a stool from the kitchen and placed it in a corner where she could sit unnoticed.

General Jackson was the center of attention. His victory over the British at New Orleans still excited public interest, and the guests were most anxious to hear a first-hand account of the battle from the General himself. Jackson told the story he had told hundreds of times before. And at the end of the story, he received the same questions he had answered a hundred times before. As usual some of the questions were straight forward and bordered on the impertinent. In more refined company such questions would have been considered a sign of bad manners, but on the frontier, they were asked for the sake of lively curiosity.

The General answered all questions with good humor. Betsy got the impression that he was thoroughly enjoying the attention and adulation.

At last, he threw up his hands in protest.

"Gentlemen, Gentlemen, please," he pleaded. "I have made a long journey to witness the manifestations of the spirit that has haunted this house. But if I continue to talk so much, I fear the spirit will flee from boredom in search of peace and quiet."

"The spirit has enjoyed your stories, General," the Voice announced.

Everyone immediately fell silent. Several looked about for some sign of the spirit's physical presence.

"Well thank you," the General said as though addressing one of the guests at the table.

"I encountered the General earlier in the afternoon," the Voice said.

"You did? I was not aware of that," the General replied.

"I delayed your wagon back there on the road so you might have proof of my power."

The General laughed heartily. "So, that was your doing?" he said with mock surprise. "I would have sworn that the wagon merely got stuck in the mud."

"I caused it to get stuck in the mud," the Voice reminded him, "and I caused it to get unstuck when the slave Dean was sent to fetch it."

"That is true," the General admitted.

At that moment the General's eye met Betsy's who was watching him closely from the corner. His eyes twinkled with amusement, and he gave her a wink.

"He knows," she thought. "He's the only one besides Richard who knows. He ain't fooled one bit."

"Am I allowed to question the spirit?" the General asked.

"Why not? Everyone else does," the Voice answered.

"Then tell me, what is to be the fate of General Jackson?" he asked, half in jest.

"You are now known as 'General,' but you will soon lay aside that title for one more prestigious. You will live in a mansion and be a lonely leader of your people. Then you will have a few years of peace and finally be laid to rest beside your beloved."

As the Voice spoke, the General's face changed. The mocking grin slowly dissolved into a look of extreme gravity.

Betsy met his stare as though she were spellbound. As the Voice spoke, her eyes grew wider, and she shook her head as though she too was unable to believe what she was saying. They continued to hold each other's gaze for another moment then the General shook his own head as though to clear it.

"Well," he suddenly exploded, "this has been most interesting. And now that the Witch has answered my question, I think I shall go to bed."

As he was about to leave the room, he signaled for Richard to follow. They left the house and walked in silence until they reached the General's tent. The General pushed aside the flap and motioned for Richard to enter.

Jackson's manservant, William, was busy arranging the General's belongings. Now he rushed forward with a small glass of bourbon. It was obvious that the General always had a nightcap before retiring. Seeing that the General had a guest, William made profuse apologies and soon produced a second glass.

"Thank you, William," the General said. "Now, you may go to bed. Senator Powell and I will talk for a little while."

Bowing profusely, the old Negro backed out of the tent. The General took a sip of the whiskey and motioned for Richard to take a seat on a camp stool.

"You are to be congratulated, Senator," he said. "Miss Elizabeth is a most attractive young lady."

"I'm not sure I understand," Richard said.

"Well, it's most obvious that the child is smitten with you. May I assume that you return her affection?"

Richard laughed. "You are most perceptive, General", he said.

"She is young, but she will get older. Does Colonel Bell approve of your courtship?"

"As a matter of fact, I have just learned that he has given his approval. There was a bit of a complication. But that has been taken care of."

"If you need me to speak a work to the Colonel..."

"No. I believe the matter is working out very well."

The General took another sip of his whiskey and cradled the glass lovingly in his hands.

"Miss Elizabeth is a most accomplished ventriloquist," he said.

"Yes, she is," Richard agreed.

"In your opinion, is she also a seer?"

"She does have visions of things happening in other places."

"And can she see into the future?"

"She's never claimed to be able to see the future."

"She told my future. It was an amazing performance but also a bit disturbing."

"In what way, General?"

"Because it cannot possibly be true..."

"Oh, I think she was just giving an answer to your question for the benefit of the guests."

"But she did know some things that no one else could have known."

"What, General?"

Jackson appeared to be in deep thought. "She said that I would change the title of General for one more prestigious. Only a few days ago, several gentlemen visited me asking if I would be willing to let them put my name forward as a candidate for the United States Senate. Of course, I refused. The last thing on earth I want is a political office. But then they explained to me a situation that makes it conceivable that things might work out in a way that would put me in a position where it would be impossible for me to refuse to run. I told them if things worked to that end, I would then stand for the office. Then I swore them to secrecy. Besides those in the house that night, you are the only one who knows about this, which makes Miss Elizabeth's prophesy rather uncanny."

"You would make an excellent Senator," Richard flattered.

Jackson ignored the flattery and continued. "But then there was that bit about me being a lonely leader of my people, living in a mansion and finally being put to rest beside my beloved. Why it sounds like Miss Elizabeth is predicting that I will outlive Mrs. Jackson."

"And you don't think that's possible?" Richard asked.

"Of course not. Just because Mrs. Jackson is a year older than me, it doesn't mean that she's an old woman."

"Certainly not," Richard hastily replied, realizing this was a sore point with the General, "When I visited the Hermitage, I found Mrs. Jackson youthful and attractive."

"There now," the General exulted while pointing a finger directly at Richard. "You saw it. And, Senator Powell, you are a most perceptive young man. Incidentally, you have excellent taste in your women."

"Thank you, General," Richard bowed graciously.

The General sighed. "Senator, I'm an old soldier. I've fought too many battles. Sustained too many scars. Doctors tell me I have enough maladies to kill a less robust man several times over. No, I shall die in Mrs. Jackson's arms, and a sweet death it will be. Do you happen to remember that grove of elm and cedar just to the west as you approached the Hermitage?"

"Why yes, I did notice such a grove," Richard answered.

"That is where I intend to build the new Hermitage. It will be the equal of any Virginia mansion. But not for me, understand. It will be for Mrs. Jackson to enjoy after I have passed on."

"I trust that will be many years into the future," Richard said.

The General cast him a quick look as though probing for his sincerity.

"Uh...You think so? Well perhaps. So, to get back to Miss Elizabeth, she is an exceptional ventriloquist, but I would say a poor prophet. But she certainly gives people something to talk about."

Here the General let out a chuckle. "Nevertheless, Senator, you marry that girl as soon as possible, and when you do, tell her that General Jackson said that it is time to start a family and put an end to all this witchery."

"General, you have my word that I will do my best to obey that order," Richard assured him.

23

DREWRY GOES ON
A JOURNEY

General Jackson left the Bell Place the following morning. But because of the other visitors, the house remained crowded. Richard found it impossible to get an opportunity to talk to Betsy. At last Betsy announced that she was going out for a ride. The announcement was so pointed that Richard knew she expected him to follow.

He overtook her at the point where the woodland path leading to the old Indian Grave joined the road. That morning, winter was showing signs of reviving so that there was a sharp bite in the air. They dismounted and hitched their horses to nearby saplings and walked together up the pathway.

"I didn't fool the General," Betsy said as an opening.

"No, but he was impressed with your skill as a ventriloquist," Richard consoled her.

"How come him to catch on when everybody else was fooled?"

"I'm afraid that the General is what Brother Gunn calls a free thinker, and as such he would not normally believe in witches and ghosts. Then too, he has spent some time in New Orleans, and that city is filled with entertainers. He has probably encountered ventriloquism before."

"Do you think that he will tell folks that I am the voice of the Spirit?"

"Oh, I doubt that. You merely amused him. But you can be sure that, soon or later, somebody is going to catch on."

Betsy nodded gravely. They walked on in silence.

"The General was disturbed by your prophesy," Richard said, breaking the silence.

"I know."

"Why on Earth did you say such a thing?"

"He asked me."

"But couldn't you have said something vague and general?"

"Look, I was just as surprised as General Jackson at what came out."

"What do you mean?"

"Well, he asked the question, and I started to answer, and you heard what came out."

"You mean it wasn't a conscious statement on your part?"

"I mean I'm not sure why I said what I did. It sorta came out all by itself."

"Well, it probably doesn't mean anything. But the General took it to mean that he would outlive his wife. He is very devoted, and that disturbed him."

"He will outlive his wife by many years."

"Now how can you know that?"

"I don't know. I just know."

"My God, you're saying you can foretell the future; that's just not possible," Richard said in a voice tinged with irritation.

They walked on in silence.

"I'm sorry, Richard, but I do know. I can't help that."

He put an arm around her shoulders and gave her an affectionate squeeze.

"I know, I know," he said. "It was nothing that you could help. But when you predicted that he would change his title for a more prestigious one, he accepted that because there are some people trying to get him to stand for the United States Senate. It was what you predicted next—that he would outlive his wife—that disturbed him."

Again, they walked in silence for a few steps.

"Richard?" Betsy broke the silence.

"Yes?"

"It wasn't the title of Senator that I was thinking about."

"It wasn't?"

"No. He will be elected to the Senate, but the title I foresaw wasn't "Senator.""

"Then what was it?"

"President."

"President? Now that *is* ridiculous. No one from the West will ever become President in our lifetimes," Richard said with certainty. "Your prophesy has failed you!"

Before Betsy could respond to that, Richard continued, "You know, the General gave me some advice that I need to give some serious thought to."

"What advice?"

"He told me to marry you and then tell you that it's time for you to raise a family and stop all this witchery."

"Oh, I like that advice." Betsy responded enthusiastically. "When do you think you could talk to Poppa?"

"I'm not sure. You are still too young for us to get married."

"But you could declare for me. Then you could come courting. We could talk without having to slip away from the house. Besides, Poppa said I could marry Josh when I was fifteen, and I'll soon be thirteen."

"Suppose I talk to your mother first and see what she thinks?"

"Would you? Would you talk to her today?"

"I'll do my best."

They turned and walked back up the path, remounted their horses, and rode toward the house. As they came around a bend in the road, they saw a buggy waiting in front of the house.

I guess we got new company," Betsy said. Richard detected a trace of irritation in her voice.

"There's something familiar about that buggy," Richard observed. "Isn't that Doctor Hopson's rig?"

They spurred their horses to a faster pace, now aware that something had happened while they were away.

General's Jackson's visit had acted like adrenalin on John Bell. Under the stimulus of the excitement of having such a distinguished guest, he had left his sick bed, supervised the preparations, and was on hand to greet the General upon his arrival.

Now with the General on his way home and the excitement gone, he collapsed while in the dining room talking to his guests. John Jr. had again gone for Doctor Hopson, and the doctor had just arrived as Betsy and Richard came into view of the house.

John Bell had lost the ability to speak and was shaking uncontrollably. He was also hallucinating. Pointing to a corner of the room, he made piteous sounds, and his eyes pleaded with the family not to allow the apparition to take him away.

Drewry was still spending most of his time at the house during his father's illness, and he was the most upset over his father's relapse into his illness. He hovered around his father's bed shedding tears of helpless rage. Betsy and Richard were forced to delay plans to their courtship.

John Bell's spell lasted into the Spring. By that time, Betsy had added another birthday to her age and had begun to fill out into her full womanly figure.

In early April, Betsy overheard Drewry trying to persuade his mother to allow him to go to Kentucky and engage the witch chaser to come exorcise the spirit that was afflicting his father. Lucy refused to hear of such a thing.

"Your father is sick, not plagued by any spirit," Lucy Bell told Drewry. Lucy knew that Betsy was behind the strange happenings around the house, and she was afraid that an exorcist might expose her daughter.

Doctor Hopson concurred with Lucy's diagnosis of John Bell's condition, but most of the community sided with Drewry.

On a sunny morning in May, John Bell awoke feeling better.

Although he still could not talk, his head was clear, and the violent shaking had stopped. He was still too weak to leave his bed, but he had improved to the point where he could respond to questions by nodding or shaking his head.

Lucy brought him his breakfast as usual, and as she left the room, Drewry was waiting outside the door. She knew Drewry wanted to discuss bringing the witch chaser into the home, but she did not have the heart to keep him away from his father.

Drewry drew a chair up beside the bed. "How are you feeling father?" he asked.

John mumbled and waved his hands helplessly.

"Are you feeling better?" Drewry persisted.

John nodded his head in the affirmative.

"Perhaps the Witch has been distracted," Drewry continued. Again, John nodded.

"Father, I've heard about this man over in Kentucky who is able to cast out witches like they did in the Bible."

John stared at his son.

"I've been thinking that maybe he could help us."

John nodded.

"I would be willing to go to Kentucky to fetch him."

Again, John nodded.

"Would you like for me to bring him here?"

This time the nod was vigorous.

"When I go, I don't want anybody to know where I've gone," Drewry cautioned.

John's eyes questioned his son.

"Mother is opposed to the idea," Drewry explained. "She believes that you are only ill."

John nodded and tried to speak. To some extent he communicated to Drewry that he understood Lucy's reluctance to believe he was possessed. But during the worst of his illness, he had seen the Spirit watching and waiting from a corner of the room.

"I shall leave early tomorrow," Drewry said. "Perhaps I can

be back early next week. I will tell no one that I am leaving, and when I return, I will bring the witch chaser."

The following morning Drewry slipped out of the house before anyone was awake. No one missed him until the family sat down for breakfast.

"Where is Drewry?" Betsy asked.

"I'm not sure," Zadock replied. "He was gone when I got up. I thought perhaps he had decided to go back across the river. Last night he said something about needing to check on his slaves."

"He wouldn't have gone without his breakfast," Betsy insisted, "not just to go back home."

By this time Betsy's suspicions were growing.

"I heard somebody leave the house before daybreak," John Jr. said. "I thought it was Zadock leaving early to get ready for his court case."

"Lawyers never get up before daybreak," Zadock laughed. "Court doesn't convene until nine. Besides, my case will be heard before a magistrate. It won't take much preparation."

The conversation ranged farther and farther afield, and the matter of Drewry's absence was forgotten by everyone—except Betsy.

Laying her fork on her plate, she said softly, "I'll go sit with Poppa so mother can come eat."

As Betsy entered her father's room, her mother laid her crocheting aside. After the two women exchanged a few words, Lucy went to have breakfast. Betsy was now alone with her father, who lay propped up on a stack of pillows. His eyes followed as Betsy moved quickly to straighten the bed covers, fluff up the pillows, and restore order to the room. When finished with those tasks, she took the chair her mother had vacated and picked up the crocheting. She soon seemed to be completely absorbed in work.

Looking up, she asked innocently, "Have you seen Drewry this morning?"

Her father shook his head.

This was technically true, since John had not seen Drewry since last night.

"Did he go back across the river?" Betsy asked.

John Bell shrugged his shoulders, but his eyes looked worried.

Betsy knew her father seldom lied, but she was sure he was now withholding information. Betsy continued her crocheting and pressed the matter no further. She was almost certain that Drewry's absence had something to do with his wish to bring in the witch chaser.

When her mother returned a half hour later, Betsy went immediately to her room. Lying across her bed, she fixed her eyes on the ceiling and concentrated on Drewry.

Slowly her immediate surroundings faded. She seemed to be flying above the road heading north from the house. Drewry had evidently covered much distance since he had left early in the morning. She looked down to see a man mounted on a horse leading another horse. As she moved closer to the rider, she saw that he had stopped in the middle of the road and appeared to be waiting for someone. The rider was not familiar, but he was holding on to the reins of another horse, and that horse definitely belonged to Drewry. In a panicky moment Betsy thought that maybe Drewry had run afoul of an outlaw who now had possession of Drewry's horse. As the scene became clearer, Betsy saw another man with his back to the road, standing amid some bushes. She knew that this man was Drewry, and she suddenly realized what he was doing. She blushed as if she had intruded into some obscene act. Drewry turned back toward the road, busily buttoning the fly of his trousers. He cast a glance at the morning sun.

"Can we make the Kentucky line by noon?" he asked his mounted companion.

His companion also glanced at the sun. "It'll take hard riding," he answered.

At that moment a small rabbit, recently out of his birthing

burrow, hopped out of the roadside cover almost at Drewry's feet. Drewry moved quickly and scooped up the young rabbit and held it aloft.

"Ho, ho, what have we here?" he called to his mounted companion.

"Can't be more'n a few days out of the nest," his companion said. "But it's big enough for frying."

"Aw, I'd never hurt the little fellow," Drewry said as he pushed the rabbit into his coat pocket. "I'll just give him a lift down the road a piece."

Drewry mounted his horse, and the two men started down the road urging their horses into a fast canter.

That night the Bell family and the remaining guests assembled around the supper table.

"We're all worried about Brother Drewry," the Voice suddenly announced.

By reflex the guests looked around for the source of the Voice that they would never locate.

"But I am able to report that he is well and has found an agreeable traveling companion," the Voice continued. "By now he is far on the road to Kentucky to fetch the witch chaser. This morning, I assumed the form of a young rabbit and rode along in his coat pocket until he released me just before the two stopped for supper in Adairsville. When he gets home tell him that Kate is grateful for a long ride in such a warm and cozy pocket.

24

THE WITCH CHASER

After asking directions several times, Drewry found a decaying house built of log and frame at the end of a country lane on the banks of the Barren River. It was several miles beyond the small village of Russelville. If he could believe those he had asked, here lived the witch chaser, Filbert G. Clogg.

An elderly female slave answered his knock, and he was ushered into a dimly lighted room that served as the parlor. It was a corner room with windows on the north and east. He had arrived in midafternoon so that the room was now in shadow. The room itself presented a contrast. The furniture was massive, but of good quality. An expensive rug covered the floor and heavy drapes hung over the windows. But there was an atmosphere of neglect about the place. A layer of dust covered every surface and there was a musty smell about the entire room.

The man who entered seemed to fit the room. He was formally attired in a frock tailed coat and ruffled shirt. Drewry noticed that the clothing was well cut and made from good cloth. But the outfit was well worn, and he saw a stain on the lapel of the coat that perhaps represented some small portion of the wearer's noonday meal. The man eyed Drewry with cautious reserve.

"Are you Filbert G. Clogg, the witch chaser?" Drewry asked.

The man's eyes showed relief, and the sullen face relaxed into affability.

"One and the same," Clogg declared in a sonorous voice. "And whom might I be addressing?"

"My name is Drewry Bell."

"And where do you hail from, Squire Bell?"

"Adams, Sir. Adams, Tennessee."

"Would you be one of the Bells from that town whose family is troubled by a witch?"

"I am."

"I've heard tales about your family troubles," Clogg said.

"I am hoping that you can help us," Drewry explained.

"You have come to the right person," Clogg assured him. "I can only be thankful that you did not fall into the hands of some of the charlatans who profess to have power over the supernatural. Won't you have a chair, Squire Bell?"

Drewry sat down in a cluttered chair. At an early age, Drewry had learned a mania for neatness and order from his mother. His own small cabin was spotless.

His aversion to the condition of the room was apparent to Clogg, who now offered an excuse.

"Please excuse the state of disarray. Mrs. Clogg passed away recently."

For the next hour Drewry related the family experiences with the Witch. Filbert Clogg listened attentively, nodding his head or interjecting a question from time to time as Drewry added some new detail of the Witch's behavior.

As Drewry finished, Clogg asked, "Are you familiar with the nature of disembodied spirits, Mr. Bell?"

Drewry shook his head.

Clogg continued. "It has been my good fortune to study abroad with the famous Doctor Gottenhaus at the University of Heidelburg. The good professor was then recognized as the world's foremost authority on theophistic manifestations. I was considered his most outstanding pupil."

Drewry's face was a study in awe. His own education had

been limited to what he had been able to learn in the one-room school on his father's farm. He had never been in the presence of anyone who claimed to have studied abroad.

Filbert Clogg was aware of the impression he was making. He cast a furtive and appraising eye over the man before him. The dress was simple, but he had an air of quality about his bearing, and he mentally translated this into a fee he felt he could safely ask for his services.

He was also sufficiently encouraged to press his claim to scholarship a bit further, "Unfortunately, some have done the good Doctor a great disservice by spreading the rumor that I have since surpassed that good man's accomplishments."

Glogg made this declaration with downcast eyes and a voice of becoming modesty.

"But rest assured, Good Sir, that I have never presumed such august distinction."

"Could you possibly banish our witch?" Drewry asked.

"We shall get to that point shortly. But for the moment I would like to expound on the subject of the nature of spiritual phenomena. The Scripture teaches that upon death, man's immortal soul is separated from his body. In a natural course of events that soul travels to a state of limbo to await final judgment. But in a few cases the disembodied spirit is unable or unwilling to break its ties with this world. In its efforts to cling to this life it develops a plasmatic presence and becomes what we refer to as a ghost, witch or spirit."

"What is this plasmatic presence?" Drewry asked.

"I'm glad you asked that question," the good Clogg declared. He now got to his feet and paced about the room. Drewry was reminded of some of the preachers he had listened to as they lectured to a large congregation.

"I may say that I am one of the few scholars on either continent who has mastered this concept," Clogg continued.

He held up two fingers. "We acknowledge that man has two forms of existence."

He held up on finger. "One is the material form that you and I have today. That form consists of flesh and bone."

He reached out and grasped Drewry's shoulder and gave it a hard squeeze.

"In the material state we have substance. We speak and are heard; we appear and are clearly seen. But now let us consider the soul. The soul is that part of our being that comes from our Heavenly Father."

Now Clogg held up a second finger. "The soul has being. But no substance. When the soul leaves the body, it loses its means of contact with other souls. We presume that it may regain a method of contact once it passes into limbo, but as long as it clings to the Earth, it may speak, but it will not be heard; it may appear but will not be seen."

"Still, the very reason the soul clings to this Earth is a need to make its presence felt. Suspended between life and death, the spirit becomes a plasmatic presence. In that state it may be seen as an ephemeral vapor that one associates with ghosts."

"But we never see our spirit," Drewry explained, "not unless it appeared in either human or animal form."

"Ah, yes," Clogg exclaimed. "The plasmatic presence may possess the body of man or beast, but only for a short time."

"It's mostly just a voice that speaks out of thin air," Drewry clarified.

"That is, of course, another manifestation of the plasmatic present," Clogg expanded, "the ability to be heard."

"And it makes knocking or scratching sounds," Drewry added.

"Knocking and scratching are primitive forms of the plasmatic presence. It often is the first indication that a spirit is trying to establish communication. Recently, I cast out a spirit that had long frequented a home in Lousiville that had no way of communication except by rapping. It would rap once for 'no' and twice for 'yes.'"

"Why does the spirit want to cling to this world? Seems like it would be anxious to go to a better place."

"Oh, there are many reasons. Sometimes it feels that it has unfinished business here. I recall one spirit that left with great joy just as soon as I discovered a will it had prepared and then hidden away during life. There was another that refused to go until his wife promised not to remarry."

"But as far as we know, our spirit has no family connection," Drewry explained.

"From what you tell me about its attacks on your father and sister, I would guess that you are beset by a lost soul well aware that it has no hope of salvation. Already damned, it has become a malevolent spirit, and because it is doomed to suffer in the next world, it stays in this world to inflict suffering on others."

"How can it be cast out?" Drewry wanted to know.

"Ah, I'm glad you asked that question," Cloog exclaimed. "It gives me the opportunity to expound on He who is even greater than witches. Are you a believing man, Mr. Bell?"

"Certainly, Sir, all the Bells are deeply religious."

"Then you need hardly ask the question. Our God is also Master of the Kingdom of Darkness."

"But Reverend Gunn prayed for the Witch to be removed from the house. Nothing happened. It just kept on with its mischief."

"To each is given according to this ability," Clogg intoned piously. "Your Reverend Gunn is gifted with the power of persuasion. He is guided to the conversion of sinners in this life. Demonologists such as I are sent to delve into the dark recesses haunted by those rebellious spirits seeking to drive men away from the light."

Drewry was impressed but confused. He had failed to inherit his sister's sharp wit or nimble mind. He was a farmer and functioned well in sunshine and among growing things, but now he was delving into things of which he had no knowledge.

As the afternoon passed, Clogg continued talking, and the conversation soon became a monolog. In time the topic turned to money.

"Ah, the Good Book tells us the laborer is worthy of his

hire," he said. Then he quoted, "Thou shalt not muzzle the ox that treads out thy grain."

Then Clogg told a pointed story about casting out a ghost for a wealthy farmer who then refused to pay for the service.

Even though Drewry was no match for his nimble-witted sister, he eventually understood that Clogg was hinting that he wanted to discuss the matter of his fee.

Drewry was not a diplomat. "How much are you going to charge us to get rid of our witch?" he asked bluntly.

As anxious as Clogg had been to open up the subject, the directness of the question caught him by surprise.

"Oh, well, let's see," he said as he pretended to make mental calculations. In reality, he was trying to guess how much he could ask without running the risk of scaring his client away.

"It would involve several days of travel," he mused.

Drewry sat stolid, giving no hint of his reaction.

"And three days in preparation for the casting out ceremony," Clogg added.

Drewy sat listening.

"The casting out would require another day," Clogg continued to calculate.

"Eight days in all," Drewry said.

"It's only fair that I receive remuneration for all my expenses," Clogg suggested.

"We'd expect to feed you," Drewry offered.

Clogg decided to make a stab in the dark. If his client's reaction was negative, he was prepared to make a fast retreat into a bargaining position.

"Most folks insist that I take a hundred dollars to do the casting out," he ventured.

Drewry nodded gravely. On the frontier few farmers had ever seen a hundred dollars all at once, but Drewry did not consider it too much to pay if his father got well. Somewhere in the back of his mind, however, he recalled that his mother believed his father to be ill rather than under a spell. Now the natural caution of one who works hard for his money asserted itself.

"Fine," he said, "providing it ain't payable until the Witch is gone from us and Poppa is up and well."

Clogg's face fell for the merest fraction of a second. Although his reputation as a witch chaser had spread throughout Kentucky and much of Tennessee, it had grown mostly as a result of his own bragging and storytelling.

He had never seen anything he considered a ghost. On a few occasions he had been called in by superstitious families who had seen fleeting shadows or unidentified noises. In such cases his assurance that the offending ghost had been chased into limbo had been enough to put anxious clients at rest.

He was not sure about the spirit that haunted the Bell house. He had heard prominent men swear that the spirit was real enough. But there was no good way he could refuse Drewry's terms. To do so would put his own claims in doubt. Now he held out his hand to seal the bargain. At the very least he would get a few days of free eating.

Late that afternoon Clogg and Drewry mounted their horses and rode south. Late on the third day, they turned into the road that led to the Bell house.

On the surface there was nothing unusual about the Bell house or its surroundings, but now its reputation for being haunted caused many to see it as sinister. Clogg considered himself a man far too intelligent to believe in ghosts, but he had dealt with superstitious people and their fears for too long not to have been affected to some degree with the same fear of the supernatural. Now as the two men turned their horses into the driveway of the Bell house, Clogg experienced an involuntary shudder.

They dismounted their horses and climbed to steps up to the front porch. Drewry pushed open the front door without knocking.

Because of the previous revelations of the Witch, everyone in the house had been expecting the arrival of the two men for several days, and as they had approached the house, slave children had announced their arrival from the moment they had turned off the road.

As the front door opened, Lucy Bell appeared in the hallway, and Betsy peered down from the top of the stairs. Lucy's lips were tightly compressed, and Drewry recognized that as a sign of her disapproval. He had not fully considered the fact that he would have to face his mother upon his return, and now he hesitated in making the introductions.

Instead of introducing his companion, Drewry said, "Well, Mother, I'm home."

Suddenly the hallway was filled with cackling laughter. "Well, well," the Voice proclaimed. "Who have we here but the world-famous witch chaser, Filbert G. Clogg."

Clogg almost jumped out of his skin. Drewry had explained to him that no one in the family had known of his mission.

A wide-eyed Clogg twisted about trying to locate the source of the voice. They only people present were Drewry, his mother and a timid girl standing on the stairs.

"The good Clogg has come to banish me from this house," the Voice continued. "His efforts should be most entertaining. I shall allow him a few days to work his enchantments, before I reveal the dark secret unknown even to Brother Drewry."

Drewry was the first of the mortals to speak. "There! You see what this family has to put up with?" he said to Clogg. "There's hardly ever a night when we aren't being interrupted by that kind of talk."

"I see," Clogg said, although he did not see at all.

Drewry turned to his mother. "Momma, Mr. Clogg here thinks he can cure Poppa."

"Mr. Clogg," Lucy said, "my son is under the impression that his father has been hexed by our spirit. As a matter of fact, his father is old and sick. This has been confirmed by our family doctor, Doctor Hopson. I'm afraid that Drewry has brought you here for nothing."

Drewry was distressed. "Momma won't you let him try?

219

Even if Poppa don't get well, we will, at least, be shed of that spirit."

Lucy cast a hasty glance at the stairs where Betsy waited. Her daughter was watching Clogg through narrow, slitted eyes, reminding Lucy of a cat stalking a robin. Suddenly she shuddered. Her former fears had been groundless. Now she realized that Clogg would never be a match for the spirit. In fact, it was now Clogg she worried about. She turned to Drewry.

"I fully realize that your father thinks he is under a spell. If he wishes to engage Mr. Clogg, I cannot deny him a hope for his cure."

Now Clogg spoke up. "A wise decision, Madam. A wise decision."

Clogg was taken to the sick room to meet John Bell.

Bell's face lit up with hopeful curiosity. Such acceptance restored Clogg's self-confidence.

"Be of good cheer, Brother Bell," he intoned. "I have come to deliver you."

Bell nodded his head vigorously and held out a trembling hand in supplication. Clogg took the proffered hand.

Betsy had descended the stairs and watched the goings on by peeping around the door frame. As Clogg grasped her father's hand, she turned away and allowed herself a small snicker of disgust.

Clogg dominated the conversation around the supper table that night. For the benefit of the entire family, he again expounded his theories about ghosts and other supernatural phenomena. Reactions around the table varied from Lucy's thinly compressed lips to Drewry's hopeful acceptance. As for Betsy, she ate looking at her plate, making no effort to enter into the conversation.

It was Zadock who intervened during a lull in Clogg's monolog.

"Drewry," he asked, "did you happen to catch a small rabbit on the road while you were on the way to Kentucky?"

Drewry was puzzled by such a trivial question, but then his face took on a startled look as he remembered.

"Why, yes, I did," he said. "A very small rabbit just days out of the nest."

"And at that time, you were traveling with a stranger?" Zadock persisted.

"Why yes," Drewry's said, his confusion growing. "I overtook a Mr. Almont who was going to Russelville, and we decided to travel together."

"And you put the rabbit in your pocket and carried it with you until you stopped for the night near Adairsville?"

"Yes," Drewry admitted. "But how come you know all of this?"

"Kate told us. She said that she had taken to form of a rabbit and had ridden in your pocket for the afternoon."

As was the custom with important guests, Filbert Clogg was given the upstairs bedroom where Richard William and Joe E. had slept in less crowded times. The boys now had pallets on the floor in the room with John Jr. and Zadock. That night, as Clogg settled into bed, he tried to collect his wits and think. The apprehension that he had felt riding up to the house had not left him. The disembodied voice was disturbing, and had he shared the same beliefs as the people in the community, he would have been terrified. He only kept his wits about him because he thought that it had to be some sort of trick.

How had everyone in the house known about his mission? Drewry insisted he had told no one, and even Drewry had not known the name Filbert G. Clogg until making inquiries in the community where Clogg lived. How had that disembodied voice known his name down to the middle initial? How did everyone know about the rabbit? Drewry, like Clogg, had been completely befuddled over these mysteries, and Clogg knew that neither

Drewry nor anyone else in the family would have the inclination or sophistication to make up an elaborate plan to entrap him.

Clogg was not ready to admit defeat. He considered himself much too intelligent to believe that ghosts really existed. Whatever was happening here had to have a logical explanation. He was sure of that—or at least ninety-five percent sure. Yet a deep inner awareness told him that for the first time in his life he was in a situation that he might not be able to bluff his way out of.

25

THE WITCH CHASER
IS CONFOUNDED

The next morning Clogg demanded a place where he could prepare for the casting out ceremony. According to Clogg the site had to be behind a locked door and have no windows where idle curiosity seekers could spy on his preparations. After some thought, Drewry decided that the carriage shed was the only place on the farm that met all of Clogg's specifications. The carriage was rolled out into the yard and the floor swept clean. Clogg's next demands were for candles, tools and some lumber. Then when these things were delivered, he took his saddle bags and locked himself inside the building. For the rest of the day the Bells heard a considerable amount of sawing and hammering. As for Clogg he appeared for his dinner and then returned to seclude himself behind the locked door. If there was any concern over what was going on behind the locked door, it was all cleared up that night at the supper table when "ol' Kate" announced to all assembled that Clogg was building an altar.

"And a fine piece of carpentry it is," she concluded. "It would seem that a man with such talent would be content to make an honest living and allow a harmless old witch to pass her time in peace and quiet."

Again, Clogg was completely mystified as to where the Voice was coming from. But it occurred to him that as a mighty witch chaser he was probably expected to challenge the Voice. It was not a task he relished, but he made a good show of bravado.

"Enjoy your earthly sojourn while you may," he admonished. "You have two more days then on the third day you shall be banished to outer darkness."

Refusing to be bated into an argument, the Voice gave no answer except a soft laughter that seemed to echo throughout the room. Somehow that unnerved Clogg more than any threat the Voice might have made. It had occurred to Clogg that the Voice had a possible human origin, and when he was in bed that night he made an effort to decide who in the household might be the source. Obviously, it could not be John Bell. The man's afflictions were real. If Drewry had been the source, it was not likely that he would ride for four days to bring a witch chaser home to expose him. Clogg had decided that Drewry was not too bright and would not have had the wits to pull off such a trick. He also ruled out the younger Bell boys, but Zadock he considered a definite possibility. His prime suspicions centered on Lucy Bell and the slave woman Nanny. Being of a devious mind, himself, he could easily believe that Lucy Bell might have it in her head to do away with her husband for any number of reasons. As for Nanny the old woman's contempt showed clearly every time she cast a look in his direction, and it was well known that many slaves dabbled in witchcraft and perfected skills to fool others.

He could be forgiven for having no suspicion of Betsy. In the time he had been in the house, she had been little more than a shadow, and Clogg was barely aware of her presence. In fact, for most of the time, he noted, she hid herself away in her room lying across her bed with her eyes staring vacantly at a spot on the ceiling.

But tonight, as Clogg lay pondering, Betsy was rummaging through her closet looking for Esther's old cape by the light of a candle that rested on her windowsill. Clogg had barely dropped off to sleep before he was awakened by what sounded like rats gnawing on the posts of his bed. He sat up in bed, groping for his flint and steel to light a candle. As his hand moved about on the table, his fingers came into contact with something soft and warm. He picked it up. Although, the room was pitch dark, he was able to feel that he was holding a small dead animal. He yelled in terror and threw the thing from him. As he did there was the unmistakable sound of someone laughing. Clogg was not a courageous man. He fell back in the pillow and pulled the covers over his head.

When Clogg awoke the following morning, his first thought was to find the creature he had flung from him the previous night. Although he was certain that whatever he had picked up from the table had been dead, he was not able to find any sign of a dead body in the room. By the time he had finished looking, a bird chirping outside his window made him aware that it promised to be an almost perfect day. With the sunshine streaming into the room, it was difficult to believe in witches, and by the time he appeared in the dining room for his breakfast, he was starting to doubt that the things in his memory had really happened.

"Perhaps, I am being overcome by the power of suggestion," he thought as he took a turn about the yard to help settle his meal.

As he regained his self-confidence, he began to think about the one hundred dollars that Drewry had promised once the Witch had been cast out of the house. With that thought in mind, he went to the carriage house with renewed determination.

Betsy watched Clogg from her bedroom window as he strolled around the yard. Once he retired to the carriage house, she went back to her bed and once more called forth a vision. That night the Voice was able to make a new progress report.

"Our witch chaser is making wonderful progress on the altar. The woodwork is finished and he is now busy with the signs and symbols. In the very center of the front panel there is a serpent. No doubt he believes the serpent to be the animal that tempted Eve and led man's fall from the Garden of Eden.

225

There're also numerous stars, moons and suns. All are painted on the wood in the brightest colors."

All during this time, Clogg had been watching both Lucy and Zadock for some sign that they were the Voice's source. He had limited experience with ventriloquists, and during that day it had occurred to him that this might explain the phenomena he was witnessing. But his experience had been with unskilled practitioners--those of limited talents who might awe frontier audiences but would have never made their way in professional performing companies. Now he watched for some slight movement of lips, or the movement of throat muscles or Adam's Apple or some other tell-tale sign that might confirm the suspects' participation in the hoax. Much to his surprise he saw nothing to support his suspicions of Lucy or Zadock. Next, he broadened his observations to include other members of the family, and at last in desperation he focused his attention on Betsy.

She had retired to a stool in a corner of the room and seemed to be nodding from a need of sleep. She seemed so bored that he quickly dismissed her. He even suspected that the child lacked some of her mental facilities.

In bed that night, Clogg reluctantly turned his consideration to the possibility that he was now face to face with a real supernatural power. He analyzed the evidence. There was no way a human eye could have seen the work he had done earlier in the day constructing the altar. After the Witch's detailed description of his activities the previous night, Clogg had gone to great lengths to secure the carriage shed from any possible prying eye. He spent an hour caulking up any hole or crack in the shed that could have accommodated a prying eye, and he had carefully locked the door behind him upon entering or leaving the shed. Yet the spirit had once again detailed every bit of work he had done in the shed, as if the entity had been standing right beside him as he worked.

And there was the matter of the Voice itself. Clogg wracked

his brain for any non-supernatural explanation of that voice, but in the final analysis, he was stumped.

His thoughts were interrupted by the sound of the gnawing rat. Recalling the previous night's unpleasant experience, he reached out with extreme caution and felt about the bedside table until his hands contacted his tender box. With flint and steel, he was able to light a candle. The minute the light flooded the room the gnawing sound ceased. Nevertheless, he got down on all fours and looked about under the bed. Except for lint balls and dust, he found nothing, not even any marks where a rat had chewed on the leg of the bed.

Getting back on his feet, he searched the room carefully. Nothing was out of the ordinary. But as he passed the door, he noticed that the latch was undone. He carefully placed the bar in its slot, satisfied that no one could enter the room. At last, he returned to the bed and blew out the candle. He had barely arranged the cover, before he heard rapping on the wall near the head of his bed. Now he pulled the cover up over his head and lay tense with dread. Sounds seemed to come from all parts of the room. At one time it seemed to come from one wall and the next time from another. Then it would be like a rat gnawing and again like a board being rent asunder. Finally, someone seemed to try the door and then as sudden as it had begun all sound ceased and there was an absolute silence.

Clogg breathed a deep sigh of relief and allowed his body to relax. Just as he was convinced that all demonstrations were over for the night, he felt the cover slide from over his head. Thinking that it must have been his own imagination he reached up to take a hold on the quilt. A strong tug convinced him that the cover was moving. Before he could react, the cover was jerked out of his grasp and flew from the bed. Raw nerves now took over and he let out a scream of terror.

When Lucy and the boys got to the room, they found the door to Clogg's room wide open and the bed covers piled in a heap on the floor at the foot of the bed. Clogg himself was lying on the bed drawn up into the fetal position. At the same time across the hall a sleep-logged Betsy was cracking open her door to see what was making the commotion.

It took them all some time to get Clogg settled down enough to leave him alone. Each member of the family assured him that his experiences were in no way unusual.

All assurance was obviously in vain. The next morning when Drewry went to call Clogg to breakfast, he found the room empty. The only thing left to testify to Clogg's presence at the Bell house was a rather ornate altar out in the shed.

Years spent with the vagaries of farming had made Drewry philosophical.

"Don't seem like a man so afraid of spirits would have much luck casting out witches," he said, "but him going so soon I reckon saved us a hundred dollars."

The real victim of Clogg's attempted scam was John Bell. As long as, he had hope of getting better, he had perked up and actually seemed much better. Learning of Clogg's hasty departure and apparent failure, he again sank into despair, and the nervous tremors again took control of his body.

The Bell family resigned themselves to the eventual demise of their father.

26

RICHARD TAKES
BETSY TO TASK

When Betsy first learned that the witch chaser was coming, she sent an urgent letter to Richard, who was away at the time on business connected with his duties as a tobacco buyer. At the time Betsy had no idea what powers a witch chaser might possess, and she had naturally turned to Richard for help.

The letter caught up with Richard in Bowling Green. Much to his exasperation, the letter urged his immediate return to Adams without saying why he was needed. Not daring to ignore the summons, he had finished up his business as soon as possible and had started for Adams the following day.

He arrived in the village two days after the good Clogg had taken flight. The town was filled with excitement, and the story of the witch chaser's flight was on every one's lips. Although there was a genuine fear of the Bell Witch, Richard detected a note of pride in the voices of those he talked to. In any contest involving the witch and a witch chaser, the local folks were glad to note that the victory had gone to one of their own.

By the time Richard arrived at the Bell house, he knew the entire story. He was determined to take Betsy to task for practicing her trickery just when the community was beginning to lose interest in the Witch. But when he arrived, he was so glad to see her that he merely took her in his arms and forgot his rebukes for the moment. Whatever joy the family experienced by his arrival, it was dampened to a marked degree by the fact that John Bell was now much worse. Not only was he unable to speak or control his tremors, but he was delirious for much of the time. Lucy told Richard that the family no longer had any hope for his recovery.

Richard realized that it was now out of the question for him and Betsy to get engaged. While he, Betsy and Lucy might be able to put such a thing into a proper prospective, in the eyes of the rest of the family and the community it would be tantamount to Betsy's dancing on her father's coffin. Nevertheless, the family now accepted the fact that he and Betsy would become engaged as soon as it was proper, and now they were able to be alone without slipping away from the house.

"Well, I understand that you have been rather busy over the last few days," he said when they were finally alone.

"Are you talking about me scaring away the witch chaser?" Betsy asked.

"Yes, I thought we agreed that you were going to phase out the Witch's appearance."

Betsy looked at him hard trying to measure the depth of his displeasure. She did feel a bit guilty, but of course Richard had not been there to advise her and could not possibly understand how things had looked from her perspective.

"But he told everybody that he was going to send the spirit into limbo," she offered as a kind of justification for what she had done.

"What difference did that make?" Richard countered, not accepting Betsy's excuse.

"What if he had found out that it was me?"

"How could he have found out? All you had to do was just to remain quiet. Betsy, what I've been trying to tell you is that just because people out here in Tennessee are completely mystified by ventriloquism, there are people who would recognize the Voice for what it is right after you uttered the first half dozen words. If you remember, you didn't fool General Jackson. With that witch chaser, you were in much greater danger by speaking than you would have been if you had remained silent."

"But then he would have told everybody that he had cast me out," Betsy repeated her earlier excuse.

"What difference would that have made?" Richard countered with his previous point.

"Well for one thing he was going to charge Drewry one hundred dollars, and he would have collected if I had let him."

That was the first time that Richard had heard about the witch chaser's fee.

"Are you telling me that he was going to get one hundred dollars just for a little mumbo jumbo over a sick bed?" Richard asked with surprise.

"Drewry himself told me," Betsy confirmed.

"I suppose that does make some difference." Richard conceded.

That night Richard was in bed in the room where Clogg himself had slept. He heard his door open. For a moment he wondered if Betsy had gotten so carried away that she was going to try to frighten him. He soon realized that she had something else in mind. When she slipped into his bed, she was naked.

"I'm tired of waiting," she told him.

He made a modest effort to do the gentlemanly thing. But the long period of waiting had made him almost as impatient as she. He pulled her too him, and their union was consummated.

Later they lay side by side in near perfect relaxation. Around them the house was perfectly still.

"You know," Betsy whispered, "it wasn't at all what I expected.

"What did you expect?" Richard asked.

"I thought it would be something I would do just because I loved you. It hurt a little, but it felt good too. I think I like it. Do you reckon I would have liked doing it with Josh too?"

"No," Richard said sharply. "With him it would have been disgusting."

The small body he held shook with convulsions. For a moment he was alarmed.

"Oh God, what have I done to her?" he thought. Then he realized that she was laughing.

"What the hell are you laughing about?" he demanded.

"You," she said. "You're funny."

"I suppose with Josh it would have all been very serious," he accused with indignation.

"You're funny because you are jealous of poor ol' Josh. But I was also remembering how ol' Clogg looked lying on this bed trembling with fear."

He was relieved knowing that she was not laughing entirely at him. Now he allowed himself a chuckle.

"I wish I could have been here to see that," he admitted.

Betsy squeezed him hard. "Then you are not mad at me for running him away?" she asked.

"I suppose not, not if it saved Brother Drewry one hundred dollars."

John Bell died on December 20, 1820. Doctor Hopson wrote on the death certificate that he was the victim of a curious nervous disorder. But elsewhere the verdict was unanimous. Throughout the Adams community and the whole of Tennessee and Kentucky it was believed that he had been killed by a vindictive spirit.

During her father's illness, Betsy had heard the stories about her father being persecuted by the Witch, but knowing the truth of the matter, the stories had not greatly bothered her. Now that her father was dead, she became depressed by the rumors. Betsy always had a fearful respect for her father, and there were never any expressions of love and affection between them. As a rule, she was not generally concerned over the welfare of her father. Now that he was gone, she became convinced that her pranks and trickery with the Voice may have hastened his demise. As her depression grew deeper, this became a certainty with her.

Why could not the Voice have encouraged her father to get well as it had done with her mother? Why could she not have once had the Voice say to her father: "Listen John Bell, I am cast out, never to afflict you again!" Would it have made a difference in her father's state of mind and postponed his death? She would never know.

During the period of her depression Richard was a great comfort. Yet he too reminded her that she had been playing with something that could easily get out of control and that could have unforeseen results. He made her promise to stop all activities having to do with the Bell Witch. In the grip of her depression and in her desire to please him she readily promised. Still, this did not bring an end to the stories about ghostly events. For many years thereafter, when anything happened out of the ordinary, people would swear that the Bell Witch was responsible.

EPILOG

Betsy and Richard were married as soon as custom would allow. In time they had children and lived happily together until Richard's death seventeen years later. When he died Betsy was still a relatively young woman. On the Tennessee frontier, it would not have been unusual for her to remarry, but she knew that she had had the one great love of her life, and any other union would have been poor by comparison.

Without Richard she never felt at home in the house they had lived in, so she left Tennessee and went to live with her children in Mississippi. It would be romantic to say that she remained true to the promise that she had made to Richard concerning her unusual gifts, but it would strain the bounds of imagination to believe that Betsy could possess such power and not yield to the temptation to use it when an occasion demanded. Perhaps this explains why, in American folklore, the reference is always to the Bell Witch of Tennessee and Mississippi.

Did the folks around Adams ever suspect Betsy as the source of the strange events that so many of them had witnessed? If so, no one ever made a direct accusation. Still, whenever some strange phenomena like a ball of glowing gas rose over the swamp, people would tremble and point to it and tell their children, "There goes the Betsy light, lighting some poor soul on its way to hell."

Printed in the United States
by Baker & Taylor Publisher Services